THE HEALING HUT

by NEIL PATRICK

For my Dad

THE HEALING HUT
First published by Touching Tales 2013

© Neil Patrick

Publisher address: 484 Oundle Road, Peterborough, UK PE2 7DF
neil.patrick1@ntlworld.com

ISBN 978-0-9576083-0-6

Neil Patrick has asserted his right to be identified as the author of this book.

Cover image: Detail from Winter Allotments by Cath Read (www.cathread.co.uk)

The end of
the new beginning

THE HEALING HUT

ONE

I remember, so vividly, our last meal before it all happened; grilled barramundi, slightly wilted green salad, and white wine so thoroughly cooled it made the roof of my mouth ache.

I can still feel the condensation on the bottle and the warmth of the late-evening sun on the jarrah wood table. I can hear the dog that always began to bark in some distant garden as we settled for supper each evening in summer under the sunshade.

Normal, everyday.

Then, out of the gathering dusk, came what felt like an earthquake. Yet the ground hadn't moved. No drink had been spilled. There had been no vibration under our sunburned feet. Even the wonky jarrah table had not budged.

The juddering upheaval was in my head. It was my life being torn apart with the uttering of a single sentence. Still unbelievable. A few whispered words and the landscape of all our lives had changed forever.

The epicentre of the turmoil was our home in the Northern Suburbs – the place Grace and I had built, the hub of our life together – but the reverberations were felt 9,000 miles away in the place that was once home.

We'd had one of our perfectly ordinary, lazy days. An unhurried start, a sandwich lunch near Whiteman Park, a drive into the city, a couple of hours at the touring exhibition Grace had wanted to see – childish daubs, unvarying desert landscape, the paint scattered with sand, I remember.

Then, coffee, a little light shopping, and home where I'd buried my head in The West Australian while Grace pottered and went to and fro watering the plants as the sun went down.

I brought out the fish, the salad bowl and some Lost Sheep Chardonnay. I recall it was the last of the case; crazy how every detail has stayed with me. I'd given it a last-minute chill in the freezer. I lowered the parasol now the sun had lost its fierceness, and set stuff out. We didn't talk as we ate. In fact we had barely spoken all day. But after years of marriage there are days like that. So much of what there is to say has been said – many times – and contriving to break the conjugal silence can seem an intrusion on, well, contentment I suppose.

It was after I'd taken a shower and Grace had spent an hour or so agonising over clothes she had spread across the bed, stuff she might need for the winter rain, that everything was in place for the drama to come.

I think of it now as resembling that hushed, expectant silence just before the curtains open and a play begins.

We'd gone outside again, onto the patio; the Perth climate let us practically live out there. It was me and Grace – and Erik, who had dropped by unexpectedly after we'd had dinner.

When he'd arrived I immediately turned on the TV so that we could catch up with the day's sport, then Grace shouted from the kitchen: "Please. Not now Kyff. Let's sit outside. We have to talk."

Erik looked distracted, I thought. He was carrying my mitre saw and my new router. Odd – normally he was so tardy about returning anything borrowed. Not only that, he had a plaster on his thumb, so he must have been pushing on alone with the sauna project.

I can't say I was put out. But Erik and me never, ever, worked solo on DIY. We were a team when it came to home improvements.

Along the way we'd survived the odd faceful of leaking water and, recklessly, recoiled laughing from unexpected sparks. Once we went into hysterics because our plaster mix turned rock hard while we broke for coffee.

Mindful of approaching middle age, we were enjoying a last chance to be boyishly silly.

Grace had said we were true blood brothers because when we were together blood was always involved – "If the tool box comes out, I look for the first aid box."

We had a routine for self-assembly. We'd speed-read any instructions – "Perusing the destructions," Erik called it once, and repeated the little joke ad nauseum – then we'd plunge into assembly, faltering as we grew confused by the various bits. Then we'd have to take it all apart.

"Ah! So those little buggers go there!" one of us would shout, half an hour into the project.

Erik, with customary conceit, swore that it was possible to be too intelligent to understand makers' instructions. He would forge ahead impetuously; I would accede, gently question, diplomatically suggest. Team work. A partnership.

So all in all it was odd that Erik had decided to work on the sauna without me. But as I took beers from the fridge and flicked the switch to turn on the lights around the patio, I stumbled across what I thought was the likely reason for the visit, and Grace's seemingly urgent need to talk.

It hit me that my birthday – unbelievably, my fortieth – was due early in the new year, millennium new year. I'd have bet any money Erik and Grace had put their heads together to plan something a bit grander than normal, maybe the luxury trip to Asia we'd talked about. They'd want me to book leave.

I suppose the forty milestone is an excuse for a bit of a fuss. But, truth to tell, I'd have settled for a good gargle in Northbridge and the usual celebration meal in our usual foursome, at our usual table.

Pathetic, I know, but we'd reached the stage, I suppose, when mellowness appeals more than adventure, and, anyway, Perth was a great place to be approaching middle age. Lots of wonderful food if you knew your way around. Places that were lively but not wild.

For some time we'd had a routine when birthdays came up. We'd get dolled up, have beers at Mamie's, move on to cocktails, then, suitably unwound and ravenous, we'd swoon over the fish at Molto Pesce, passing round forks so we each had a taste of all the dishes. The wine would flow and we'd always top the night off, a bit giddy and loud, back at Mamie's.

I did also wonder, as I carried the beers out, whether Grace had secretly planned to get me tickets for the Waca cricket; there was a Test in my birthday week. For Erik and me, every Waca Test was a must. Could this be the year that the girls finally came along?

Of course, my absolute, sublime dream present would have been the Kawasaki - Gracie knew which model, and we had the money, but she said she'd always be fretting over my safety.

Oddly, when I brought the beers out to the rustic table - recycled timber, design by Erik, construction by me, and unsteady as hell - they both still looked po-faced and neither showed an interest in opening them.

Maybe someone had got some nasty medical news? Erik had mentioned Becky's blood tests.

No, Becky was fine now, Erik said. But he looked at the floor and not at me. Perhaps he had a health worry.

I was mystified. One thing was certain - Grace was useless at sustaining hoaxes, so this weirdness wasn't some elaborate tease. I'd had enough.

"OK!" I demanded, popping open a can and taking a long, welcome slurp. "Come on you two - what?"

There was a scarily long silence and then Grace made a couple of false starts: "I know that it will be a shock but ... This is hard for me..."

Cripes, I thought. This really is something dramatic.

Grace slowly reached across for my arm. She was trembling.

It was then, with a quickening of the heart, I realised: it was Dad. Only Dad, I thought - then felt ashamed. Only Dad? How could I think like that?

So the moment had come, after years of straining against the fraying tether: we could finally cut it, and let England drift over the horizon.

I recall thinking fleetingly how kind it was of Erik to have come along to give us a bit of moral support. But then my mind began to race with all the implications – work commitments, late availability flights to England, funeral arrangements made at such a distance. Everything practical, nothing emotional.

"No, Kyff, it's OK. It's not Dad," Grace said.

Not Dad? Then who could it be? Please God not Grace's mother. That would stir up Grace's grief over Lizzie all over again, set Grace back months.

She began to swallow hard, then started crying, making a small, continuous whining noise that I remembered from the first days after Lizzie. Suddenly a wail bounced off the house walls and echoed in the darkness over the rooftops. She was so distressed it was difficult to make out her words.

So it was her mum.

Erik went inside and came out with kitchen paper, and Grace plunged her face into it as if to shut out the world.

"What, Gracie, for God's sake?" I shouted.

There was just enough, barely-audible, information for me to understand.

It was not Grace's mum – but I was right about there being a big surprise for me. It was that my blood brother, Erik, and Grace, my dear wife of fifteen years, had decided to spend the rest of their lives together.

TWO

"I'm so very sorry, Kyff," Grace sniffled, rocking to and fro as if to comfort herself.

Her face was bloated and flushed. She was finding it difficult to speak and weep at the same time, and every so often she blew her nose with a trumpeting sound into the paper towel.

Evidently it would be "best all round". Things "hadn't been right for some time." It was if she was quoting from a script someone else had written. Or did I not know her?

I have since likened the sensation of being told about Erik and Grace to what a patient must experience when the doctor announces that, despite appearances of good health, there really is absolutely no hope.

I've heard that when a cataclysmic verdict like that is delivered, it's simply too ghastly to absorb, too big and too shocking to fit into our field of comprehension.

I suppose little diversionary concerns scurry about, giving that giant, black fact time to force its way in and settle...

"I must cancel that dental appointment ..."

"Who'll look after the budgie? ..."

"Well, now at least I don't need to cut down on the drink."

For me, Grace's news was simply incomprehensible. Surreal. And, like a man rendered near-comatose by a handful of well-rehearsed words delivered over a doctor's desk, I took refuge in the peripheral details of the situation.

How would we tell our friends? They'd never believe it...

Who'd get the car? What would Grace's mum think?

Victims of accidents or violence often say that the moment of infliction wasn't really painful at all:"It was only later, when I felt a warm stickiness, that I realised I'd been stabbed several times..."

Even several minutes after being told, I didn't fully realise how horrific the news was.

Mundane consequences flitted through my head.

Now there'd be no Test tickets. No birthday bash with linguini and Morton Bay Bugs. Absolutely, certainly, no Kawasaki - but then I realised I could have one now anyway as there would be no-one around to worry about me smearing myself on the back of a truck.

Oh, and of course it sank in that I no longer had a best friend. All that all seemed bearable.

But sweet Jesus - *no Gracie?*

I remember sitting bolt upright in my chair, my bowels churning. The big black fact had now settled inside me and I could feel its weight. I am losing Grace. No, I have already lost her. I stared with disbelief first at her and then at Erik.

My erstwhile cobber sat chalky-faced under the string of garden lights. He was stock still, staring at me with an expression that might have been shame, or fear. The eyes were wide and anxiously alert.

Maybe I looked as if I might kill him, an option that flashed as an enticing impulse across my brain.

"I know you'll never, ever ... Forgive us ... Kyff," Grace blurted out, as yet more improbably huge tears brimmed and fell, and streams of clear mucous ran from her reddening nose. She clung to the soaked corner of paper as if her life depended on it.

Just as friends learn exactly how to please, they also know precisely how to cause most pain.

"Judas," I said quietly to Erik.

It hit the spot. He lowered his elbows onto his knees and his head into his hands. For once, for the first time in all the time I had known him, Erik was speechless.

I believe that inside all of us lies an embryo holding the genetic code of primeval savagery. Within seconds it can muscle-up and go on the rampage, fangs gleaming and eyes bulging, if the inner cage is rattled hard enough.

I've known this since one scary day at fourteen when I had been pulled away by the scruff of the neck - growling, biting and crying - halfway through killing a fellow pupil.

From that moment, I'd understood that it was the mildest, the most gentle, who have the greatest potential for carnage.

"You mean Kyff did that to him? *Kyff?*" Mrs Power had exclaimed with disbelief as my bloodied victim was patched up in the staff room, while I waited at the door for the consequences, my fists still clenched.

And now my fists were ready again, under the lip of the table. In a moment my right would swing and land like a wrecking ball and that face, especially that nose, would yield like damp clay.

That nose...

Erik's nose tapered to a point, shooting out from beneath the promontory of his flat forehead. His aerodynamic profile was completed by a smooth wad of combed-back blondish hair that spoke of his Scandinavian forefathers.

I'd once shown Becky a magazine photo taken from Kings Park on the historic day Concorde flew into Perth, and mischievously asked her to guess which person they'd modelled the plane on.

She was not pleased, and neither was Erik, I suspect, despite the half-smile. But to be fair he was amused on another occasion (Becky not being around) when I claimed that his ancestors had evolved sharp noses for grub-hunting.

As my hair receded, and I took to wearing my glasses almost all the time, he began calling me Bald Eagle.

That was the way we were - our affection channelled through

banter, play fighting and mutual enthusiasms. Until a few heart-stopping minutes ago.

I took a deep breath, struggling now to rein in my fury. I was quite literally seeing red and I could feel my heart thumping beneath my ribs.

Erik correctly read the danger signal and got up. He looked at Grace pityingly and walked away.

As he reached the side gate of the house he turned back to me and said imploringly: "Look Kyff, I feel terrible. It's unforgivable. But we just know it's right for us all."

"Judas," I called out to him in a calm, level voice that I knew he would keep hearing in his mind for a very long time.

Same weapon, same wound – but satisfyingly deeper now for that second plunge and twist. Not as cathartic as reshaping a face, I'll admit, but I saw his head go down, as if he'd taken a low blow. It had landed somewhere vulnerable.

Grace's eyes followed him. She was no longer crying but at intervals a sob would make her shudder.

Erik disappeared into the dark beyond the garden gate and then, silently, we went inside, knowing we were moments away from the fight of our lives.

We were barely in the house before I landed the first punches, making the kitchen cupboards bounce. We filled the night with shouts and taunts, threats and scratches, tenderness, recrimination, tears.

After what seemed like hours we retreated briefly to separate rooms before we were drawn out to tangle again.

By dawn we were spent, hoarse and red-eyed but I still didn't have the answer to the question I kept bawling into Grace's face: "But for Christ's sake, Gracie, *why?*"

I sat on the carpet, my back against the wall, and rambled aimlessly once more over ground we had gone over again and again during the last hours.

Grace was lying on the settee staring at the wall. When I looked up she had lowered her head onto the sofa arm and fallen asleep, her arms encircling a cushion on her belly.

As she drifted off, had she imagined she was holding Erik? Or me? Or the bump that had sheltered the unborn Lizzie?

The grass was cool under my bare feet as I slunk away to decamp in the summerhouse, a pillow under each arm. Twice I picked my way back under a canopy of stars to the house, first for sheets then to dig out a sunbed from the hall cupboard.

Pathetically I searched the cupboard especially noisily, hoping that Grace would wake and call me through to say it was going to be all right after all, that we should go to bed and start again tomorrow.

But when I looked in she was still curled up with the cushion.

Grace had slept this way on the day she'd come back from the maternity hospital and each afternoon afterwards for a week or two. She didn't get dressed, barely ate, hardly spoke, always holding on to the cushion.

As soon as she settled, I'd find her dressing gown and cover her up, sometimes kiss her forehead. And that was what I did before going back to the summerhouse.

"Many waters cannot quench love, neither can the floods drown it," we had sung in the fourth form, showing off our brand-new post-pubertal voices, but blithely unaware of the profound truth of the words. I was sure I was about to find out how true they were.

As I trudged out I knew that I could never forgive, and never, ever forget. And I had been left with the insoluble problem of how to drown my unquenchable love.

THREE

When would the old boy go?

It was a recurring question that could only be answered by death.

For me, it was not a matter of fearing the news, more a case of having to re-bury the subject each time it worked its way to the surface, like a dog's bone. Any concern I felt seemed to centre not so much on how Dad's death would make me feel but more on how the news would reach me.

Maybe I'd be at Ascot – Perth's imitative Ascot. Or perhaps a message would be waiting as I came back in to the quay from fishing with Fraser. Or I'd be woken by the phone on a hot summer's night.

Would it be at a "good time"? This was the question that seemed to loom large.

I guessed it would happen when it was mid-winter back home with one of those freeze-ups culling the old and the weak.

Mum had gone like that, killed by an unrelenting meteorological siege laid by invading Siberian winds.

"They've been going down like flies here," Dad had said matter-of-factly, in a call breaking the news.

"There's long queues for funerals, so no hurry."

His accent had more of that indelible Welsh sing-song to it on the phone; altogether too much sing-song in his voice, I thought, given the circumstances.

I'd been called away from a lecture to the phone in the bursar's office and, as soon as they said it was Dad ringing, I knew it was about Mum. Only the Grim Reaper had the power to spur Dad into ringing me; the last time was when his brother had gone. "Bit of a cough, then her chest. Then heart," he had said without emotion. "I blame the fags. She wouldn't be told. But don't worry, if you can't make it, you can't make it."

If I can't make it?

Was he handing us an excuse, believing that flying back would be difficult for us as well as expensive?

Or was he testing us, secretly wanting us to show we'd be rushing to support him at the funeral? Maybe he simply didn't want us there; he was expert at masking the message.

Of course we made it, Grace and me, leaving the just-tolerable heat for godforsaken Britain, which cowered under sleet showers.

There was an uncomfortable, awkward week-long stay, overlaid by an oppressiveness that invaded even the musty bedsheets we huddled under. We tiptoed around Dad's ill-disguised unease at having us around.

"Is it me, do you think, Kyff?" poor Grace had asked on the second morning. But of course it wasn't her, or me – "it" was Dad.

As the taxi arrived to take us to Heathrow – and bring merciful relief all round – Dad came to the door with us and offered me an awkward handshake. I tried to break through his reserve with a bold clasp of his forearm. It was just bone and sinew beneath his cardigan sleeve and he eased it away slowly.

As usual, Dad also chose to shake Grace's hand, even though this time she stooped to kiss him. Icy droplets swept into the porch, wetting Dad's glacial cheeks. We turned to wave but he was already shutting the door. We hauled our cases to the taxi.

I was sure then that it would be the last time I saw him; and he must have known that, when I next came home, it would be for his funeral. As it turned out, we flew back a year later, on a healing trip for poor Gracie after we lost Lizzie and she pined to be with her mother.

The flight home had seemed endless this time. Sleep on the plane evaded me; I kept seeing that final image of Dad being lashed with sleet, and turning away without a long, last look.

As Grace and me chatted groggily over coffee at Singapore airport we were not quite honest enough to admit to each other that Dad's longevity was a little cloud hanging over our sun-filled lives but were surprised by the objective tone we'd struck.

We speculated about when we might have to make the next flight.

"It'll be years!" Grace said with a laugh. "Taff's as tough as old boots."

Grace always called Dad Taff, not to mock but to humanise him, to get behind the façade. She always had a teasing, provoking way with him. I think he liked that, though he would never let it show.

I knew that once Dad had gone, we'd continue to become less and less English, with "home" slowly melding into the fog of memory despite Grace's token resistance to what I called our Ozzification.

Once, during one of my recurrent colds, she overheard me ringing the uni to say I would not be in because, in local parlance, I was "real crook". She had winced then looked at me with disdain. I was also sworn off "strewth" and "bonzer" in her hearing.

But Grace and I had agreed, and Grace had indicated to her mother Mary, that there would be no going back. Perth really was home now.

The problem was the not knowing the when, and the how, about Dad.

Grace had said that when his number eventually came up we'd probably be blissfully unaware, on a blanket at our favourite shady hummock near the river, or down at Cottesloe Beach, while back at the house the phone would be ringing.

"We'll have to be found and fetched, you'll see. Taff won't make it straightforward," Grace said with amused affection.

When we left for Perth, Dad had vociferously demanded to know not why we'd been so selfish as to emigrate, but what in heaven's name made us choose the most isolated bloody city on the bloody planet to bloody well move to.

Being unreachable when he lay dying would prove Dad's point,

Grace said, and it would cheer him immensely in his final hours.

As to the messenger, I knew I'd get the news from someone whose name I wouldn't recall and whose face I would be unable to conjure up.

We Pughs are pegging out fast.

There are no close relatives, though there is Aunty Megan, the remaining sound Welsh bough of the fast-withering family tree; she might relent and do the honours, I conjectured.

There had been some sort of stand-off between her and Dad for as long as I could remember but surely death has the power to re-unite for the duration of a funeral?

"And how long will it take you to get back for the arrangements, *cariad?*" I imagined Megan asking on the phone – in that voice that was as sickly sweet as Llandudno rock – as if she were talking to the little boy I'd always be, in her mind.

When word did eventually come, I knew Grace would be wonderful, supportive, organised.

We'd work on getting the maximum leave from the university, do as much of the official stuff as possible while we were there for the funeral, then set up arrangements to allow me to deal with matters from Perth.

Finally, we'd clear the house and close the door on England.

Of course, there would be the matter of grieving. I'd already done the rehearsal when I'd mourned for Mum, or rather mourned her wasted life, but I understood that this time grief might prove to be problematical.

Maybe I wouldn't have to try after all. Perhaps a defrosted orb of love for the old bugger would bubble up from deep inside me and fill me with warm endearment.

Casting my mind forward to "the moment" usually happened when I'd just put the phone down, having heard Dad's increasingly reedy voice answering, giving his near monosyllabic answers.

Going back to bed, I would be kept from sleep by that familiar unease: we'd talked, but we'd not really talked. But then we had never, ever really talked.

There he was, half a world away, in his eighties and alone – stubbornly, wilfully, bloody-mindedly alone – and unreachable in a way that had more to do with our accustomed remoteness than the thousands of miles that separated us.

And there was me: secure in a job that was as comfortably tolerable as most but better paid, with autonomy and plenty of time for me to indulge myself in the areas of historical research I cared to dip into.

I had a roomy home. Friends. Sun on my back every day as I biked around the campus across swathes of greenery, knowing that the sparkling ocean was near enough to reach that evening, any evening.

We had prospered here but without drudgery, yet there was a grain of sand in the oyster of content, a tinge of guilt – a sense that Dad regarded me as an escapee. And the more we prospered the greater the feeling of guilt became.

I didn't quite know how exactly we'd become so comfortably off. Two people working, no children, modest ambitions and sensible spending I suppose. Unlike some of our friends, we had an old and inexpensive car and we didn't own a boat.

But one day we would buy one. The shiny, red Japanese four-stroke outboard – a second-hand bargain buy from a repatriating colleague – in the corner of the garage stood as a symbol of our prosperity and future hopes. That thing packed some real oomph and we were happy to wait until we could get a boat big enough to match it.

A boat. Now Dad would be sure to take the edge off that pleasure – "There's flash for you!" I could hear him saying, with a sourness that was hoarded to pour on pleasurable things.

Bloody Dad! Stubborn, proud and independent to the point of stupidity. Still tottering along to the demands of the seasons. Probably still filling in his weather log each day with a pencil stub held by fingerless gloves. Still packeting his seeds and trying to keep snug in that creaking shed, resting occasionally in that old dentist's chair nursing his mug of tea.

Solitary, his face set in a mask that revealed nothing; absorbed and unaware of the bomb that was ticking somewhere inside him.

FOUR

I was woken by the dazzle of the sun hitting the interior timber of the summerhouse, turning everything glowing amber. I was stiff, disorientated, and then suddenly fearful: nothing had changed in the night.

Padding through the dew to the house I left a note for Grace to drop in at the department saying I was having blackouts, that I'd been ordered not to work until "they" knew what was causing them, and that I'd be in touch.

Grace was no longer on the couch and for a moment I wrestled with an urge to go to the bedroom, wake her and plead, wheedle, grovel, promise that I'd learn to forgive.

Instead, I took coffee back to the summerhouse and lay on my back staring at the timber ceiling. Light sliced through a crack between boards. Erik had been the roof man. Once (it seemed a lifetime ago) I would have teased him about his faulty workmanship.

But finally I had absorbed the reality of my situation. The shockwave had passed through and I was left with emotional dregs of self-pity, fury, and the terrifying thought of life without Grace that manifested itself in an ache of loneliness.

Maybe there was a single scintilla of consolation on the horizon; surely having your world collapse around you provided a good enough excuse for going back to smoking?

Coaxed and comforted by Grace, I'd spent eight difficult months wrestling with the nasty Mr Nicotine and figuratively pinned his shoulders down, a manoeuvre that in real life would have left me gasping and dizzy.

Now, with newly-laundered lungs, I could enjoy guilt-free self-destruction – and there was a bonus: Grace, who had been so proud of me, would always know she was to blame for my cruelly early death from lung cancer. If it happened I vowed to croak down the phone with the diagnosis.

Our little local store was 200 yards away. It was liberating to walk barefoot in the fresh morning sun.

Mr Christakos served me, smilingly as usual, but he seemed to look at me longer and more closely today.

Obviously my haggard face, tousled hair and vagueness suggested domestic drama, and this was confirmed by my greatly revised early-morning order – normally a loaf of grained bread (small), six eggs (medium) and a copy of The West Australian. Today it was sixty cigs, six cans of Emu Export (ironically sometimes known as "wife basher") and, as an afterthought, a bottle of Shiraz. No bread thanks. No eggs.

For the next couple of days I could not bear to be in the same room as Grace, yet I hated to see her go to work. I was constantly seeking her out so I could vent my anguish and parade my self-pity. The more I bullied her into the tearful confessions that inevitably came after relentless grilling, the more I knew. The more I knew, the more excruciating the pain; the greater the pain, the less I understood.

In fact my interrogation sessions seem, in retrospect, to resemble self-harm. I couldn't resist unsheathing a new and shiny verbal scalpel as soon as I ambushed her.

Grace had taken to anticipating my movements and hiding away but on Saturday afternoon I left my can-littered patch beneath the water gum tree and cornered her in the bedroom.

She was dressed to go out and was reaching for her bag when I gently took her arm and launched into another cross-examination. She was afraid of me now but maybe, as the guilt-ridden betrayer, she felt that I had a right to abuse her. Perhaps being punished eased the guilt.

I had become a cruelly lethal inquisitor, and despised myself for taking on the role. But I was good at it – slowly peeling away protective layers to reveal the sweet kernel of truth that always turned out to taste bitter.

Today I was brimming with ill-will. A new and urgent suspicion had sprung up this morning when I looked at the calendar for the past weeks. It was burning inside me now as Grace, half turning to go, stopped and braced herself for a renewed assault.

"Grace. Just one thing. Remember your IT For Archivists weekend?"

"Yes," she said, looking at the door so our eyes didn't meet – and, perhaps, to assure herself that there was an escape route if she had to make a break for it.

"Was there one? A seminar?"

"Of course," she said.

(Let the record show that the accused appeared unruffled.)

"Really Grace?"

"For God's sake leave it, Kyff. I've got to go."

(The accused became flustered and evasive.)

"I just wanted to know. Just tell me; I don't mind, now we know how things are."

"For God's sake! Please drop it Kyff."

(The accused moved to leave but was restrained.)

"It's just that Helen would have been on the course with you and when I bumped into her coming out of a shop in Hay Street a while ago she didn't know anything about any seminar. Zilch. So it made me wonder at the time. But of course I trusted you."

(There was no chance encounter in the shopping centre but a little lie can have the compensating merit of uncovering the bigger truth.)

"Helen wasn't asked to go. She wouldn't be involved. Now I really have to get off..."

"But Grace. I rang Martha, asking for details of the tutors she'd hired, just in case the department ever wanted some help with IT."

(Yes, another lie. But all's fair in love and treachery.)

I went for the soft underbelly.

"Grace. Martha, your boss, your bloody boss, didn't know what the hell I was talking about! So say it, Grace. You were with him."

(The accused put her hands over her face, reminding the prosecution of a medieval painting of Eve being ejected from the garden.)

"All right! We went to Freo for the weekend. We had to talk things through. We needed to be sure."

(Collapse of prosecutor. Having that confirmed was excruciating. I should not have asked. And now I'd never be able to "un-know" it.)

"OK, Kyff? Happy now?"

"Happy, Grace? Happy? Just think. Just think of me back at home reading motorbike magazines and watering your precious plants and getting the stuff together for your welcome home dinner while that very afternoon you and that Swedish streak of shit were holed up in some Fremantle hotel room…"

(The accused moved to leave the proceedings.)

"…bunked up together in bloody Freo, working on the timetable for the destruction of my world."

"Happy Grace? Happy?" I bellowed after her but heard the front door slam. She had gone.

The hearing was adjourned to a later date.

FIVE

On Monday morning, Grace came to the summerhouse with coffee. She looked fresh, cool and beautiful.

She had always woken with skin that was translucent and downy. Even at an age when women turn to rejuvenating creams, she needed only a night's sleep to replenish every pore.

She passed the coffee mug down to me, using her elbow to hold open the wonky door that Erik the Bastard and me had never got round to realigning. Sunlight sliced through the lattice, striping her forehead with bars of bluish shadow.

The fuller face she had developed when she was expecting Lizzie had remained, along with the thicker hips and chubbier upper arms.

Her little breasts had kept the new fullness that she had always wanted. But her unstated pleasure in being curvier was soured by the association of how the change had come about. The ragged pink etching on her hips and belly provided an enduring reminder. I thought of the marks as regretted tattoos. Lizzie's little legacy.

Grace was as English as they come, a Wiltshire girl, but her mum said there was a sketchy link in family lore to Malta. This was given credence by Grace's colouring.

When I was a child, at Easter, Mum used to boil onion skins with white eggs Dad brought home. They came out of the pan wearing a glowing tan. That was the precise tint of Grace's shell-smooth skin – the visible bloom of inner good health.

I had been appalled when she became hollow-eyed and sallow, her hair oily, in the days after we lost Lizzie. But now she was back to her old self, at least in physical terms.

She had always been pretty but now, at thirty-eight, to me she seemed handsome, although there would always be a girlishness about her. Her hair – straight but wayward, a shiny, conker shade, with no trace of grey – was topped by an untrainable tuft that had always defeated hairdressers.

"Boing!" I would go, playfully flicking it.

"Bloody hell Kyff – stop doing that!" she'd say, reddening with anger and shying away like a spooked mare.

The spring-laden tussock, cocking a snook at maturity, was silhouetted against the sun now, as she looked down at me coiled in a foetal crescent beneath a sheet on the sunbed.

"Kyff," she said, "I've put out some clean clothes. There's cereal and stuff near the cooker. You need to start eating properly."

Then, with a note of exasperation: "Kyff. We have to make plans. We can't just stay like this."

I sat up and jabbed a finger at her.

"You decide to go off with my best friend and suddenly you find me inconvenient!" I yelled. "This is my place too, so go and shit in his nest instead!"

"But Kyff, we'll have to sort things out…" she said fearfully, retreating, letting the door swing shut.

I got up suddenly, tripped on the leg of the sunbed, cursed, then lurched out of the summerhouse, swathed in the bedsheet. I hobbled after her like a crippled beggar pleading for alms, holding my scraped shin, my sheet flapping round me.

Grace quickened her pace down the path to the front fence and the road. I struggled to keep up, the sheet getting under my feet and exposing my underpants. I guessed neighbours would be about at this time of day and for some bizarre reason felt ashamed that they were my least flattering pair. All support and restraint had gone many washes ago.

As I reached the road, the tangle of sheet made me fall heavily, face down. I lay spread-eagled on the drive, but before Grace could get in the car I managed to shout:"Just remind that beaky bastard he's still got my bloody band saw!"

The man had my wife – and there I was believing I could get back at him by curtailing the loan of a saw. Yes, pathetic.

On the opposite side of the road, Mrs Henderson was out, stowing her briefcase in the back of her car. She was the sort of woman who had always been vigilant about the "tone" of our "executive" estate.

I saw her eyes widen. She then turned away as if to digest the surreal spectacle she'd stumbled upon: that quiet, bookish Mr Pugh, in a shroud, rising from the pavement as if resurrected, his wedding tackle lurching unpleasantly.

Grace was flushed and fumbling with her car keys, desperate to get away. I was within a pace of her when she slammed the car door.

As she revved the engine my pitiful mewling reached its climax. I found myself bellowing through childish tears:"And tell Erik that when he tries to wire up his sodding sauna, I hope he ... fucking ... well ... FRIES!"

SIX

Grace drove off with wheels screaming.

After checking with painstaking care that the way was clear, Mrs Henderson eased her car from her house-front into the road and past me, keeping her focus straight ahead. But for a second, as she drove off, I saw her look back in astonishment through her driving mirror.

Going back inside the house, I paused in front of the hall mirror.

I was a grey apparition, still slightly breathless. I despaired at the indignity of what had happened, and now looked with self-loathing at the ageing body, incipient beer belly, the lardy big girls' thighs and ragbag underpants.

"You creep. You child," I told the hapless reflection. But, then, I felt just like a child – spiteful and vengeful.

I found my cigarettes and collapsed onto the settee and lit up. Kippering the furnishings would remind Grace that she had put me back on the path to an early death.

Watching a skein of smoke rising to coat the ceiling, I saw another tiny glimmer of comfort in the enveloping blackness. Surely this chaos was a valid reason to leave work?

For the last couple of years I had been looking for a get-out. Lately, even the balm of researching had not soothed the irritation I felt at having to teach.

I'd begun to grow intolerant of students, finding many of them prematurely cynical, inured to wonder, incapable of being enchanted. In short, they were unforgivably young – and they had been coming at me year after year like an autumnal high tide.

I was proud that I didn't drop my standards; I still believed that history could be living, breathing, that we could go back and really see. I would sprinkle pearls before them but if they turned up their snouts, so be it. I would reserve my passion for the clique of true enthusiasts I thought of as my Chosen Few.

So – that's decided. I will never go back. Never read the essay on the Sumptuary Law of 1363 that I'd set dear Lily (already donnish at 20); never again send Sharon (the only punk medievalist in the southern hemisphere) on an academic treasure hunt.

I knew they would flourish without me and the rest could sink or swim.

Comfortingly, I'd still be there in academic terms, even if only as an indexed name. In fact a final contribution to my chosen discipline was gathering dust on the bookshelf above me – the ring-bound tome of my academic paper, Hue and Cry: *Public Policing and Other Expressions of Mutuality in Medieval England.*

It had been a labour of love involving three weeks in Europe, trawling for tiny gems of detail that had lain in deep and dusty recesses for hundreds of years.

I remember the sleep deprivation, the headaches from eye fatigue, and hours of meticulous indexing and cross-referencing. Yet at this moment I could bin the entire thing without a second thought.

Out again in the blinding light, I shook out my blanket beneath the water gum tree and tumbled into a deep sleep that came over me as suddenly as concussion.

It was dusk when I woke, feeling a little stronger. On the radio at my ear was Our Song, a programme based on dedications to loved ones, and on the music they held dear. I'd sometimes tuned in before, when I was feeling low, to be reminded of what wonders can result when a sublime melody is overlaid with lyrics that tug at the heart.

I was unaffected by a couple of upbeat numbers and found myself sneering at the saccharin dedications ("It was when they put this on that he asked me to dance…").

Then, as my mind had drifted, Sinatra pulled me back as he eased into the first bars of *I'll Be Seeing You.*

I was startled when the tears came. The top had come off the bottle. I lay face down and very gradually the sobs that came like hiccups subsided and I experienced the warm glow that comes from the release of tensions that are too great to bear.

Radio hosts must be callous bastards, I thought. Surely it must have occurred to them that for every hand-holding middle-aged couple snuggling up as their requested track is played, there must be hundreds of love's losers nursing their pain in lonely rooms?

The DJ spoke intimately, almost in whispers, as if his entire audience was a friend he had known for years. Later he would say "Goodnight. Wherever you are, sleep tight," tucking in a few thousand widows with words that, with a little imagination, might indeed have been for them.

It is all calculated, I said to myself. It's their job. There they sit, nicely isolated in their glass cubicles, striving to find the songs that will tease even more tears from thousands of eyes that have already cried themselves dry.

As if on cue, by way of illustration, over the airwaves came the breathy, almost womanly, voice of Chet Baker, rising out of the hiss of the drummer's brushes and understated piano…

"I get along without you very well … except…"

Could there be a sadder song about lost love? Certainly. Many. And the radio sadists will be sending more our way soon.

I sat up, drawing my sleeve over my wet eyes and trying to haul myself out of the bath of self-pity I'd been soaking in.

Maybe I could write my own heartbreaker now.

I allowed myself a little hoarse laugh at the thought… "Since I lost you, baby, I got those beer-and-Tim-Tams suppertime blues…"

The tear-shedding had relaxed me enough for me to acknowledge my hunger. It was indeed Tim Tams time.

I'd disliked Tim Tams, Grace's - and Australia's - favourite. So I'd never have guessed that chocolate cookies and Emu beer would taste OK together but now, as a garden hobo, I was easily pleased. Starve long enough and they would have the allure of fillet steak.

The truth is I needn't starve. Grace keeps putting out plates of nutritious things for me, just as she would if she needed to assuage her guilt for leaving a dog alone all day. But where she is concerned, I'm on hunger strike. It's so perversely pleasurable to think of her coming home and finding the food untouched, the little paper note with the word "Kyff" still lying on the foil cover!

Bringing out my beer and biscuits I find my head playing flashbacks from my student days. My predicament keeps leading me to think about the path my life has taken, and for the first time I've been struck by the good fortune that has followed me. Until now.

I'd escaped from family claustrophobia when so many of my fellow school leavers were destined to be eternal home town boys. Then there was Cambridge that gave the feeling of being on the set of a classic film. Running alongside was a frantic college social life, spent in the company of brilliant oddballs, Old Etonians, the sons of Yankee millionaires, earnest working class boys from northern towns. Then there were scintillating women with soft bodies and scary intellectual power - a heady combination...

Part-way through, as if by magic, Grace came into my life. Then - without much effort - I walked into a well-paid job that I would have taken, unpaid, as a hobby.

I'd been fascinated by the Middle Ages since I'd read an Everyday Life history book when I was eleven. It was strong on contemporary clothing and food, and hierarchies of power but shied away from the walkways of flyblown entrails, the brutality, the infestations, the unrelieved agonies of disease and daily reminders of mortality.

There was no mention of famine, everyday brutality, the terror of hell, the little boys turned overnight to men, the horrendous punishments for wrongdoing.

Punishments...

Unsurprisingly, I seemed to be thinking a lot about right and wrong at the moment, and the attraction of pure vengeance as an element in law enforcement – the reverse of what would have been my position a fortnight ago.

Tugging open another beer, I found myself harking back to a time when justice was swift and unerring: to an England where thousands of gallows dotted the country. A place where bastards like Erik could, as a result of a whispered word or two, find themselves sans blood, sans eyeballs, sans wedding tackle, hanging out (quite literally) with crows and buzzards.

Insisting, on pain of death, that a miscreant eat his own shoes on the spot no longer seemed quite as comically cruel as when I first came across the incident in research. Now it held a certain charm: I pictured Erik and those exclusive orange designer trainers, an indulgence bought out of his sales bonus.

But for a moment I felt able to put aside my rancour towards Grace, and, retrospectively, grudgingly admit the notion that she may have been more a victim than a partner in crime.

Looking back over months, I could see now how much she had been changing: the waning enthusiasm for life, indifference over things she once would have thought of as treats; the daytime sleeps, the silences, her uninvolved acceptance of my sexual needs.

It all added up to depression, probably, and of course it went back to Lizzie.

Erik could be dominating, persuasive, charismatic, even; it was comforting for my pride to believe that Grace had been indoctrinated and, blinded by her infatuation, had trashed all she'd held dear.

Not that Grace was naïve; she had no illusions about Erik's power. "Erik the Ego" she'd once called him after he'd regaled us all evening with tales and jokes that all seemed to lead back to him.

She'd once remarked to me that, although we were around the same age, I seemed to regard him as senior.

"You feed Erik's insatiable appetite for worship," she said. "Your friendship works because you're undemanding and a bit admiring."

For me, Erik was simply good to be with. His humour and brightness easily compensated for the times he was overbearing. Away from his wheeling and dealing he was likeable and good company. He could be like an electrical charge. He made everything crackle. No wonder he had flourished in sales.

"You old bugger – you could sell tree pruners in bloody Nullarbor!" I'd told him once over late-night drinks, when he'd bombarded me with the detail, abundant detail, of his latest sales coup.

He conceded that the lack of a single tree in hundreds of square miles might present a bit of a challenge but was undeterred: "I'd have a pop at it." And he would have had a pop. In fact within seconds he had his sales pitch.

"Sell them as chicken jointers. Yes! You know, for cutting up a roast chicken into portions," Erik said decisively.

"Knock, knock. 'Madam – don't waste time carving that chicken while the vegetables are getting cold. Give them neat, even portions, on the bone for extra tenderness. All the rage in Sydney restaurants. They're quite literally a snip – normally thirty dollars but if you buy today, twenty…'"

Telling people what they wanted, and then selling it to them, seemed to come naturally but his triumphalism when he'd made a mug out of the easily-persuaded was deeply unpleasant to witness.

Occasionally he read disapproval in my face.

"Well, if I don't take their money, someone else will!" he would say brightly, in mitigation. "You'd never survive out there, Kyff. Not in the real world. You've still got that nasty streak of honesty. Out there, away from cosy academia, it's a croc pit. You'd be eaten alive."

Still, it was incredible that he had pulled off a coup with Grace. Stolidly down-to-earth, immune to flattery, conservative, she had listened to the patter, lost her way, and actually believed in the illusory future he'd held up in front of her like a catalogue of bright and beautiful things.

Grace fancied (a word she would have recoiled from) conventionally good-looking men, pretty men even, gentle, introspective men – at least that seemed to be her taste in actors and singers.

So how did she fall for that wind-tunnel profile? That big mouth on legs – spindly ones at that. This polar opposite of her, this man my old granddad, on the strength of one meeting, would have marked down as "a bit of a gobshite"?

But then, Grace somehow fell for me – crazily and completely, as I remember it. I would never have believed that possible before it happened. No-one would have called me good looking, conventionally or otherwise, though I suppose the lolloping crop of Celtic black hair I had then, and good, even teeth, saved me from being totally unremarkable.

Grace seemed to be tolerant, affectionate even, about my many imperfections, including the white, porcelain thighs that did not change shape with exercise, and the stubborn roll of back fat above my waist.

Once, on her little bed in the halls of residence, we had put on a record, shared baked beans from the can, and decided to use what remained of a lazy Sunday morning to make lists of the qualities and faults we found in each other.

My list, I recall, was a light-hearted paean of praise; any irritating traits were laughed off lovingly, little intimacies of our love-making encoded in sentimental baby-talk. Grace's list was deeper, more serious, more of a pledge.

She had been two-timed in her first long-term relationship in her first year at the university, and I suppose that's why she had added a footnote that said: "Joni M is right!!! We DON'T need no piece of paper from the city hall! Love and TRUST will keep us tight and true!"

I remember thinking: people who love each other shouldn't really need assurances about trust. I had never for a moment thought twice about the need to trust Grace.

But we live and learn.

SEVEN

Today – or was it yesterday? – I should have been giving a lecture on the role of women in medieval England. It was mainly for my new students but others doing history modules were invited, and there would be my clutch of second-year disciples.

I had conceived the session as an appetiser for the new intake – to ignite them and demonstrate how thrilling their chosen subject could be – but to be frank it also gave me a chance to share some of the new stuff I'd unearthed, to validate the work – and yes, to show off a little.

There was a certain piquancy, after the hours of lonely research, to put up on the screen a document extract or a picture of an artefact and say: "I was digging around recently in some documents when I stumbled across this, which I think illustrates the point…"

It was to be the sort lecture I'd have liked to attend.

I'd planned to explore how the Bible influenced medieval attitudes to women; I'd be looking at dress as a class indicator, fascinating as a subject in itself with those sideless frocks and foxtail bustles to rivalling fashions seen on the streets of any modern-day Australian city.

I'd incorporated references to the role of women as wet nurses, as dildo-sellers, as brewers – and accounts of what happened to some of the poor devils if the beer was bad.

I'd even managed to get a Scandinavian colleague to send me facsimiles from a rare medieval fight manual showing women in pre-arranged, life-and-death battles with their husbands. Women versus men, the women swinging lethal weights wrapped up in their veils.

Yet as I'd drawn it all together I'd stopped and wondered: Why the hell am I bothering?

The answer was that I was really pulling out the stops for my Chosen Few – and to remind the faculty why they were paying me, and giving me so much time, and helping me travel, to breakfast well at decent hotels and then spend hours in soft white gloves in sepulchral silence with crackly manuscripts for company.

The magenta flash of Sharon's hair in the front row of the lecture room, face alight with interest, would have reassured me that there was still a purpose in what I did. She would have been there, hanging on every word and in fact writing most of them down, scribbling vigorously while the sleepy herd ambled to graze in the refectory.

Lily, ever loyal, would inevitably have come up at the end of the lecture, begging extra leads for further study, her eyes shining with a light that I'd put there.

So. Instead of having to get up in front of a white board today (yesterday?), here I was, free to rot away to my heart's content, sour of breath and unwashed, on my blanket in the shade of the water gum tree.

Free, yes. But having no sense of release, because one dead weight had been replaced by another. I'd begun to experience an empty feeling not unlike hunger. It gnawed at me like my ulcer used to ("Suspected, ulcer Kyff," Grace would have said).

It wasn't like the anguish over betrayal. It was the feeling of common loneliness, and it was new to me.

By night I would writhe around on the sunbed in the fug of the timber summerhouse and it was then that the scary feeling of being set adrift invaded. During the day I languished, venturing into the house only to hover at the fridge door before carrying biscuits back to my lair.

Having no purpose, I lost my grip on the passing of time. One day I wondered why Grace's car was back so early in the afternoon, then found it was already early evening.

In states of half-sleep I planned vile acts of vengeance. Arson. Loosened wheel nuts. Untraceable poisons. That favourite of TV pathologists – blunt instrument trauma. In my head I saw the mallet in my tool box pop up, cartoon-style, and volunteer itself for the dirty deed. What is it they say:"While the balance of his mind was disturbed..."?

I grappled, in deadly seriousness, with the detail. Disposal for instance...

Maybe I could stow him under the patio?

That patio. Erik and I had slogged long and hard under a crucifying sun one ANZAC Day to lay it to form the frontage of the summerhouse, all to please Grace, who watched us from beneath her sunshade.

"Keep at it boys!" she had shouted with a giggle, turning a page of her magazine. With her iced drink and parasol, she'd looked like a starlet in a Hollywood movie from the Sixties, and she was relishing the role. At that moment she looked years younger than her age, and I had thought the coquettishness was for my benefit..

But now I wonder. Was betrayal already being hatched then as, stripped to the waist and struggling to keep the sweat out of our eyes, we manhandled the hexagons of reconstituted stone while she took occasional glimpses over her magazine?

I'll never know. Under sustained interrogation Grace claimed she wasn't sure when "things started" and I believed her because I knew – hoped really – that what happened was for her an affair of inertia, convenience even, and not passion; it was something she had drifted into.

The patio was a landmark in our friendship with Erik and Becky, and so was the summerhouse. Last year we'd soldiered on manfully for several fiercely hot weekends, ignoring blood blisters and the splinters to build the summerhouse, even though such a structure was an unnecessary facility in Perth.

Grace and I persuaded ourselves that we needed the extra space but knew, really, that summerhouses are for countries where sunshine is a scarce luxury, places like home. Hadn't I read somewhere that George

Bernard Shaw's den turned on a base, to follow the sun's path so he didn't miss a single ray?

Of course, we had to have an official opening. One Sunday, Grace and Becky were summoned to admire the finished job. We brought out tinnies, and between cans Erik and I hazarded exaggerated estimates of what cash had been saved by not calling in professionals.

It was good to have rough hands for a change and a few aches in underused muscles. Sentimentally, I would think of my weekend graft as homage to my horny-handed ancestors.

Grace once asserted, perhaps not entirely facetiously, that Erik and me embarked on the projects to bond in a way that was intimate but acceptably manly.

"Homoerotic DIY?" Erik had countered, laughing. "More like Laurel and bleeding Hardy!"

As for Becky, I always suspected that she was more relieved that we – or, rather, Erik – had not been electrocuted than she was impressed with the results of our ventures.

She encouraged us, appearing pleased to see Erik happily occupied. Poor Becky – she must be feeling that there's nothing to live for now. Her selfless mission was to make sure Erik was content, and my boyish badinage with him contributed to that and so, in turn, I was valued.

"Right – I'm just going to check we've got a tourniquet," she had announced with a motherly smile over her shoulder as she went in to make coffee while we laid out the timber for Erik's grand sauna project.

Meanwhile we shared the "team specs" (my spare reading glasses) to pore over Erik's blueprint.

While I retreated into self-neglect, somehow Grace was managing to keep up appearances, going to the university library as usual, evidently convincingly fielding concern about my extensive "medical tests".

Back at home she was turning herself into a stranger, probably to make this last phase of coexistence more bearable. She would respond to me on practical topics but had cut off any communication that involved feelings.

Was she braving things out, fearing that if we talked of our emotions she might lose her nerve and question her future with Erik? I knew that she was also trying in her compassionate way to wean me off loving her.

Meanwhile I was tortured by opposing extremes of emotion. One minute I'd want to cradle Grace's face and plead: "Can we try again Gracie?" The next I would want to disfigure her, especially when she appeared not to be sharing the agony I was feeling.

I pondered endlessly on the tight-knit friendship we had just blown apart. Me and Grace, Erik and Becky. Couples, but more than couples. Over the years we had become a bigger, single organism... Kyff-Grace-Erik-Becky.

Me and Grace were their sounding board, they had been ours. We fought poor service, bad cooking. We railed against politicians, and criticised any aspect of Ozziness we chose to dislike, we lambasted "home" in equal measure. Our lives ran in parallel but the lines were close and sometimes blended, as at railway points. For the last two or three years especially, the friendship had become pivotal to all our lives.

Of course, there were other couples, university people, new colleagues, whose company we could enjoy socially but there was no continuum. We always seemed to fall short of converting the jolly dinners into lasting bonds. We steered clear of the clubby campus gatherings, preferring to hand pick people to unwind with.

Fraser, my sailing mate, was always good value – especially if there was plenty of wine about. You had to tolerate his jovial but dominating presence and re-telling of stories. That said they were good stories that were always enhanced by new embellishments.

The problem was Fiona. She was the frail little dinghy being pulled along in the wake of the jet boat that was Fraser at full throttle.

Grace found her feeble, and irritatingly finicky over her food: inevitably, towards the end of the meal there would have to be some acknowledgement of her digestive problem.

Diverticulitis I think she said it was, and it couldn't have had a more appropriate name – by dessert she would have diverted the conversation to what was on her plate, and the health threat it represented. It was her way of saying "I'm here too you know."

For a couple of years, we'd had days out and meals with Tim Buchanan from the engineering faculty, after we'd got to know each other in squash games. He was a deep thinker, easily amused and likeable and we loved his wife Bonnie. But his fixation over money robbed every occasion of spontaneous fun.

Tim – skinny, freckly, gingery of head and beard – wore clothes that stoked up his colouring rather than cooled it down. His wardrobe of bright and uncoordinated items recalled shop clearance items of ten years back, bargains he hoped would serve him for another ten.

And he carried a purse. It was made of some indefinable animal skin, a small, mean envelope with a closing stud. I saw the looks he got. All right, maybe it was unmanly but that wasn't my objection: it advertised a mean mentality.

Another thing: Tim ate much too carefully, chewing longer than necessary as if to ensure every vitamin and mineral must be extracted at source. Not only that, annoyingly (no, unbearably) Tim never, every failed to comment on the price of anything he bought.

He had a way of screwing up his face after a waiter or shop assistant had given him his change, sucking in air and whispering, in an appalled voice: "Ouch! ...Fifteen dollars?!"

Tim's frugality inhibited our own spending when we were together, and one day Grace said:"Can we give Scrooge a rest? I know he's a sweet man, and Bonnie's brilliant, but if I see that bloody little purse come out again, I'll do something unpleasant with it."

The university friend whose company I never tired of was Ellie, and she was the person Grace probably liked least.

Ellie's office was a short step from mine. She shared my healthy cynicism about aspects of the university administration and my sense of humour. At thirty-five she was the damaged veteran of two marriages, now very much alone.

I told Grace about her and twice she came round for drinks and snacks. She was ill at ease, excusing herself with expressions of shame several times to smoke outside.

Ellie was scrawny, wore loud lipstick, and had big dark eyes that seemed always to be anticipating something alarming. She reminded me of a wounded deer but Grace claimed not to recognise Ellie's tremulous manner as vulnerability.

"She's just highly strung, that's all - hence the smoking and the roaming eyes, and the way she gulps her drink," Grace said, after we'd had supper at Ellie's rather chaotic flat. She added, ungraciously, I thought: "I do wonder how good she can be at her job. Did you notice that she says 'somethink' instead of 'something' - not what you expect from a lecturer in Eng Lit surely?"

The slight was undeserved. It was Grace being uncharacteristically catty. Ellie was highly regarded. Now I realise that in Grace's eyes, her real crimes were: being a woman, being needy and available, of having an office near mine, and of being able to make me laugh.

Eventually Ellie went to Sydney in search of love, or even something resembling it. I saw Fraser only when we went sailing, or when he needed a listening ear, and we had an excuse ready for when Tim finally threatened to crack open the family safe and splash out a few dollars on a barbecue supper.

Erik and Becky began to fill any need we had to socialise. Once we had consolidated out friendship we felt no need to put out social feelers or seek to make acquaintances more than that.

I'd met Erik in the squash club bar after a cup competition when he'd knocked out my usual partner, Sabeer Bhatia from the philosophy department. Sabeer knew Erik quite well and somehow, over beers, I was drawn into a "wives included" plan for a pub crawl.

Sabeer failed to show up on the night, so me and Grace, and Erik and Becky, drank and laughed our way round half a dozen pubs in Northbridge.

That was the beginning. Now we've reached the end.

Now there would be no such thing as a fresh start for any of us; we'd remain enmeshed historically and haunt each other for life, no matter where we went, or who we ended up with.

Everything had been tainted by what happened. It was as if the infidelity manifested itself as some corrosive liquid that moved through the house, seeping into our photo albums, our bookcases, destroying as it flowed.

The lethal gas it gave off permeated Grace's make-up desk, her underwear drawer, our car. It would soon befoul other old friendships and stink out the places we'd frequented together.

Every treasured incident we'd laughed over and re-lived, every Sunday barbecue, every boozy boating trip, was smeared with the stuff. The stench had seeped into CDs that could never be played again, eaten away at the pages of books that we had passed from one to the other, poisoned the memory of the many meals we'd had together at waterside tables at weekends.

If Grace really had to break away, it would have been a blessing if she had taken up with a stranger.

EIGHT

But what of Becky?

Poor, nice Becky – most people who knew her would have said that the word could have been coined for her. But I discerned a steeliness, and she would certainly need it to recover from losing Erik.

Erik had been everything to her since she met him soon after arriving in Perth. She was doting and possessive to a point that, I suspected, left him feeling suffocated. There was a prickliness about my relationship with her because I could tell she resented the affection Erik showed to me.

One night, as we were leaving after a session at Mamie's, Grace had patted my tee-shirt to point out the beginnings of my beer belly.

Becky had gone behind Erik and looped her arms round him and with a tipsy laugh boasted:"Well, this one has the waist he had ten years ago, so I don't think he'll plump up now!"

Erik was trying not to writhe. I'd spotted that tight, false smile before, when Becky was being particularly cloying.

"You never see a fat greyhound, even an old one, do you?"

Letting go of him, she had nudged him with a little hip-flick, looked up into his face and said playfully:"I think I'm going to have a lovely slinky husband into old age."

42

The poor girl would be devastated by what had happened – if indeed Grace and Erik had performed their joint confessional for her.

Surely she had been told?

I'd find out.

Judging that Erik would have left for work, when I heard Grace's car leave, I rang Becky.

The voice at the end of the line was not hers, or rather I thought not, but the Geordie accent was the same.

Perhaps someone was with her, in support?

"Who is that?"

"It's Kyff. Is Rebecca there?"

"Becky speaking."

Her voice was hard-edged and there was a hoarseness that comes from a night of drinking and smoking, or prolonged weeping.

"Sorry, I didn't recognise the voice. Just wondered how you are."

There was a pause, and then: "How am I? How do you think I am?" She spat out the words.

This was not the nice Becky.

"But how are you," she added with heavy irony. "And that devious bitch with the little-girl smile?"

Bitch. In seven years I had never heard Becky be anything but timorous in speech. When she was riled enough she would say "Shoot!" – to her, still daringly close to "Shit!"

"Look, Becky, I just want you to know..." I began, not really having thought about what I wanted to say.

"And I want you to know something, Kyff. I think you must have been blind or stupid not to know that Grace was stealing Erik. You were a damned coward to just sit back and let her go, for not doing something about it."

"So I'm culpable for what Erik's done? And what Grace has done?" I protested. "That's very unfair Becky..."

"I despise her," Becky croaked. "Sweet as honey to my face and all the time tempting Erik away. Two-faced bitch."

So finally the mouse had roared. Becky's own inner beast had broken from the cage. The timidity had gone, her Geordie blood was boiling.

Her deflection of guilt from Erik on to me and Grace infuriated me but I should have known that in Becky's eyes, Erik - up there on his pedestal gyrating his bony whippet's arse - would emerge blameless.

She'd turned Grace into a seductress, a grave miscasting. Despite the deceit and the pain Grace had caused me, I felt a defensive anger.

"Anyway, Becky, why didn't you suspect what was going on under your nose?"

She needed to face the truth.

"You say I've been blind. I take it you didn't smell a rat when Erik went off for a weekend early in October?"

"A weekend...?" she asked huffily.

"Yes. In October. Work would have been his alibi, I bet."

Silence. Thinking time.

"You see," I said, welling with pleasure, "in fact Erik and Grace went off to fucking Freo. Grace told me. He hid away for the weekend to decide how he could humanely dispose of you - and to help Grace decide how to get shot of me, of course."

There was no response.

I allowed a few seconds to pass because I knew Becky would be reaching over with her spare hand to the calendar, the one from home with the photo of Durham Cathedral on the front.

She would be turning back to the October page, and to that weekend, marked (I'll bet) with the words "Sales Conference".

"It's probably down there as a conference, or something similar," I said but there was no reply.

The click as she put down the phone spoke volumes.

NINE

I'd taken to coming into the house when Grace had gone to bed, for a catnap on the sofa. But well before dawn I'd be wide awake. I'd carry my coffee out into the dark and trudge back to the summerhouse with my cigarettes and a book, which inevitably remained unread.

When the sun was up, I'd go out and lie on my blanket. My al fresco pitch was feeling more like home now: I had the pocket radio, and each morning I'd surround myself with cushions from the house.

But Grace was right. We (I) couldn't go on like this. We (I) had to make plans. I already had one this morning: I'd have a drink.

We had kept a special bottle of red, Fotty's Pool Merlot, separate from the rest in the wine, at the bottom of the rack, stowed away for a celebration meal, something we'd never enjoy.

I poured a glass to the rim, then took out our document file and emptied it onto the dining room table – bank statements, certificates, notifications of interest, investment documents, insurance.

It all added up to a comfortable situation; financially, I'd be fine. But totting up only served to remind me that money was no substitute for what I was losing and raised the dreadful question: "Now what?"

An hour later the wine bottle was empty, my head was swimming, the ashtray was full, and the paper bearing my speculative sums had been screwed up and discarded.

I traipsed to the summerhouse, wrapped myself tightly in the bedsheet and put the earphones into the radio.

"We were so inseparable…"

Billy Eckstine. Passing Strangers.

"…now you're acting very strange…"

I re-tuned to the classics band. A sublime tenor aria, a lament for his dying lover. The voice soared over plangent strings.

They were at it again, those radio people. Keeping us mired in heartbreak. It was enough to make you think of farewell notes, of stored-up tablets, of tow ropes and rafters.

I changed channels and to the drone of the stock market report I fell asleep.

Lunch next day was a picnic, as usual: two pies and a packet of Tim Tams, supplied, along with a six-pack, more cigs and the newspaper, by the ever-cheerful and diplomatic Mr Christakos, who still acted as if he hadn't noticed that within ten days I'd changed from a kindly spoken middle-class academic to a drunken, chain-smoking tramp with leaves in his hair and no conversation.

It felt like lunchtime but as I went in I saw Grace's bag. So she was home; the day had gone and I had missed it.

She came into the kitchen from upstairs and gave me a cool "Hello". She took a boxed meal from the fridge, kicked off her shoes under the table, just as she always had, and flipped open the tin of Earl Grey teabags, just as she always did.

Erik would grow to know and love these foibles, unless he was too wrapped up in himself to notice.

I hadn't appreciated how dearly intimate they were, and how viciously jealous I was at the thought of someone else growing accustomed to her ways, especially those that dated back to when I first began to love her and even back to her childhood.

There was the way she cleaned her teeth by moving her head from side to side, rather than the brush. And her curious habit of watching TV on the floor, lying on her side with her head on a cushion.

On Sundays, she always had a boiled egg (three-and-a-half minutes from a cold start) with toast soldiers. She never failed to say "bless you" when someone sneezed – even if it was a stranger on the tram. She was a sublime eater of potato crisps, the only one I've known who could eat them crunchlessly, as if they were marshmallows.

Today she looked downcast as she filled her little floral English teapot. To my shame, her wretchedness gave my spirits a lift; so she was suffering too.

As I paced around the kitchen she became vigilant. She had begun to look at me as if I were a pet that had disgraced itself once and might just be reverting to a dangerously feral state. But when she sat down at the kitchen table to my surprise she gestured with a slight movement of her head for me to take the other chair.

"Stay a minute, Kyff," she said, then: "There's some news."

She announced this with the neutral intonation we'd both adopted lately, as if a spark of emotion in our speech might reignite embers we'd damped down.

"News?" I said. "Bad, I expect." I turned away with professed disinterest though inwardly I quaked with morbid curiosity.

"Go on…" I said. "Tell me you're having the baby we couldn't have, and that it's with that long-nosed bastard."

"No, Kyff," she said calmingly, and now with warmth.

"No. And we could have had a baby. You and me had a baby. We had Lizzie. Nothing changes that. And we could have tried again if … if things had been right…"

"So – are they cutting up rough over me at work?"

"It's not that Kyff."

She reached for my hand, a gesture that made me buckle. A reconciliation? Had Erik repented?

"Kyff," she said earnestly, squeezing my fingers. "I'm sorry love but it's your dad." So the moment had arrived.

We sat in silence for what seemed a long time. She still had her hand on mine and I wanted it to stay there.

"It shouldn't be happening to you now, Kyff. The timing's so cruel," she said. Of course it would be cruelly timed; it was so like Dad, and Grace had predicted it.

But strangely I had no feelings about the news. None. Grace might as well have announced that the cat had just been spayed.

What I felt was the imprint of Grace's fingers on my hand, and the tenderness of her words. "I'm sorry love…"

Her eyes brimmed as she tried to read my reaction. She was looking at me quizzically, expecting me to be shaken I suppose, but I felt almost indifferent.

"Aunty Megan rang the house half an hour ago," she said. "I couldn't bear to just wake you and tell you then and there, out there."

"Well, they say it never rains but it pisses it down," I muttered inanely, simply for something to say.

Grace stood and went upstairs quickly.

I believe she was afraid that if she stayed a moment longer she would have hugged me, out of pity. But a loving embrace, even for old time's sake, was out of the question. Things had gone much too far.

TEN

When the moment came, Huw Pugh exited with a dull thump that no-one heard. It was probably painless, certainly clinically swift, and the most private of deaths for the most private of men.

Mercifully he had been unaware of the indignity involved.

As Madge Jennings, with her customary muddled logic, declared: "If Huw could have seen himself straddled on the edge of that stool like a discarded ventriloquist's dummy, he would have absolutely died."

"And there I was thinking he was just having a nap," she told the huddle of mourners beneath the rimed thatch of the church lych-gate a fortnight later.

The bleakness of the day of the funeral presented the perfect backdrop for what became a performance. Madge shone out of the grey fug with her crimson beret and rouged cheeks – as vivid as a poinsettia against a wintry window. The captive audience prompted her with vaguely encouraging noises as she doled out titbits of detail. Madge blew into her gloves, and warmed to her role.

"What happened was that I knocked on his shed door and shouted 'Let's have that manure money!' Just teasing him as usual – not that he ever let on he was amused.

Then I poked my head in and... found... him..."

She was pleased with the way she managed to get her voice to trail off just like one of those actresses in the old films she still loved to watch.

"Poor old lad," a bobble-hatted member of the group mumbled, with a note of pity, from behind a scarf. "OK, he was a buttoned-up old bugger but you had to respect him. Huw was never a people person. That hut was everything to him."

Madge could see her own breath and through it an assortment of attentive, watery eyes, most peering back at her from behind glasses.

"His kettle was on the ring boiling away like billy-o," she resumed with inappropriate brightness. "But when I put my hand on top of his, to wake him, I saw that his eyes were open and when I felt his hand it was ... icy." "Icy" was pronounced with a suspicion of a tremble.

"But, Madge, what about, what about doing the kiss of life?" asked a massive man with bucolic slowness.

He towered behind the semi-circle of mourners. He had broad shoulders but hips that were even wider so he appeared as a looming grey pyramid topped by a yellow knitted hat stretched over an alarmingly large skull.

"Didn't you try it on him Madge?"

There was a heavy, childish persistence in his voice and his blubbery cheeks and wet, fleshy bottom lip gave him the appearance of an over-nourished infant.

"They learned it us on the Scheme."

"No, Yeti," said Madge testily. "No, I did not. Not with Huw. Anyway, the paramedics said I did all I could by turning his gas ring off and going to phone them."

Mouth-to-mouth with Huw? Perish the thought, she said to herself, regardless of that business of his teeth. She would have shuddered but it seemed disrespectful. Just in case Yeti was hinting she'd been negligent in any way, she chastised him with a look.

"What matters, Yeti, is that he's gone. We've lost somebody special."

Yeti was well aware of his place in life and there were plenty of people around to put him back in it if ever he had doubts. He reverted to his accustomed role of mute onlooker, casting his eyes down and searching for interest in his feet.

His pudgy nose was glowing pink and from it hung a crystal-clear droplet that twinkled, reflecting what little light there was.

The group beneath the lych-gate shuffled like penguins to accommodate two slight old men, arriving in slow motion in overcoats that had grown too big as, with the passing of the years, they shrank within them.

Madge gave in to the urge to fill the silence.

"Another thing I noticed..." she announced. "There were envelopes all over his bench and the poor old lad had got spilled seeds stuck all over his forehead. Like blackheads they were."

She added ruminatively: "Brassica by the look of them, or they could have been...""

"It'd be Jellicoe's Pride," said a pipe-smoker out of the side of his mouth. "Victorian. Reddish outer leaves. Stand all winter. Somebody had sent him some seed."

"You can't beat wossname in my book," offered a voice from under a hat with earmuffs.

"The good old Savoy, eh Ray? It's still the one for me," said a gaunt, bowed man on a shooting stick.

Yeti's curiosity spurred him to risk another contribution. He asked sheepishly: "Did you brush them off, Madge? The seeds? Because we could have grown them for Huw."

Madge offered no response, so Yeti again sought distraction in his feet and, with dinner-plate palms, smoothed his already smooth hat. The sparkly drip dropped.

Yeti tried to picture Huw's head with his forehead peppered with seeds but was waylaid by thoughts of that fancy bread with poppy seeds on top. The cold and the long wait were making him peckish. Breakfast was a distant memory. He heard his cavernous stomach moan restlessly.

"Any sign, Prof?" asked the pipe-smoker, with a moist sucking noise. No-one smoked pipes nowadays so those who did, he believed, should be seen, and heard.

An intense-looking man with long, unkempt hair and bottle-bottom glasses that turned his eyes into beads of jet peered round the lych-gate corner post and down the road.

"Not yet, Johnny. But then Huw wouldn't be bothered about keeping God waiting, never mind us."

He gestured towards the church, with a shake of his stringy mane, and said sourly: "All this religious claptrap would leave him cold."

The clump of mourners shuffled again as one.

"Well, he's leaving us bloody cold, Prof," said the man on the shooting stick. His face was ashen except for tributaries of red threadlike veins. "We'll be bloody well joining him in a box unless he puts a spurt on."

"He'll be here when he's ready," declared the pipe-smoker. "You know Huw."

He leaned forward to check that Huw was indeed intent on being late for his own funeral, that he had remained doggedly independent to the end, the very end.

"No sign yet."

Madge was pleased; there was time for her to conclude her forensic monologue.

"Actually," she said, "you could see from his teeth that whatever it was had hit him right out of the blue."

Yeti, feeling an itch that could only be scratched at the risk of another rebuke, tilted his head inquisitively, like some gigantic canary looking for millet, and asked: "But what was wrong with his teeth, Madge?"

"Don't be so damned morbid, Yeti!" she said, then: "Can't you guess?" She breathed again into her gloves.

"Well, if you must know, they were hanging half out."

Yeti made a silent "O" with his mouth and struggled to compose the full picture in his head: the chilled corpse; the staring eyes; the forehead peppered with seeds, possibly brassicas of special provenance. And now the teeth. Hanging out. It was simply too much to hold together; if he captured the teeth he lost the eyes, if he summoned up the seeded forehead, the eyes went.

Not only that. A disturbing new image had just sprung into his mind – of Madge moving Huw's teeth aside to get into the classic resuscitation position he'd seen demonstrated on the Scheme. It was all too much.

He was distracted by the noise of someone deep within the gathering breaking wind. It was a mournful bleat, muffled by multi-layered clothing. No-one seemed to notice; perhaps even the perpetrator was unaware.

There was an unstated consensus among the more elderly members of the group that these things were inevitable in later years. No need now for embarrassment, for speculation about the culprit … certainly no youthful pride now in claiming ownership.

Yeti's stomach groaned again but then he was startled by a sudden shout that came from behind him.

"Aneurhythm!"

The belated diagnosis was bellowed out by a tiny man wearing hearing aids and spectacles with tinted lenses. He appeared to be nestling beneath Yeti's bulk.

"You mean aneurism, Wilf. A localized bulge in an artery," Prof said flatly, adding, under his breath, "unless it was an algorithm. They can be bloody lethal." This was not meant contemptuously; he knew that Wilf would not have heard his reply.

Prof had a reputation for knowing something about everything, and did. But in taking care not to parade his knowledge he sometimes made little under-the-breath jokes to amuse himself. It helped to alleviate the isolation that came with having an encyclopedia for a head.

"That's it – aneurhythm! That's how my sister went. Fit as a fiddle," he barked, "laying out one of her fancy cream teas. Then – bang! Down on the table like a bag of spuds! Scalded the poor neighbour. A right mess."

Yeti's mouth made another "O" as he pictured it – the flying kettle, the crash, the squeals, the flying crockery. The look of surprise on the face of the corpse, on her back on the coffee table, her legs (he chose to imagine) well and truly akimbo.

He felt compelled to check the detail.

"Did she actually fall on the cakes, Wilf?" he enquired, talking into the nearer of the two hearing aids (what a shame it would have been if cakes had been wasted on top of it all).

There was no reply. Wilf's conversations were essentially one-sided nowadays. He simply said things, never expecting the answer to reach him.

"Aneurism, eh? Poor old Huw," said the man with the pipe, absently, in response. "Well, I'm just glad he never hung on in a bad state. Damn sure he wouldn't have welcomed our pity if he'd lingered."

He tamped down the tobacco ash with his thumb and added thoughtfully: "Talk about every man being an island! Strange, the old beggar didn't seem to need anybody. Maybe because he didn't really have anybody.

"Well," he said, with a sweep of his pipe towards the rest of the group, "I mean, just look at the turn-out today. No family, no relatives," he said.

Madge snatched at the chance to clarify, and reassert her place at the centre of things.

"Well, not quite, Johnny..." she said. "Kyff's come all the way from Perth, and there's two ladies from Wales, a cousin and a half cousin."

She indulged herself in a half-smile of pride.

"Actually, I've been very involved. They got me to be the link at this end because I knew Kyff when he was a little lad, and I had him traced. And then I tracked down the Welsh side for him."

"Kyff? Oh, so Huw had a son did he?" said Ray. "Kept that one dark didn't he? I didn't know he'd ever ... wossnamed."

"Yes, he'd been married," Madge confirmed, then changed tack, cutting him off. "Just imagine though – what if I hadn't popped to the allotments, and hadn't seen his windows steamed up, and hadn't called for his manure money? It could have been so much worse..."

"What, worse than him dying?" asked Prof with a tinge of sarcasm, keeping his tiny bird-like eyes on some distant point down the road. Madge was stung.

"Well, no, Prof, but just you think. There was his gas bottle and that wonderful old shed might have caught fire and it would all have gone up – his notebooks, his cupboard full of seeds and all his little relics..."

"Hell's bells! Did you just say Huw's shed's gone up?" shouted Wilf, cupping one of his hearing aids. "It'll be bloody vandals!"

"No, Wilf!" said Ray, mouthing the words. "No, it wasn't vandals this time and it didn't actually go up but it could have done, because he'd got a, got a, wossname in there."

"Gas bottle," said Madge.

"Oh I see," said Wilf, though he had neither seen nor heard.

The fog was closing in rather than clearing now. So many mourners had reached the church that they spilled down each side of the street. In the gloaming under the thatch of the lych-gate watches were consulted at arm's length, scarves adjusted, feet stamped, shoulders hunched.

An angina spray hissed. A mourner coughed himself to tearfulness then took off his glasses, mopped his eyes with his handkerchief and reached into his pocket for a sweet.

In the growing restlessness, Madge began to lose her audience – just as she was winding up for a last-act climax. Undeterred, she blethered on, like a loop of tape playing in an empty room. Ray tried to stem the verbal tide: "Any sign of the wossname yet Prof?"

But Madge was unstoppable, remarking to no-one in particular how cruel it was that these things always seemed to happen just before Christmas; and wasn't it a shame that Kyff had to come all that way from Australia for such a sad occasion; and wasn't it a shame that the poor old Pughs seemed to be nearly extinct?

As she began describing what a devil of a job they'd had finding a Welsh flag – "He was so proud of being Welsh!" – she found that she was now addressing Prof's back.

Undeterred, she explained how difficult it had been to find a way of fixing the leek to the coffin, and what a brainy idea the undertaker had come up with ("You'll never guess – velcro!").

The words were still tumbling when Prof leaned forward from beneath the lych-gate to scan the horizon one more time and, spotting slow-moving headlights piercing the fog, looked over his shoulder and muttered, almost inaudibly: "He's here."

ELEVEN

This morning I remembered why we'd emigrated. It was to escape the bloody freezing British winter. And the eighteen hours of daily darkness that goes with it.

By the miracle of flight, over two days I had left the almost monotonous tee-shirt sunshine of "home" to the shock of what I've just recalled we used to call brass monkey weather.

Whoever wrote "In the bleak midwinter..." had it right.

Leaden skies, oily, ice-coated puddles, inky figures plodding along half-dark roads. I had forgotten how deprived Britain is of daylight, and how you don't need a funeral to imbue a winter's day with post-apocalyptic desolation.

Yes, it rains in Perth in winter but we're generally at the other end of the thermometer; it's more often enough to melt, rather than freeze, the balls off a brass monkey. Only the Fremantle Doctor bringing the balm of a constant breeze makes things bearable when it really hots up. Here, I was being reminded, the cold is bone-achingly disabling.

I'd slept deeply and healingly in the crisp cotton sheets of a new and nicely impersonal hotel on the edge of town, but that first view from the third-floor window – planes of grey and black, a cold sheen on every surface – had wiped out any feeling of having been restored.

Despite this morning's drabness, later there were reasons to be cheerful.

They got me to the church on time - and the coffin looked terrific. The leek had survived the journey in its improvised harness, looking for all the world like a great anaemic limb. The Welsh flag with its hissing red dragon had turned up in time. And the hymns had been chosen, the tributes arranged.

Madge had thought of everything. My only request to her had been for *Ar Hyd Nos - All Through The Night* - to be sung at some point, and there it was on the order of service.

I knew I'd probably be thinking of Madge, rather than Dad, when it was sung. After Dad died, she had rung us in Perth several times, always disregarding the time difference.

The night after I got the news about Dad I had been asleep in the summerhouse. Grace appeared at my side like an apparition and shook my shoulder. It was just after 3 am.

"It's that lady on the phone again. She says it's urgent," Grace said, disappearing into the dark.

I stumbled inside. Madge told me excitedly that she had been in touch with Aunty Megan and they were sorting everything out. But she was really ringing, she said, to say that she was about to bike into town and if I dictated the wording for a death notice she'd call in at the Chronicle office.

"Don't go to more trouble, Madge. It'll wait. But thanks for ringing, and for sorting out the church and the hall and everything. I'll sort out what I owe when I see you. Goodnight Madge."

"Goodnight?" she said. "Oops! It's afternoon here, Kyff. Oh - sorry!"

Dad would never have let on but he would have been touched by Madge's efforts to acknowledge his Welshness. His national pride was fierce, though increasingly it had teetered on the edge of maudlin.

Thinking about his stubborn, old-school nationalism reminded me of those thoroughly Australian cobbers donning hired kilts and sporrans and rallying in Perth at Scots pubs for Burns Night booze-ups.

Grace always said: "The main reason Taff's so damned grumpy is that he can't forgive himself for settling in England and he can't forgive England for not being Wales."

One day soon I will tell her that "Taff" got his leek, and his Welsh dragon at his send-off, and that the spray of white chrysanthemums she had ordered had arrived –

"Dad Pugh (aka Taff), dearly missed. Grace, X, Perth."

Grace had always reminded me, whenever I grew frustrated over Dad's self-imposed isolation, that I should show more understanding, that he was the product of a hard-done-by generation, always at the wrong end of economic vagaries, rendered secretive by the distant echoes of Victorian ways, imbued with guilt by chapel.

Grace was right, of course about Dad's generation. As a boy during the school holidays we returned to the villages Dad knew and saw men, old before their time, coughing and spitting in the street.

Faces were different there. You could see the bone structure. Necks were muscular. Every man seemed to have broad hands, and as a child I was fascinated by the spidery black tattoos most had, where injuries had sealed in coal-dust.

I thought of my uncles (small, dark-browed, black-eyed) as moles who spent most of their time burrowing but who were forced to emerge now and again to blink in the daylight, quench their thirst at the pub and then stoke up on corned beef hash kept hot in black-leaded ovens.

That everyday hardship – the sweat-soaked pants, the wearying weight of the pick axe, the plunge down in the cage while the town slept – lay at the foundation of Dad's nationalism, and was carried over into his life far away from Wales.

Now, wimp that I am, as Dad is laid on a metal trolley by six men who look like the Mafia in their black suits, I shiver in my pew and incline towards a cast-iron radiator that is barely warm.

Megan is next to me, the chubby, rosy-cheeked teenager of long-ago holidays in Wales, now grown to maturity and motherhood and beyond. The chubbiness has resolved into stoutness, the cheeks now topped by bulging little bags beneath tired eyes. Where did the sparkle go?

"You OK, Kyffin?" she says kindly, giving me a sidelong glance. If she is looking for tears, she will have a long wait.

The echo of footfalls in the church and the rustling of hymn books began to abate and, as the vicar took his place in front of the altar, my mind raced back to when I was thirteen, on holiday in Dad's village, and had strayed into the wrong bedroom.

There was Megan, starkers, reaching inelegantly into the wardrobe.

In one eye-popping, mouth-gaping second everything that I'd theorised about – having been steered in the right direction by some kid's clandestine, thrillingly evil naturist magazine – was proved to be true.

The image of that moment had a double-page spread of its own in my mental album but it had been impossible to enjoy it. As I grew up, shame marred many pleasures, most of them furtive and unmentionable, so the pink apparition of Megan with one leg raised balletically was a perfect blend of sweet and sour.

Ludicrously, at the time I also worried that there had been a breach of manners.

Did the incident call for a note saying "Don't worry about today Aunty Megan. I didn't see everything"?

Gauche as I was, I sensed that this might be making a mountain out of a molehill – and through my hungry teenage eyes what amazing mountains they were and, even more amazing, that molehill.

Megan had always indulged me; her most severe chastisement was to say "There's cheeky, our Kyff" if I crossed behavioural boundaries. And this is how I rewarded her, by stealing an eyeful.

"All meat and no taties that one," my uncouth Uncle Glyn would say, to Dad's disapproval, if he saw a comely woman. That summed up Megan – then. Alas, now the meat had been joined by several helpings of potatoes.

Next to Megan on our pew is Gwyneth, a girl with a raw-pastry complexion and the big black Pugh eyes, a concave chest and an unfortunate overbite. Poor kid had also been cursed with the Celtic monobrow, branding her a true Pugh.

She looks lost, wondering what she is doing here, so I lean forward and smile at her. As she smiles back sweetly I count myself lucky that I inherited Mum's eyebrows.

Gwyneth is wearing a slightly distressed look and unsuitably summery clothes. She must be perished, I think, just as I am, in my lightweight suit designed for the sunniest city in Australia.

The church is full, mainly of old men with a sprinkling of women of similar vintage – Dad's allotment friends. Friends? Dad wouldn't have been comfortable being linked with such an intimate concept – it was always "them down there."

Breaking the uniformity of grey-heads is an enormous red-faced chap, much younger than the rest of the company.

He is on a front pew eating a chocolate bar while the vicar deals with a few pre-funeral "housekeeping" matters about car parking, the venue for the refreshments and the forecast for more dense fog.

I can tell that the snacking giant is not being disrespectful. His eyes are fixed almost adoringly on Dad's coffin. In his shadow is a little man wearing two hearing aids, large glasses and a solemn face.

Near the altar, alongside Madge, is a tweedy chap of middle age, with a kindly, weathered look. By the look of the weight of badges on his lapels, he must be the allotment overlord. Dad is being accorded full horticultural honours.

Above their heads is the big brass lectern in the shape of an eagle. I remember it as a child – at Harvest Festival, having to stand on a kneeler up there, to read a text with Dad and Mum in the congregation.

"…*the trees are bearing their fruit … He has given you the autumn rains in righteousness … He sends you abundant showers…*"

As instructed, I didn't hurry or mumble, and stepped down relieved that I'd been word perfect. I'd learned that whenever pride appeared Dad would organise a fall, and it came.

"You said that a bit posh didn't you Kyff?" Dad had said, as I crept back beside them in the pew.

The formalities over, the vicar cocks his ear to Madge who has lurched forward to whisper something, no doubt an invitation to food after the service. The wattle overflowing his modern, abbreviated dog collar suggests that he does not live by bread alone.

"Thank you again for braving the weather to say farewell to Huw," he begins.

"Let us think of this as a celebration of his life and start with a hymn which, although unseasonal, could not be more apt for a great gardener. We Plough The Fields And Scatter."

I find the words in the hymnbook – I know them anyway – but haven't the energy to sing. I look at the coffin, imagine Dad lying inside.

"Thank God it wasn't me who found him," I say to myself.

What if I'd had to cradle him and say comforting things as he passed away, or hear a croaked confession, like those dying dudes did in the cowboy films?

Dad and me had always been like repelling magnets, drawn together so far then sent spinning away into our own worlds by a force we didn't understand. Our separateness was unbridgeable and it showed in little ways.

When I was a boy he took me to see United for the first time. He led me, hands on shoulders, through the crowd to the urinal at half time but wouldn't go in himself until I had come out. He was embarrassed to pee with me there.

I found a space between two gabardine macs and tinkled against the tar-black wall, eyes firmly ahead, the steam rising into my face, while towering men with black-and-white scarves round their necks put their Park Drives in their mouths to free their hands for shaking themselves and buttoning up.

"Now don't you move," Dad said, as I came out and he went in.

There's a saying: "The family that prays together stays together."

What hope had there been for a father and son who couldn't bear to be together, let alone pee together?

TWELVE

The lingering wheeze of the last chord from the organ pulls me back into consciousness.

"...*All good gifts around us are sent from Heaven above, so thank the Lord, O thank the Lord, for all His love.*"

The vicar takes off his social face and dons his pious look. His strained delivery suggests that his dog collar, or rather the modern, groovy adaptation, is two sizes too small.

"All of you here, I know, knew who," he intones. "I mean, all of you here knew Huw Poo. Pugh. And respected him. *Respected* him."

I suspect that the reverend has been trained to say key words twice for emphasis, and because of the echo the effect is doubled. Doubled.

"A son of the soil, a son of Wales. A history lover. Weather watcher. An enigmatic character who never found the path to God but could easily have been mistaken for a Christian. A one-off. A one-off. "

I am no longer sleepy, intrigued by the vicar's castrato delivery (was it that collar?).

"Huw Pugh could be outspoken, brusque. Yes, brusque. And I can confirm that at first hand!" Two or three mourners chuckle.

"But he offered a hand to those in trouble. Those ... in ... trouble," he repeats with affected thoughtfulness. "Of course, few knew what good Huw did because…"

The vicar stops mid-sentence to watch (we all do) as the tiny man with the two hearing aids shuffles past his huge companion.

"I'm bustin'!'" he says in a stage whisper. "Are they round the back?" ("…round the back?" echoes around us.)

The vicar tries to pick up his thread.

"…few of us knew what good Huw did because he was such a private man, and so very prickly on the outside. Because the good he did he did…" ("he did … he did" echoed back like a phrase from backing singers)"…by stealth. By stealth."

Megan nudges me and whispers:"He's right. Deep inside your Da was fab'lous. Fab'lous. Inside."

"You know…" yodels the vicar, lodging his elbows on the lectern and leaning forward as if to share a secret. "You know – Huw makes me think of that parable of the mustard seed. Perhaps you know the story of the mustard seed? One of the smallest of the seeds…"

("That's wrong for starters," grumbles a well-spoken man in the pew behind me.)

"…in fact, Mark calls it the smallest of all the seeds," says the vicar.

("Smallest?") The posh old man taps me on the shoulder and confides into the back of my ear: "Never! Some seeds are like dust."

"Yet this little seed – and let's think of Huw as that little seed – grew into a tree. A tree…" intones the vicar. "Yes, perhaps we can think of Huw as this towering tree. Deep-rooted. Unchanging. Strong for his gardening friends."

In reaching his oratorical climax, the vicar begins to sound as if the trendy clerical collar might see him off.

"And didn't Mark, speaking of that mustard tree, also say:'All the birds of the skies came and lodged in the branches'?"

"Yes!" he wails, with a shake of his wattle.

He pauses as the man with the two hearing aids toddles past him to his seat.

"Huw certainly had something of the fiery tang of mustard about him! But … but … like the mustard tree," he says, letting his voice plummet,"he was a refuge providing for others a safe place to lodge. To lodge. In safety."

(Room for all the birds of the skies was there? Shame I could never find a perch on Dad's branches.)

An emaciated man of perhaps fifty, with an almost skeletal face, long wispy grey hair, unkempt beard and circular glasses, joins the vicar and begins to list Dad's attributes.

"I know that funerals are not occasions for truth-telling. When we see someone off, we make great efforts to find only praiseworthy things to say," he begins.

"But Huw wouldn't have wanted us to focus on his qualities today. He'd have said: 'Go on Prof, if you must – but just tell it true' ... And so I will."

He has the congregation in his hands.

"Yes, Huw Pugh could be ungracious, ill-mannered, detached. Cold. Could be. He held fools in contempt and showed it. He stamped on insincerity as if it was a slug after a prize plant and he wouldn't budge an inch on a principle."

("True. True," Madge whispers breathily as Megan turns her face to me to check on my tear ducts).

"Huw was a crusty old devil and I believe that this was because he was angry. Angry that people were becoming philistine, turning away from simple, basic fundamentals of life: a sense of community, the joy of changing seasons, nature.

"He feared for the future. It infuriated him to come across school kids who didn't know that potatoes grow underground. He hated corporate greed. He once said: 'Today we all seem to be trying to con one another.'"

The congregation listens, absorbed, as do I. This man is illuminating Dad for me, shining a light into hidden corners of him I had not even known were there.

"When Huw read of scientific advances that would make everything in life go even faster he would ask: 'Why?' and then despaired and turned back to the rhythm that his veg plot dictated.

"Yes, he was angry – over huge organisations manipulating the lives of ordinary people. And I suppose, most of all, he was also permanently displeased that the Welsh, Britain's ethnic people, had been tamed by the English and only allowed the ritual of rugby to get their own back."

There is a pulse of nervy laughter at this and when it dies down I think of Grace, picturing her next to me instead of Megan, and I know that she would have been dabbing away tears now.

Madge has a paper hanky to her crimson lips, and the chin of the gigantic man on the front row is trembling in his attempt at self-control.

"People turned to Huw but he didn't seek to be a leader. We seemed to make him one. But for others, this man was Horrible Huw…" he says, with a smile that reveals smokers' teeth.

"Like a coin, he had two sides. On the front, a fierce profile. On the shiny reverse, rare qualities. Generosity. Humility. Reliability. Brotherly concern.

"Huw Pugh was the man who supplied the night shelter people with vegetables, who filled the church with produce at harvest festival, the helper on the scheme for those with learning difficulties. The historian with empathy for underdogs."

Prof looks across at the vicar, as if to signal that he has nearly said his piece.

"This might seem the wrong place, the wrong time to make an appeal…"

The vicar looks edgy, sensing that something inappropriate, maybe even dangerously political, might be coming. This is God's house after all.

"But the best memorial we can give Huw as he says goodbye is a pledge take up the fight that he started, the fight to save the bit of ground he loved."

After some uncertainty as to whether it is good form to applaud at funerals, the congregation clap. Madge cries, then Megan.

The giant on the front pew is looking down at his feet but there is a tremor in his neck that shows he has been overcome.

When the organ strikes up with *All Through the Night,* Megan and

Gwyneth sing fiercely in Welsh, warbling a descant.

Then the vicar indicates that it is time.

The Mafia men are back and, as they stoop to take up their load, the little man with the hearing aids makes another scramble past the legs of his minder. He hurries as best he can to the coffin.

I wonder whether he is going to give it one last embrace. Instead he takes out a penknife, hacks through the harness of the giant leek and gathers it to him like a child who has been lost and found again.

"This one was runt of the litter, Yeti," he says. "But they start to feel like family." The giant, red-eyed and looking down at his shoebox-sized feet, nods.

As we wait to troop out into the fog, the massed voices of the Treorchy Male Voice Choir come over the sound system, caressing *Calon Lan* to a climax. Perfect, Madge.

Calon Lan is the Welsh supporters' song that turned dad into a statue as he waited, in front of the TV, for the Welsh rugby team – red-shirted, red in tooth and claw – to pile into the lilywhite ranks of English players. Figuratively, in his wingback chair, he was standing to attention.

"That's never, ever sung in English," I heard him say contentedly to himself once as, absently, he drank in the words. "It's ours."

Ten minutes after the final note and the last elderly mourner has left the church, Dad is part of the earth that he had been so attached to. I am an objective spectator, as cold and unfeeling as the clod I threw down on the coffin.

What I really feel is the desperate craving for a fag.

THIRTEEN

"Straight through, flower," says the doorman through ill-fitting dentures. "You're all signed in."

Flower. The grittiness of the area, my home town, contrasts starkly with this apparent delicacy in addressing people.

As I recall, the floweriness can be quick to wilt, as in: "Say that again, petal, and you'll be up at the infirmary getting stitched."

The doorman wears a dark suit – albeit a shiny one – as befits his rank.

He guards the tiled lobby, perched behind the little table on which lie his trappings of power. They are pencil stubs, rule book, and his little wad of tear-off tickets that give full and official permission for non-members, on a discretionary basis, to enter and enjoy temporary access to the facilities of Benton Working Men's Social Club but on no account to buy drinks.

Madge had negotiated, in advance, for our group to circumvent the bureaucracy and go straight to the inner sanctum of what used to be called "Clubland".

In short, the concert room had been booked for the post-funeral refreshments.

"Funeral people straight through the bar!" the committee man shouts, more warmly now, as if he were bestowing a gift, although he peers through smudgy glasses at me, and then at Madge, to double check that we are genuine mourners, and not black-clad interlopers trying to infiltrate without appropriate paperwork.

The din and brightness of the front bar, and the over-excited air of a lunchtime drinking session that for most started three pints ago, comes as a shock.

It's been the last morning of work for some before Christmas. "Work" is being flushed out of consciousness.

Knots of men are gesticulating, shouting the punchlines of jokes, hailing one another with raised glasses, feeding coins into the tinkling fruit machines, all competing against the clicking of snooker balls and clattering dominoes. It's a relief to shut the hall door on the clamour.

The hall has barely changed since I was last here, what seems a lifetime ago. What strikes me immediately is that the ceiling has lost its patina of cigarette tar. But the melancholy atmosphere goes deeper than a coat of paint; it is in the brickwork.

All in all, it's a sublimely funereal venue for a funeral despite the cheery foil Santas hanging from the lights, and the tinsel trim pinned across the stage front.

The stage itself, flanked by faded plush curtains and empty except for a wire globe containing bingo balls, suggests a place of pleasure abandoned when a travelling show moved on.

There is the old committee notice board, its once-green felt now bleached to a dusty grey, but still bearing notices of the exact sort I read a generation ago – a notification of the annual meeting, the winning numbers of the Christmas meat raffle, the date of next year's club outing, the darts team fixtures.

A recollection stirs, of a notice I copied down years ago and, in doing so, memorised:

"Owing to Stain's and possible Cloth Damage wives of member's are not, repeat NOT, allowed on the snooker table's – The Committee."

As the first mourners arrive, in slow motion, they see me smiling to myself. I'm savouring again the delicious positioning of the apostrophes but my conscience is pricked when I remember that I created a mocking anecdote out of it to take back to Cambridge and share with my guffawing fellow freshers.

Dad would have been appalled. Right now I can feel him looking down and twisting his mouth in disapproval.

Shaking hands at the door with each of the mourners, all of them anxious that I don't feel alone, I feel lonelier than I have ever done.

It strikes me that I am now an orphan. How odd that, at thirty-nine, the very word should make me feel child-like and vulnerable.

The queue to commiserate seems endless.

"Now he was a character…"

"We had our differences but he was straight down the line…"

"It was Huw got me started down there…"

And still they come.

"Ray," says a thin man, stooping down slightly to introduce himself. "Condolences, Kyff. Your dad had real wossname … real…"

"Charisma?" I offer.

"That's it. Charisma. In buckets."

The tweedy man with the kind face grasps my arm and then holds my hand firmly.

"Cecil. Sorry for your loss Kyff. I'm proud to say he was my friend," he tells me with obvious sincerity before Madge calls him away.

Bringing up the rear is the gentle-looking giant I'd seen in church. His size, close up, amazes me. He fills the door-space and has to dip his head as he comes in.

He pulls off his bright yellow hat and crumples it in huge hands as he stands in front of me like a penitent, blushing and awkward.

Gormless, Granddad would have called him but I warm to his child-like demeanour. He extends an arm like a tree bough and, with what for him must have been a gentle squeeze, disrupts the internal bone structure of my hand.

He beams a big, slobbery grin and says: "They call me Yeti."

"And I'm Kyff," I reply, glancing down at his feet, as Madge takes my elbow and leads me into the throng.

Her face is alight.

"Bet this hall brings it all back Kyff..."

She's still gamely lifting the mood, making sure death doesn't get us all down.

"My God it does!" I say with too much conviction. The temptation to add the word "unfortunately" is almost too great to resist.

I tap a glass with a fork and thank people for coming, praise Madge to the skies and say that there will be no charge at the bar.

Instead of the drinks being on you, I say, they'd be on Huw, whereupon several people laugh, some a little too generously, and those waiting at the bar hurriedly, and happily, put away their wallets.

Madge is fussing, urging people to "come and get stuck in". Several tables have been set, end-to-end, on the dance floor and she moves in like a conjurer's assistant to draw off white net curtains to reveal pyramids of food and piles of paper napkins.

The man with the grudge about the size of mustard seeds touches my arm and points at the food.

"How's that for a demonstration of old-fashioned domestic preserving," he says. "All is safely gathered in – and now you're damn well going to have to eat it all winter!"

He was right. Here is a pickle-fest. Bowls of pickled beetroot, pickled red cabbage, piccalilli and pickled onions sit alongside chutneys in jars with frilly cotton tops. Only the celery, in jugs of water, and the pies are unvinegared.

The Wilkie's pies are lined up on trays; each has a little glistening eye of jelly in the centre. The shape is still the same as when I was a boy, the crisp sides bellying out, the finger-wide crimp at the top, the crusts crumbling just as they had when we'd had them for tea, with salad and long, agonising silences, after I came home from Sunday School.

Back then, if a wife called out to a husband "Fetch me a medium!" as he left for the shops, he knew that she meant a pie, a Wilkie's pie.

I wondered whether they still had that peeling painted picture on the shop side, showing fingers shaping a pie above the slogan "Hand-raised by Wilkie's since 1935"?

There were fruit pies too. Madge had identified them with cards – "Gooseberry (Careless)", "Bramley and Blackberry" and, with a nod to her hero, "Cambridge Gage (from Huw's tree)".

The man with the badges approaches me. His tumble of hazel hair gives him a boyish look, at odds with the crow's feet round his eyes, and his rounded, tanned face and bright brown eyes combine with his russet tweed to give him an autumnal air.

"Kyff – Cecil again," he says, offering his hand once more. "Hon Sec of the Allotments Society, and for the region. But, much more important, a friend of your dad's. Can't say how sorry I am that we've lost him."

I soon warm to Cecil. He is kindly, unstuffy, warm and open, and I see that his eyes have moistened with the mention of Dad.

I put down my empty plate and pick up my beer as he steers me to a half-circle of elderly half-pint drinkers flanked by Madge and another woman, younger than the rest by far.

"Bill…" Madge says, gesturing to a man whose weathered face is vaguely familiar. He could be from another age with his white moustache, rosy face, boxer's nose and fleshy red ears.

He must be in his eighties. There is something about his rusticity that for me recalls old photographs of fresh-faced village boys in World War One, aged overnight by what they saw at the front.

It dawns on me that this is the Bill who had an allotment when I was a boy, and who seemed ancient then – a farm worker with one bowed leg who rode up on summer evenings on a big black bike.

I recall being fascinated by the fact that he always had string round his waist keeping his jacket shut, and that his bike was so big that when he stopped he had to fall from it onto one leg.

He regards me through milky eyes.

"Remember you as a shy little scrap. Couldn't get a peep out of you," he says with a wheezy laugh.

"And you've met Ray…" says the Hon Sec.

"I didn't know about you until this morning!" says Ray, a tall spindly character with a predatory stoop, like a heron, and pitch-black, slicked-back hair.

"Absolutely no idea!" he says, as if there had been a conspiracy to keep my existence secret. "Never even suspected that Huw was wossnamed. He never let on."

Madge moves forward and plants a wet kiss on my cheek. She smells of pickled onions with a sub-note of flowery scent.

"We need no introducing! We go back years don't we Kyff? This is Pat…"

Pat is freckly, with sad, greyish eyes and cropped grey hair; her black coat provides the perfect foil.

She leans towards me and above the din says in a near-whisper that Dad was her favourite down at the allotments, and had been very good to her.

"I'll miss him a lot of course," she says with a break in her voice.

I escape for a cigarette. Madge walks with me towards the door, past the vicar who is into the fruit pies, and says out of the side of her mouth: "She's still very fragile from losing Terry. Big sweet pea man. Inseparable."

In the fog enveloping the entrance I see a pinpoint of red light. Behind it is the man they all call Prof, drawing in hungrily on an untidy roll-up. The light from cigarette turns his wayward hair into an aura against the early evening blackness.

"Huw's lad!" he says. He holds out his roll-up so I can light my cigarette from it.

"Thanks for your words today … Prof," I tell him. "You had Dad summed up. You knew more about him than me."

"Nobody really knew your Dad. He was unfathomable. Put it this way – I think that, after years, I'd finally prised the back off the watch and even seen the cogs move but I still couldn't tell the time," he says, opening his palms in a gesture of resignation.

"He never really let me get near him," I say. "And to be honest I think he was something of a stranger even to Mum."

"One thing, Kyff. In the unlikely event of there being a celestial Head Gardener up there, he'll have already demanded a sunny spot to start his onion seed off."

We tread on our cigarette butts and with a nod to the doorman move from the din of the bar to the hum of the concert hall. I buy Prof a drink and we sit on tall stools.

"Challenge!" Prof declares, surveying the room. "See if you can spot our world champion."

There's a twinkle behind the pebble glasses.

"World champion?"

"In this room there's a current world champion," he says enigmatically.

There are perhaps half a dozen people here who are under fifty, and who might possibly excel at international bowls or archery. Maybe Yeti's a weightlifter, or a wrestler?

"Give in," I say.

"Hail the champ!" Prof declares, turning his thumb towards to the little man with the two hearing aids and the large tinted glasses. The man in church who had the water problem. The man sitting on his own, staring into space and holding a glass of fruit juice.

"Go on..." I say, intrigued.

"Longest cucumber."

Prof slides another pint in front of me.

"A bloke from Milwaukee just pipped him for heaviest radish last year. Wilf's was like a bloody cannonball. Had to be taken to the weigh-in in a pram. But it's all serious stuff..." says Prof, immediately contradicting himself with a manic laugh, revealing tombstone teeth the colour of tea.

There is a long silence, then I hear the vicar braying.

"...Well I think we have to agree to disagree. But could we find it in our hearts to forgive the Apostles for getting their facts wrong about the size of seeds...?"

The posh man is staring challengingly over his drink.

"It was Wilf's leek today, the one on the coffin," says Prof. "A baby one. He's going for longest carrot in the new year. It'll be all root, as long as a bus, thin as a hair, grown in a tube, nursed like a foundling ... That's if we're still down there..." he added.

I sense that Prof has a hobby horse that he is about to saddle up.

"Chances are that by summer we'll all have been turfed off to make way for a superstore. The council's in cahoots with the supermarket and they're selling us down the river."

He looks downcast, turning his pint glass round and round on the wet beer mat.

"It's hard to convince anybody that little bits of ground tended by Joe Soap to keep him sane and exercised, and in touch with what matters, are as important as yet another bloody great, impersonal hangar full of over-packaged goodies."

He motions towards Yeti, who is piling a quarter of pie into a big, flat mitt and says: "He'd be lost. The allotment's transformed him. And it would finish Wilf off.

"Wilkie's would go, and some of the other old shops. By this time next year, the best bit of greenery round here would be under a car park."

Prof's ears have reddened. He is becoming agitated, so I make sympathetic noises and say I need the toilet.

Coming out, I almost collide with Wilf. I say hello but he doesn't hear. I tap him on the shoulder and say: "Thanks so much for the leek. The leek!"

"It's OK lad, I've been," he says, nodding to the toilet door.

"No, I wanted to say thanks for the leek," I say, holding my arms apart. "The leek."

"That? Oh, it was just a straggler."

I mingle, and drink, getting to know my father better through the anecdotes of others.

Then, suddenly, it is all over. Madge is on stage announcing that we have to be out of the hall to make way for the club bingo. She supervises plate-clearing, and the moving of chairs and tables.

We are all getting our coats and saying our goodbyes when Yeti looms. He is like a mobile wall. He is holding a pint of beer. There are crumbs round his top lip.

"Cliff," he says.

"It's Kyff," I say.

"Kyff," he says. "They call me Yeti. I've got something."

He goes into the kitchen area alongside the stage and comes out with a huge head of celery wrapped in wet newspaper.

"For you Cliff. It's best with the muck still on. It's off my plot."

"That's very kind," I tell him.

"I really loved your Dad, Cliff," he says in a pure, even, child-like way: "He used to come to the Scheme."

"Everybody loved him, Yeti," I say and then ponder on what I had said.

I walk in the fog past the Top End gates to the allotments, and head for the cheerless haunted family home.

There's something truly heart-rending about the bouquet of celery. As I lower it into the kitchen sink I think of Yeti's devotion and, for a moment, finally feel what I think normal people are supposed to feel when they've just buried their Dad.

FOURTEEN

The chill fog has lifted at last leaving everything dripping. There's a sparkle on every link of the high wire fence bounding the allotments at the Top End.

I am heading to the Post Office to send papers I've signed for Grace. The allotment gate is open and instead I find myself taking the crumbling asphalt path that wends through the plots all the way to Bottom End.

Thyme fills the crevices and pockets of the path and as I walk I pick up a herby waft.

I remember when the path was laid. It was summer and the smell on the breeze was of tar that glistened at the edges where none of the scattered shale had landed.

I stop to light a cigarette and watch a few dark figures bending, lifting, standing. The "season" is unending on the allotments, even though the plots seem to be at rest when the winter closes in.

Dad hardly missed a day here, whatever the season, whatever the weather. Those who are out and about today are gathering sprouts and parsnips ready for Christmas Day, and maybe a last surviving lettuce from under cloches.

I'm reminded of those early-winter routines – easing leeks from soft ground, taking a handful of carrots from the box of sand, twisting onions off the plaited stems hanging crisp and dry in sheds.

Midwinter onwards was what they called "the hungry gap," when the allotments were at their barest. Kale and hardy cabbages were precious stand-bys.

Other memories flood in. Because he grew so many things, Dad would mark his rows with the name of the variety written in indelible pencil.

I'd been intrigued one year by the name "Gravedigger" marking a row of peas that produced tightly packed pods with a bloom that disappeared as soon my young fingers touched them. Names intrigued me.

"Why do they call these sprouts Fillbasket, Dad?" I'd asked one frosty afternoon as I watched him in his fingerless gloves snapping off solid green globes the size of ping-pong balls.

"Because they'll give you plenty. You can pick them for a long time, all through winter. Important if you're skint. That's why there's tomatoes called Moneymaker and broad beans called Rentpayer. But that sort of thing won't be important to you and your generation..."

He made it sound as if we eight-year-olds were already showing a negligent disregard for future crops of sprouts.

I walk on and gaze at the Old Hall, which is now pristine and resplendent, even in the dullness of winter. It was built as a replacement at least two hundred years ago and, in the English way, for most of that time it was known as the "New Hall".

The trees between the plots and the hall are leafless now, so the starkness of the freshly whitened walls makes it almost luminous. The hall used to look its age, and denoted old ways; now, as swish offices, it speaks of new money, sharp dealings.

It was said that at the turn of the century the head gardener had twenty helpers, providing vegetables every day of the year, growing grapes and peaches and even raising pineapples under glass using the heat generated by rotting compost.

Lady Benton would expect fresh flowers each day, mistletoe and holly at Christmas, asparagus and strawberries in season, and stored fruit from the orchard in winter, along with walnuts and the summer's bounty captured in preserving jars.

The elderly Lord Benton, it seems, was especially partial to cobnuts, eaten fresh and green with a sprinkling of salt, and after enjoying them would ease out the Vulcanite palate of his false teeth to clear out the rubble.

Two of the estate hazels still flourish in the little clump of trees behind Dad's hut and I remember bringing home their catkins for Mum as a child.

Lord Benton donated this corner of his estate to the town council "for the benefit of the townsfolk" as a token of gratitude after his only son had survived diphtheria and, by the time of the Great War, the allotments were well established.

His lordship had decreed that townsfolk must have "free passage" through the land and one thing that had always puzzled, and pleased, me was that the paths through meandered.

It was as if someone, perhaps a council renegade, following the dictum that there were no straight lines in nature, had refused to take the shortest and easiest route from A to B.

This meant that those walking along either path – especially children – were given a sense of being enclosed in a world quite detached from what lay beyond the gates.

This feeling of being in a verdant oasis, I remember, was strongest in summer when you couldn't see out of the allotment because of the wigwams of runner beans and sweet peas, the waist-high broad beans, the sheds and fruit trees.

Directly across from the hall, perhaps a hundred yards away, over the three lines of allotments ranged along this path and either side of another roughly parallel, is the embankment carrying the mainline railway and forming a raised boundary.

As a boy I loved watching the trains go by. I was always amused that if the wind was blowing towards us, or we were at the railway side of the allotments, everyone stopped talking and looked at each other until there was just a distant clickety-click.

But the best sound was during thunderstorms when dad would call me in as the first giant spots hit the soil, and I'd sit in the dentist's chair, while dad busied himself at his bench, and hear the drumming of the rain on the shed roof.

That was an even better feeling than when gales slammed the shed door behind us and – in my imagination – drove us out into a raging sea.

I drew on my cigarette, walked on towards Bottom End, and ruminated.

How odd that in all those years I never saw the allotments from the train. The passengers' view in spring or summer, I decided, must resemble a Breughel painting – hordes of peasants digging, sowing, chatting, transplanting, hoeing, tying up, cutting down.

They would appear to populate a natural hollow broken into patterned oblongs of varying shades of green, interspersed with tiny dwellings.

It would have appeared from the train that the gardens were there to provide for the residents of the hall, and once this was the case.

Ten years back Dad trawled through old newspapers and documents and even got first-hand information from locals whose grandparents had been in service at the hall.

He created a little booklet, amateurish in its production values but capturing perfectly the flavour of the times. He had leavened the factual framework with graphic anecdotes. He had tried to make history live.

Could it be that Dad's bitterness came from a feeling that, as a natural historian, he had not fulfilled his potential and yet, through him, I had been able to?

Today the bare bones of the allotments are on show, unadorned by greenery. I find it hard to imagine that this still and silent place will come to life ever again; that the earth will warm up, the plants will flourish, the flowers will bloom.

Rationally, I know that of course it will come alive again but in my dark mood I seem to be seeking out validations for my feelings of despair.

I feel another emotion pass through me – precisely what emotion I can't decide – when I see Dad's hut. It is beyond Madge's, which is unmistakably the garish one with the sad, sopping flags and plastic toys nailed to the front.

I turn back, towards Top End and home.

There's a noise of bike brakes behind me and I turn to see Bill, ancient Bill, fall onto one leg from his bike, which was built to be ridden by someone a foot taller.

He has string holding his mac shut, and various other bits of twine on his crossbar.

He is happy to see me, and points out Dad's hut as if I'd never been to it – and as if anyone could mistake it.

It is the biggest. It has a pipe chimney, a modest lean-to greenhouse. Weather gauges. It is three times bigger than any other hut here, although Dad had cannily extended backwards so that a passer-by might not see the full extent of his empire, which had grown unchallenged by a succession of intimidated honorary secretaries.

Of course, Dad had made sure it was on a prime site, nestling in a bend and backed by trees that spill out of the grounds of the Old Hall.

I am not up to small talk today so I wish Bill a happy Christmas and head for the Top End.

"Don't be fooled by today, Kyff," he shouts after me. "This lot'll be under water by New Year."

As I near the Top End gate, Yeti waves to me and the posh man, who I think of as a retired major, lifting celery on the plot adjoining, touches his forehead in a saluting gesture.

Yeti is beaming, standing beside a shed that looks too small for him to get into, and in his fist he's carrying a spade as if it were a badminton racquet. He is draped in something knitted and bright green and wears a matching bobble hat, giving him the appearance of a giant vegetable from a TV advertisement.

My heart falls as I see Cecil walking towards me. I feel like fleeing from the prospect of chatter. It is simply too demanding but he is too nice a man to rebuff.

He raises his hand in pleasure on seeing me and hurries to me, tapping my elbow and offering to walk me round the plots. I say I'm expecting a phone call.

"Fair enough but hang on, Kyff," he says. "Something you'll need."

He strides down the path to the hut nearest the gate and, after much unlocking, emerges. "Your dad's keys – your keys – to the hut."

I mention the threat of torrential rain. Cecil says: "So Bill's down is he? You ought to know that Bill's forecasts are famous. For being wrong. Always start watering if he says rain's on the way."

Cecil turns and waves to someone in the direction of the first plot on the opposite side to his. It's the woman who was at the funeral, the attractive grey-eyed woman who was so fond of Dad.

She wears bright red wellingtons and red gloves, at odds with her solemnity as she sprinkles fertiliser by the handful from a plastic bucket. She pauses, waves back and gives us a wan smile.

"Pat," he reminds me.

"Isn't it a bit early for fertiliser?" I say.

Cecil leans forward and mouths the words: "It's not fertiliser. It's Terry."

"Terry?"

"Her husband. His wish."

Cecil brings his forefinger to his lips. "Not sure how we stand with by-laws."

I nod and turn to go, wishing Cecil a happy Christmas, when he calls after me: "I'm being treated to Christmas dinner so I can't invite you but how are you fixed for New Year's Eve?"

"Well, I…" Failing to think fast enough, I sputter: "I think, in fact I know, I'm free."

"Well come and have a drink or two. It'll be me, my daughter and three or four of the allotment lads, and Pat if I can persuade her."

I'm making my getaway again when Yeti approaches, his long woolly flapping as he hurries up with cupped hands.

"Hey Cliff!" he says.

"Kyff."

"Kyff. Just look at these little buggers…" he says, opening his big, flat hand and revealing his treasure – beans, tiny white beans to be precise, with liver-coloured patches.

"They're special. From France. Your dad gave me them and I put them in my shed in my hiding place and I've just found them. I'm going to grow them for him."

"He'd be glad about that. Anyway, Yeti, must be off now, so have a happy Christmas."

"Yea. Happy Christmas, Cliff!" he shouts, lumbering off on those big rolling haunches, his bright green, chunky hand-knit jacket buttoned up round his belly, his earth-smeared chipolata fingers closed gently round the beans, as if they were as fragile as birds' eggs.

FIFTEEN

"Come on, Kyff – you're not dying!" Grace used to say when I was under the weather and complaining more than she thought necessary.

Then she'd relent, indulge me, fetching her special grated ginger concoction if my stomach was bad, hot whisky with lemon if I had a cold.

"Bloody men. They're all the same!" she'd say, exasperated but smiling, allowing me to feel that I was not singularly pathetic.

Instead of ridiculing my tendency to hypochondria, something Becky always took pleasure in doing ("Just a common cold, Kyff, or pleurisy again?"), Grace would listen to my health niggles and allay them with reason.

I'd known since my teenage years that I exaggerate the chances of some little ailment being serious.

At thirteen or fourteen I had once gone to sleep cradling my plums, convinced that I had some terrible testicular disease. The thought of asking a pal "What do yours feel like?" to check, and the unthinkable prospect of mentioning my worry to Mum, ensured I fretted with no prospect of reassurance. Then there was the time I'd swayed back in shock from the toilet bowl at the history department Christmas party, appalled to see that my pee was exactly the colour of the kir royales the girls drank at Mamie's nightspot.

After a couple of hours of growing anxiety – fear that made me leave early so I could worry properly, away from the merry-making – I let out a gasp of relief as I remembered that at lunchtime I'd pigged out on Grace's beetroot salad.

Whenever I contemplate the human body I conclude that it is absolutely impossible for it to work as well as it does. More than miraculous.

Just think of the physiological cogs that have to move in near-perfect synchrony! That balance of finely measured juices, trace elements. The timing of internal churnings and squirts from glands.

Think of the heat exchangers, the energy generators, the transport systems carrying chemicals, blood, liquid, waste. And there's even electricity in there somewhere. It shouldn't work but miraculously it does. For a time.

Life seems to be a matter of waiting until one miniscule fault – a lazy nerve, an errant enzyme, malicious cells getting together to hatch a plot – makes the whole shebang pack up.

That's why, for me, statistical long-shots can became terrible certainties. I'm waiting for some single-minded cell to spread chaos in my bloodstream, expecting to spot some sinister misshape in the shower.

It takes only half an hour of eye-strain for me to begin to visualise the sawbones holding up an X-ray and saying: "As you see, Mr Pugh, it's now about the size of a satsuma…"

An episode of trapped wind will become inoperable bowel cancer within the hour. Once, a bout of wooziness that turned out to be caused by excess earwax – and, according to Grace, self-induced constipation – threw up the terrible certainty of neurological disease.

Becky used to laugh openly about my health fixation, and I could tell this mocking attitude rattled Grace.

One insufferably hot afternoon, out to watch some water sport on the coast, I'd got a headache (dehydration probably) and we'd been forced to take cover under a shop awning. We were all sweltering, waiting for the Fremantle Doctor to make the 100-degree days more bearable but there was not even a suspicion of a breeze.

"They said on TV the Doctor will arrive tomorrow. Thank God," Becky had said, drawing her hands down her damp cheeks. Then she'd added, sweetly but with a note of mockery, "Better book an appointment, Kyff."

No-one had laughed and, although Grace's cheeks had turned even redder than they already were from the heat and she had glowered at Becky challengingly, the reaction went unnoticed. Grace could call me a whinger but she didn't extend the right to anyone else, especially Becky.

Last night's terrors took my anxieties up several gears. If Grace had been there (if only!) and had seen me thrashing about like a diver who had lost his air hose she would have known that I was not crying wolf.

Today there is a new alert when I creep from the enveloping eiderdown into the unheated bedroom and find that I can barely straighten up.

Slipped disc. Or worse, maybe; after all, back pain can mean all sorts of things … lung trouble, kidneys, liver.

But, after adopting a Groucho Marx gait and lowering myself gingerly into a warm bath, I am able to convince myself that it is just muscular stiffness, from all the flying and Dad's jangling trampoline of a bed.

Then, half an hour later, as I put my trousers on, I get a definite feeling of compression on my inner thigh. The right thigh.

The air stewardess on the second leg of the flight had talked us through little foot-turning exercises to keep the blood moving. This is the first thing that comes to mind when I look down, appalled to see a pronounced bulge.

Should I move, or would this send the clot whizzing round my body to lodge somewhere vital? Should I creep to the phone, dial 999 and then lie doggo?

Bracing myself, I lower my hand and am in eye-rolling ecstasy to find that the swelling is simply yesterday's bunched-up underpants lodged in my trousers.

"Bless you oh merciful Father," I find myself mumbling, then wonder why, as a C of E agnostic, I'd invoked such a Catholic-sounding phrase.

All is well for the moment, except for a residual pain, a real pain, in my chest – a pain strong enough to force me to sit down.

I am huddling over coffee and toast I cannot bring myself to eat. It was produced on a museum piece, the toaster that Mum got with coupons that came with her cigarettes. I turn on the gas oven and leave the door open so the heat wafts round me.

Gloom overwhelms me as I look around the kitchen.

There's Mum's old ironing board with its cotton cover burned brown, her timber clotheshorse folded and empty. The shelf in the dark corner beside the sink where Marguerite Patten's World Cookery (a long-ago Christmas gift from me), discoloured now and probably never opened, lies beside matches, a torch, a candle, a biscuit tin, a rolling pin and pastry-cutters.

Even here, with the radio reminding me that it's early morning, I'm already dreading tonight.

I need help. A knock-out tablet. But most of all, of course, I need Grace.

It is not the best tonic when, turning up that afternoon at the surgery our family has used for fifty years, I am told by the receptionist that, having lived in Australia, I might have blotted my copy book with the health service.

"I'll check whether we can accept you," she says, frowning to show that this is not likely, as she laboriously eases herself off her high perch behind the counter.

She returns, carrying forms.

"Is it an emergency?" she asks, hardly moving her little, hard mouth, surveying me over the counter, looking for leaking blood, I suspect.

Emergency? Not sure where anguish ranks with embarrassing itches, inverted nipples or encroaching warts. It certainly feels like an emergency, this dreadful certainty that tonight I will be snuffed out as the eiderdown is transformed into engulfing waves.

"Yes," I say.

She sets off again to consult.

"Dr May will see you," she says grudgingly on her return, then, with obvious pleasure: "But there's a very long queue." I wait in case she adds: "So there!"

"I suppose Dr McLaughlin's retired now," I offer, as Little Miss Grumpy scans her computer screen and enters my details. The cheery tinsel draped round the machine contrasts starkly with her bleak features.

"Gone three or four years," she says tartly, withholding eye contact.

"Retired?"

"Dead."

"And Dr Malik?"

"Ditto."

Charming, beaming Dr Malik wiped out. Whiskery Dr McLaughlin lost without trace; silenced, the deep burbling voice that suggested he was full of gravel.

How terrible it must be for mortally sick doctors to be excluded by their knowledge from resorting to self-delusion, or hope. They can see the train coming and just have to lie on the rails knowing that it will not stop.

At last a red light beckons me to the corridor lined with consulting rooms. But the person who comes out to usher me in can't be old enough to be the doctor. A first-year student, perhaps, doing the greeting. Work experience. He looks to be one of those lads who in their late teens put on a sudden spurt of growth leaving him gawky and angular as if crane fly genes had been infused and were taking an upper hand. But, unbelievably, he is fully formed, a proper doctor. The certificate just inside the door says so.

A floral shirt covers the string-bean torso from which Dr May's long, thin white neck emerges, topped by a bespectacled head from which sprouts a wiry tangle of black hair, as if he's indulging in a youthful experiment in self-image. Generations of dads have said to lads looking like him: "You'll have to smarten up if you want a proper job."

Dr May gestures for me to sit down and, with a gleaming toothsome smile, introduces himself, bemoaning the bad weather, apologising for the wait.

"But this is the winter of their discontent…" he says, extending an arm theatrically and again showing horsey teeth as he smiles from ear to ear.

"Their" discontent suggests a mutual exclusiveness. What was it about me that made him think I'd get the Shakespearian reference, I wonder?

Grace always claimed that out of twenty people on a Perth tram she could pick out those who followed TV soaps, those who would be able to name three government ministers, those you wouldn't want to share a lifeboat with, and those who'd rather have the seven-dollar Bellybuster at Fat Mick's than tempura oysters at Chanterelles.

"We give off invisible clues," she insisted. "We don't know what the clues are, beyond dress and such," she said, "but they're there, Kyff, and I can tune into them."

Her instincts were almost always right which, in retrospect, makes the Erik business all the more difficult to understand. It was as if – urged on by Erik – she had driven up to a red light and then thought "What the hell!" and gone straight on, without looking left or right.

Dr May looks away and leaves the quiet space that doctors always allow for patients to fill; for them to launch into rehearsed descriptions, to step nervously on to a meandering route leading to the point of mentioning the unmentionable.

I'm fascinated by this man's neck with its bulbous Adam's apple that rides up and down like a shopping mall lift when he swallows. It takes me back to childhood and that comic strip ostrich that used to eat alarm clocks.

I'm also struck by the Tottenham Hotspur badge pinned to his shirt pocket.

Is this little enamel cockerel to help male patients "vocalise"?

Is it to ease the patient's discomfiture at being invited to drop his pants, crook his legs, and stay nice and relaxed while not so much a doctor but a fellow football fan inserts a rubbery digit, all this just two minutes after they've first met?

"Any chance of them getting in the top four, doc?" I could imagine a de-trousered fan, on all fours, asking over his shoulder, in an attempt to normalise the surreal routine of the haemorrhoid hunt.

"And so Mr Pugh..." says the Peter Pan of general practice, bringing me back to the little consulting room with its thank you cards, posters showing innards, the framed photo of his child bride, the (presumably) post-pubertal Mrs May.

I bluster about a bit of pain in the chest, going a bit clammy, sleeplessness.

Dr May's searching gaze is intense; I must take my eyes off his Adam's apple, I say to myself.

He listens to my chest, feels around my front, then takes my pulse and reaches for the blood pressure monitor. As he puts on the cuff he stops and grips my bicep.

"Wow! Tension. You're all primed to spear a mammoth. Or run like the clappers."

His probing gaze makes me uncomfortable.

"Smoker?" he asks.

Has he heard something suspicious in my chest?

"Just in the last few weeks," I reply, my voice lowered in shame.

"You mean you've just taken it up? At this time of life?"

"I'd been off them but I had a bit of stress and strain and I started again."

There's a hiss from the machine. He looks at the reading and utters something about an error. He tries again and then grimaces and takes in air.

"Not good," he says, shaking his shaggy head. "Not good at all."

He asks me if "anything" has been going on in my life lately and coaxes from me the fact that I've come from Australia for the funeral, that I'd had a bit of upset before that and that I'm not sure what the future holds.

I steer well clear of marital mayhem and the nocturnal feeling of suffocation, subjects much too private to broach, even with someone wearing a cockerel badge.

"First, you've had the upheaval and stress of having to rush here, you've probably been unsettled by the flight. That can upset your system. And that pain. A bit of reflux, I think, acid coming up and trying to digest you. It can feel like a heart attack."

He lowers his voice for the more serious message.

"But we mustn't discount grief. We tend to minimise the effect of emotions on the body, things like grief. Some men think they can tough it out, put it to one side. But it won't go away until the process is over."

He spins back round to the desk, scribbles on a pad and holds up a prescription.

"This," he says, "will give almost immediate pain relief if you get that burning feeling. And with it there's a little something, something mild, just to take the edge off things for a week or two."

He turns his chair so that he is square on, and says quite gravely:

"I want you to come back immediately if you feel you need to, and I'll see you in a fortnight anyway. Meanwhile, don't be surprised if you feel that you're struggling to get your head round the finality of your loss. It's quite natural.

"You might get angry and not understand why, or get feelings of remorse, and dwell on things you'd have liked to have said. It will all ease over time."

He pauses to smile sympathetically.

"You'll probably find yourself wrapped up with memories of the person who has gone, and might even imagine you can see them. That's surprisingly common."

He looks straight at me, searching my face to see what is going on behind it.

"And, look, do have a blubber! Quite normal. Big boys do cry, and they're better for it."

Whippersnapper that he is, he talks sense. I'm touched. I feel tears tickling behind my eyelids, wanting to be released, so I concentrate hard on Doc May's mesmeric voice box, and wonder how much static electricity his hair must generate.

I stand up. He finally hands me the prescription and pats my shoulder.

"Remember – feel free to come back any time," he says, with disturbing sincerity.

"Oh, and exercise will help."

Once outside, I take a deep breath, feeling better from having had a health problem validated – a rare treat.

He was right about the desolation that comes from being bereaved, and it wasn't his fault that he was wrong over a single detail.

How was he to know that my grieving is not for Dad?

SIXTEEN

"Oh, my dear Kyff, I was so very sorry to hear the news!"

I bolt down my half-chewed toast and pull the old stool up to the phone table.

It's Grace's mum, sounding appalled.

"I would have phoned you earlier, Kyff, but Grace only let me know in the night."

Mary has a sweet and sympathetic nature and I know she means what she says. From the moment Grace took me home for the first time and Mary showed off by serving her famed steak and kidney pudding, then proudly walked me round the village, we had enjoyed an open, supportive relationship.

We were on a joint mission, of course – caring for Grace – and on our visit to Wiltshire just after we lost Lizzie we grew close, colluding to find ways to ease Grace's pain, to bring her back.

Mary will be deeply sorry to know that it is all over.

I am ready to offer a few anodyne words – something philosophical about our having grown apart over the years – but luckily the split second spent forming a sentence left time for Mary to say: "Dear Huw, bless him! I didn't even have the chance to send flowers, or a card."

So Grace had rung her mum about Dad's death but not mentioned the break-up? Perhaps she had no way of making it sound anything but crazy.

"I just can't believe that Grace didn't ring me straight away. Poor Huw," Mary says.

Mary wants to know of any other news but she especially wants to know how Grace is, whether she's getting back to being "the Grace we know and love".

She says: "It's so hard to judge in phone calls. I would be able to tell by her face."

The lies come easily. She seems brighter, I say, more interested in life, not retreating into herself so much.

"Anyway, Kyff, please come down if you've time on your hands," Mary says warmly. "Why not get a train down on New Year's Eve? I'd have the Scrabble board ready!"

I was to count on her, she says, if I need any loose ends tying up after returning to Perth.

"Oh, and Grace told me to tell you she's going to ring tomorrow night when it's two-ish here – if you can stay up! The phone lines will be hot from Oz."

So Grace will be ringing.

Staying awake might be a challenge. The "mild" tablets have not only taken the edge off things. They have deadened me, not unpleasantly, and kept me unconscious through the night.

Yet I feel a terrible heaviness this morning. I need coffee but can barely find the strength to get out of bed to make it. When I do, I take it back to bed and it goes cold while I lie, eyes open, in the half-light.

I suspect this is not the effect of the tablets; it's me. Over the past few days, when I stay still, I've had feelings of being weightless and untethered, floating away from the world. The tablets haven't made this go away.

The feeling is back now but it passes, and the space pictures I once saw at an exhibition in Perth flow in front of me.

It was called the "Our City of Light" and it was celebrating the time that Perth was discovered by the rest of the world.

It was in the early sixties, when the Empire Games were held there, and when John Glenn looked down from space on what was then a smallish city and saw it as a shining patch in the blackness.

The residents had switched on all their lights to make him feel less alone. This gesture warmed the communal heart of America and overnight for them and the rest of the world Perth became the City of Light.

I remember the photographs of Apollo, and a vast mural of the craft, tiny and white, showing against a night sky. A recording of Glenn was playing...

"Thank everyone for turning the lights on will you?" he was telling mission control matter-of-factly. He sounded as composed as if he was driving the family car.

Why wasn't he beating his fists against the walls of his prison, soiling his spacesuit and pleading to be brought back to earth? I'm more scared here under the eiderdown than he was of being vaporised.

Even thinking about the mural now I get a vivid sense of the enormity and emptiness of space and it gives me palpitations. My appreciation of it is unbearably real.

I put on the radio to distract myself and have a cigarette, which flutters in my shaking fingers.

Perhaps I am going mad.

"Can I help?" asks the receptionist briskly, signalling by her tone that she doesn't really want to help at all.

I tell her I would like to see Dr May, whereupon she tells me that there isn't a spare appointment and I tell her that I will see him, and will stay until I do. I sound like a psychopath. I stop just short of telling her that she has all the charm of the open grave.

She scuttles off, looking back, wide-eyed with alarm, as if I'd brought rabies into the surgery. Maybe I should have checked my chin for foam.

She returns.

"Half an hour. Please watch for your name."

Truly, the spirit of Christmas is about, wreathing the winter's day with twinkling smiles and goodwill...

Dr May only has time to greet me at the door, say my name and, hand on shoulder, lower me on to the chair before I belatedly accept his invitation to blubber.

It turns out to be the blubber to end all blubbers.

He sits and watches silently for what must have been a minute. I can't speak anyway, heaving and gasping, my elbows on my knees, trying to stifle my sobs with the paper handkerchiefs he is passing me.

The tidal wave of tears begins to ebb away and, looking up, I see Dr May – in a very Christmassy floral shirt, complete with his Spurs badge – regarding me benignly.

"Good!" he says at last, offering me a final hanky.

"I fancy that was long overdue, Mr Pugh."

Now all dignity has been lost I feel free to sing like a canary as he starts his nice-guy interrogation.

I'm amazed to hear myself talking about Grace, my regrets about Dad and the way we had been, my new and frightening feeling of aloneness. I begin to try to describe the night terrors but falter because I fear what he will think or do. Mental hospital? Psychiatrists?

I dry up. He nods to encourage me.

"Well," I say, "it was as if I was a goldfish flapping on the kitchen floor unseen by people around me and having no way of telling them that I was dying."

Judging by his expression and approving nod, Dr May seems to find this description memorable.

He lets me ramble, occasionally guiding me one way or another into corners of my mind I hadn't been prepared to visit.

"Just one thing," he says firmly. "Tell me honestly: Have you had any ... well, thoughts about freeing yourself from all this? I think you know what I mean."

"Suicide? No, just despair I suppose. A feeling that I don't belong here – or down there in Perth, as a matter of fact. I'm in limbo. I just don't fit anywhere. I feel orphaned in every sense."

"Everyone needs to feel they belong," says Dr May almost under his breath.

Turning to his prescription pad, he announces - superfluously perhaps, but possibly to bestow on me the label I crave, so that I know I'm legitimately ill - that I am depressed. That I need a course of tablets, that I must be patient. That I should try to make plans, find a hobby, and exercise every day.

"Some philosopher said that the cure for hopelessness lies in giving form to something, and he was right," says Dr May, handing me the prescription, shaking my hand, and urging me to come back early in the New Year.

"Despite everything, I wish you a happy Christmas," he says with a kindly, toothy smile and a slow, sliding upward elevation of his voice box.

As he opens the door for me he touches my shoulder.

That touch should go in the medical school training manual. It felt, well, not really like hope being passed on, but something I was sure the tablets would not match.

Home is where the heartache is

THE HEALING HUT

ONE

Of course we never know how we'll go – we don't get a say, except when we choose to go for a planned exit and choose the departure date and the means.

Pushed for my preference, I'd want to go like Dad did, zonked by a flaw in his internal plumbing. But not, please God, by drowning.

Just about any other means of departure would be preferable – and I've thought a lot about it.

Turned to steam in an exploding aircraft, accidentally overdosing on headache tablets, falling under a train. Being lulled to sleep by exhaust fumes, or even something exotic like being restrained and playfully inflated by air hose-wielding garage mechanics; amazingly, there are precedents.

("How did Granddad die?"

"He was blown up, dear"

"In the war?"

"No, at Tyre Swop")

Naturally, a high-speed dispatch would be appreciated e.g. falling from a height, maxing at the optimum 125 mph, if I remember my physics. Not too great a height, mind. I once read a news report of an inquest into an airman's death. His parachute had failed to open and the air force people told of finding deep scratch marks from fingernails round the pack. Much too much time to think.

So, when my time's up, any of the above would be acceptable. Anything, anything that is, but drowning.

Here, in Dad's bedroom, I feel hollow and utterly alone. Being in limbo has stirred up my anxiety.

I no longer smoke cigarettes, I devour them. I sit on the bed under the weak light from a dust-laden shade and think about death – Mum's, Lizzie's and Dad's – and, disturbingly, feel genuine envy that they're out of the fray.

Hence the vivid imaginings of the various ways of dying. In my present state of mind I can weigh up each objectively (though fearfully) – except that terrible slow suffocation by water.

Tonight my most-feared phobia came out for an airing and here I am, hours later, still in awe of the terror it generated.

I ask myself the question I fancy a therapist would be sure to use as a key to my unconscious and answer it :Well, yes, there was an incident involving water.

The close encounter happened when I was at Cambridge.

We'd been to the summer ball and at dawn a rowdy bunch of us were staggering round the Backs carrying champagne stolen from a caterer's tent.

We ended up wrestling and rolling in the dew beside the Cam and childishly shouting meaningless phrases in the way that the most eloquent and cleverest young people in the country tend to do.

Evidently, I passed out on the bank and slowly slid unnoticed into the shallows. I came round half in and half out of the water, gasping and throwing wild punches. It felt as if someone was trying to pull my head off; in fact it was Charlie saving my life.

Drunk as I was, that terrible feeling of being denied O_2 by H_2O remains pristine, encased in a bubble of memory.

"Ten seconds or so and then you can be unconscious," declared Charlie in the pub a few days later.

"That's the time you have for self-pity and religious conversion when something stops oxygen reaching the brain," he pronounced from behind a cheroot, with all the gravitas befitting a second-year trainee medic.

"But theoretically," he added, propelling smoke from his nose, "some really fit drowning people might hold their breath for a minute or more, I suppose.

"That's an untidy drowning, when the whole business takes longer because they're snatching the odd mouthful of air. Of course they get exhausted, or get cramp. And they take in water when they shout. That's what tends to get them."

Killed by a cry for help. Ten seconds. Time enough, while you're taking in water, to comprehend what is happening or, like a mortally wounded soldier, to surface and with your last gasp call for your mother.

But a minute of struggling? That's enough time for hope to flicker and then be dowsed by the frantic thrashing. Then there's still time left over to know that all is lost, to picture faces, regret shameful acts, even time to promise God that if you're spared you will devote your life to Him – and time enough to know that the offer has not even warranted an acknowledgement.

"This business of going down for the third time…?" I asked.

"Pure balls!" said Charlie, decisively, through a curtain of smoke. "How would they organise scientific observation for that idea? 'Right, that's twice, now let's see if the bugger comes up for a third time…'"

Charlie took out the cheroot and laughed so much he began to cough uncontrollably.

I think that back in Australia there was a better-than-average chance of drowning – if you weren't nailed first by a snake or killer bee, the two most popular ways of dying by what goes under the official title of "misadventure".

When we first came to Perth, Grace and me spent our holidays exploring and learned that Oz has got more lethal nasties than anywhere on earth. That includes sharks and crocs.

Just before I left, in The West Australian, there was a small news item about a boy who had been blissfully gliding on his board in Bunker Bay when he was bitten in half by a shark. Unthinkable. But in my book he was spared a fate worse than bisection: drowning.

I had wanted to tell Grace about it (and, out of habit, had almost called out to her) but the days of reading out news snippets to each other had passed.

But, months before, we'd shaken our heads empathetically over the report of the poor girl who had taken a quick dip in a billabong in Kakadu Park to cool off and was killed by a croc.

Butchered. But at least she didn't drown.

Saltwater crocs have the common decency to hold their victims above water level until they have torn them into bite-sized bits.

In fact I've just discovered what drowning is really like – and don't let anyone try to tell you that you can't experience it in a bedroom.

My heart is still racing. My cigarette is wobbling between my fingers and there's a ripple on the surface of my whisky. Dad's whisky, Penderyn brand, "the spirit of Wales" – I came across it yesterday on a low shelf sharing space with copies of Garden News and Wales of Yesteryear.

I was dog-tired and my head was filled with all the activity and emotion of the day. I wanted just to sit in Dad's old winged chair and think, blur things with a drink, and then sleep.

When I looked round I realised that, if eventually I sell the house, this entire stage set where silent, daily rituals have been performed for more than forty years – tea-making, fire-stoking, rug-shaking, clothes-airing – will disappear.

Like many terraced houses built in the twenties it has languished in permanent semi-darkness, surrounded by walls that are too high. The sunless backyard has a sub-climate – permanently moist and gloomy where brave ferns find sustenance in the crevices of dividing walls.

Things could have been improved but Dad was not an improver; he was the ultimate functionalist. If it still served a purpose it didn't need replacing. Hence the chipped Formica-topped table, the wooden breadboard that had suffered ten thousand cuts, the jazz cassettes with their faded covers, and the deep, echoing, chipped sink that is older than me.

His obstinacy over such things had been one of many running sores with Mum.

She was ashamed of the yellowing touch-up dots that covered chips on the bath; she hated the pale green glassy tiles above it. She wanted rid of the solid inner doors with their ball catches and to have glass replacements that made the best of what little light there was.

Dad had the perfect defence: silence. He simply didn't respond. He shut his ears and put on his favourite Parry Band cassette, or his Sidney Bechet CD, or he made a big thing of trying to find something worthy and self-improving on the old TV.

Eventually Mum became silent too, about most things. The marriage seemed to have declined and, with anger exhausted and passion spent, become co-existence. I saw them as cell-mates who had agreed that it was mutually beneficial that they follow a routine that had courtesy and function at its heart.

When I try to retrieve memories of being in their company the pictures have no soundtrack. I do not remember what they said to each other because everything they said was mundane.

There was just one day when they were shaken out of their sullenness.

I was perhaps seven or eight and came downstairs, after changing out of my school uniform, just as Dad came home. I'd broken up that afternoon for half-term.

Mum said very quietly: "Have you heard?" and Dad replied grimly "Yes."

Nothing more was said then, but I knew this was about death.

Mum was nearly ready to serve dinner. It was always fish on Fridays.

Dad went towards the wireless and said, more warmly than usual: "Can we leave it till we've heard the news?"

Mum nodded and said: "It'll all be on the TV..."

Dad turned to me then gave Mum a look that, I suppose, was meant to say that I should be shielded from some horrible image but I've since wonder whether Dad himself was too afraid to see pictures of the disaster.

Dad turned on the wireless and sat down in his wingback chair; Mum switched off the gas under the pans and sat on the edge of the settee with her hands bunched in her pinny.

The announcer said that a huge mudslide had covered a school in Wales and more than a hundred children and their teachers were trapped underneath and hope for any of them was fading.

"Pantglas, Glenys," Dad said, shaking his head. "It was Pantglas School!"

He was staring into Mum's face intently, as if he could not believe what the newsreader was saying and needed her to tell him that what he was hearing was true.

To me, as a child, Dad's look was worrying. I had never seen him show a trace of weakness but at that moment he seemed no braver than me, a child.

Mum had tears in her eyes.

"The poor little souls," she said, then I remember her looking startled, and saying:"Trefor's Gavin will have known some of them. Dear God."

"And Glenys's kids," Dad said.

Two other things stuck in my mind from that time. Someone came on the radio and said that the mudslide was higher than a house, and that the children had just come out of assembly where they'd sung All Things Bright and Beautiful.

When singing was mentioned, Mum started to cry properly and Dad got up. I thought he was going to put his arm round her but instead he went to the window and said: "Suffer little children to come unto me..." and then let out a sound I can't describe.

When I lay in bed, there was a droning noise downstairs. It was Mum and Dad talking, something I was not used to.

Next morning, after breakfast, Dad went out and returned with two newspapers. He sat in his chair and read silently and then put on his jacket and hurried off without a word.

On Sunday morning, again he brought newspapers home. This time he spread the pages on the dining room table, devouring every word, his face a dour mask.

Suddenly, with a sweep of his hand, he clawed together the papers, screwed them up and threw them on the floor. Mum looked frightened and led me into the kitchen.

"Bastard," we heard him say, under his breath. I knew the word because Ken at school always said it.

It was only when I grew up and read up about the disaster that I realised his target must have been the Coal Board chairman, Lord Robens, who failed to rush to the weeping parents of Aberfan. Evidently his officials lied as they tried to cover for him. That would explain why when Dad stormed off, slamming the back door, he used a word I'd never heard before.

"Toadies!" he shouted.

I took the tumbler of whisky upstairs and had a last cigarette, then gathered the eiderdown from Mum's bed and, shedding my trousers, slipped into the chilled bed.

I was dreaming when the cold woke me.

There was a young teacher, with a skull-cap of dark hair and severe fringe (Becky, I think).

She was at the front of the class and I was a pupil, the only one in adult form, and the only one with a bare bum. We were cross-legged on the floor. My friend Col was rubbing his knees as he always did when he was excited.

She held up a piece of card. On it she'd written: How We Used To Live.

"When we go to the old house I'll be asking you to look out for lots of things. Tick your boxes as you find them." She then gave out sheets of paper.

I feel I'm going to wet myself so I hold up my hand but the teacher ignores me. When she spots me, she stares disapprovingly at my big, white cottage-loaf thighs, throws her head back and tut-tuts in disgust.

Yes, it was Becky.

I woke with a gasp, as if surfacing from the escape hatch of a submarine; the bedroom had become airless. I hurried to the window and checked that it would open if I needed to take a breather. I sat in the dark trying to compose myself, the eiderdown round my shoulders, having a cigarette, taking a few swigs of drink, then tried to settle again to sleep.

My next sensation was of careering out of the bed as if fleeing for life itself. I was choking, tearing open my shirt, throwing myself towards the window, then clawing at the glass while the last precious air left me and my lungs imploded, or that's how it seemed.

I gasped in the vacuum around me and somehow managed to open the window. But even the beautiful astringent shock of the cold night air didn't ease the very real feeling that my heart and lungs were shutting down.

I knelt at the window, head on the windowsill, trembling and overcome by a sense of being beyond any help. I was unable to move for perhaps ten minutes. I clung to the window ledge, frozen through, shivering and whimpering.

Now, eventually, I dare to crawl to the light switch, gathering the eiderdown and the whisky and my cigarettes, pulling the window to but not daring to close it.

Maybe I can escape into my head? I concentrate hard on picturing Cottesloe Beach, the ridiculously huge sky, and of enjoying a relaxed Sunday feeling.

And I think of Grace, on her blanket reading, lying propped up on one elbow, at our favourite spot, the little patch of lawn – a corner of a hotel garden really – almost enclosed by trimmed hedges but allowing a clear view of the rays of sun zig-zagging on the ocean.

Silent but content, reading together and each in turn looking to the sea when we wanted to give our eyes a break.

Sleep comes and the rest of the dream of school begins to play in my head.

We are holding our pens and sheets, and Becky has led us into our kitchen. I still have my maroon school uniform jumper on but nothing else. No-one seems to be concerned but I am ashamed.

Dad is sitting at the table, motionless, his back to us, his head in his hands.

"What's that next to the gentleman's elbow? Look at your drawings children!" Becky urges.

"Yes, it's called a tea strainer. Now, when we go upstairs look for an eiderdown and a bolster and a big hot water bottle made of clay."

I hesitate to go up because of the view my bare rump would present to the classmates behind me, so I bring up the rear, so to speak, tugging my jumper down as far as it will go.

When I come down the old man is still there, head clasped round his forehead. He looks as if he has been rendered near-lifelike by a taxidermist.

"Now, look carefully children. Do you notice anything about the gentleman?" says Becky.

"He's very sad, Miss," offers a small gingery pupil, mournfully lowering her eyes.

Colin steps up and puts his arm round the girl, who has begun to cry.

"Well done, Suzy! Yes, the old man is sad," says Becky, adding that annoying chirrup of a laugh she has.

"That's because he's dead," she adds matter-of-factly. "He's called Kyff. Now isn't that a funny name?!"

TWO

"Sorry. Were you asleep, Kyff?"

"Only dozing."

"Sorry."

"No problem. I've got out of the habit of sleeping. "

"You spoke to Mum?"

"Yeah. Difficult. I'd no bloody idea you hadn't told her, Grace. I nearly blurted it out."

"I've been putting it off. She'll be heartbroken."

"She won't if she knows you're going to be happier."

"Heartbroken for us. For you, Kyff"

"I'll keep in touch. There's no reason not to. She's done nothing."

"But I have ... Did the funeral go OK?"

"As funerals go. Madge had sorted everything, bless her. I noticed your flowers."

"I should have been there."

"I managed nicely."

"All the same..."

....

"How hot is it there?"

"Usual. About thirty-six degrees. Usual bushfire reports on TV. Have you got snow?"

"No. It's quite warm. Abnormal. But cloudy every day and there's going to be a hard frost."

"Frost. It makes me envious. I've been thinking a lot lately about the weather back home."

"I have too. Perth 'home', I mean."

....

"Did you manage to get a list of stuff you want me to ship?"

"Not yet. Not really been up to doing it. Not been so well."

"Flu?"

"No, a bit of … well, a bit of a breakdown actually."

"A breakdown? Kyff – a breakdown?"

"I suppose as usual you'll think it's all in my head. Well, it is. This time, evidently, I'm pretty ill (I was nearly going to say crook). In the head."

"But Kyff. A breakdown…"

"Well, the doctor calls it depression but when you're crying all over the place and hallucinating and wanting to curl up and die it amounts to the same thing. A breakdown by any other name."

"Kyff, I did it to you. How will you manage?"

"I've got tablets."

"No, I mean, you need support."

"The tablets will do the job."

....

"We'll have to get computers sorted Kyff. I know we've always been Luddites but the web really is brilliant. We could exchange emails."

"I've got no messages to send."

"It's just that there's going to be so much we're going to have to deal with over the next few months. You haven't ceased to be a human being I care about."

"I don't really want to communicate."

"But Kyff…"

"No offence. Ignorance is far from bliss but it's better than knowing details. Knowing things can be agony."

"But the phone's no good, the post takes an age and there's so much to sort out. I'm not sure what to say to people, how to answer letters you're getting."

"Well, Grace, none of it was my idea. Just tell people that they found my clothes on Cottesloe Beach but no sign of me."

"Not funny, Kyff."

"You can tell them that I'm sliding irrevocably into insanity if you want."

"You've every reason to be bitter."

"In fact you can tell them that I'm on the wrong side of insanitary too. I still can't work the bloody washer."

"It's simple, Kyff."

"Everything white is as grey as buggery. Or fawn. Lots of things have turned fawn."

"You need help, Kyff. You know, I didn't realise so many people cared so much, mainly about you. And I didn't realise we have so many good friends."

"Had so many good friends. People who cared. Past tense."

....

"The thing is, Kyff, the letters keep coming and people keep ringing. A couple of students keep pestering me for news of you."

"It will be Sharon and Lily. That touches me in a way that nothing else touches me at the moment."

"You'll know work's suspended your salary. Now they've written to me, because you haven't answered them. And those people from that European history conference thing have been nagging about dates…"

"Just cancel. Tell them I went off one night in a car with a dodgy clutch, and turned off the Connie May Highway, and while they were searching for me in the desert you found my water bottles at home…"

"Talking like that doesn't help, Kyff."

"And what does help, Grace?"

"Seriously, what about your stuff, personal things…?"

"I'll put a list together when I feel less of a zombie. Honestly, Grace, right now none of it matters."

"I'm planning to sell eventually if that's OK. New start somewhere."

"Fine. But listen. Once we've settled things, you and Erik can do what the hell you like. But in the meantime I don't want him touching anything, repeat anything, of mine. Obviously you excluded yourself from that some time ago."

"He won't."

"I can't bear to think of him there."

"Don't worry. He's not."

"He's not what?"

"Here. He went back to Becky."

"Oh."

"She took tablets. Twice."

"Oh dear. So it's over. You and him."

"Yes."

"Oh."

"I can't believe it ever happened, any of it. I think that I must have gone insane for a bit."

"Join the club."

....

"So you're on your own for Christmas?"

"Yes. Just going for long walks at the beach. And doing a lot of thinking. What about you?"

"Trying not to think. Bed. Trying to keep warm. Trying to do some washing that doesn't come out dirtier than it went in."

"Don't mix things, Kyff. Do white things together."

"Then a bit of oblivion would be nice. But I'll certainly not be doing any thinking. Doctor's orders. I've done too much thinking."

"Kyff. I can't forgive myself."

....

"Talking about forgiveness. Tell me something Grace. Do you ever blame me for Lizzie? For not getting you to hospital quickly enough? I think about it..."

"No Kyff! No. Don't ever think that. It was one of those things. Nobody's fault."

"Just needed to know. I just had this feeling, especially as you changed so much after Lizzie."

"God no!"

"You see, Grace, I thought Erik might have been my penance, that without knowing it you were punishing me."

"No. No. Erik was a terrible, unforgiveable mistake."

"Yes."

....

"I have a theory, Kyff - not an excuse mind. A theory about me and my state of mind. About the way you cared for me exactly the way my dad used to care. Unconditional love. That I reacted against it."

"Isn't a lot of love a good thing?"

"Yes but I think I felt guilty about always being on the receiving end of all that, well, cherishing, especially during all those months after we lost Lizzie. And especially as I failed to give you the reward of her."

"It was given freely. I thought that's what it was all about. Caring for each other."

"I know. But that wasn't enough to stop me wanting to cut off that, well, dependency, to see if I could cope without you holding me up like a sodding lifebelt. You know Kyff - now it feels as if it was me who took a fork in the road even though I knew it led to the desert."

"I understand."

"It's not easy to analyse, Kyff, but I had this sense that I should free you up, out of love for you."

....

"Are you still there Kyff?"

"I'm here."

....

"Well. I suppose it's ridiculous to be saying happy Christmas. But happy Christmas anyway. Get well, Kyff. And remember - keep things separate."

"Too late - there's nothing left that's white. Everything's spoiled. It's all fawn. Or grey. Anyway, happy Christmas."

THREE

Cecil doesn't need to keep trying to convince me that Dad's hut is special but he does. I'm not the only one to think of it as a shrine. After all, it's where Dad's real life was lived, in effect, and going into it now is like opening his diary, reading old love letters.

He's soaked deep into the timbers like preservative. It suddenly strikes me - those floorboards have been creaking to his tread for the best part of a lifetime.

It has been his winter refuge, his office, his workshop, his thinking space, his seed bank, his archive, his library.

It's the coalescing of person and place that makes Dad's hut special in an indescribable way. Any warmth I can generate for him seems to be channelled through the medium of this edifice of bomb-damage timber hammered and screwed together.

In fact, I can't for a moment separate the man from his priest hole, his safe house – his true home.

When I think of the hut, I see Dad, when I think of Dad I only ever picture him in or around his hut. Dad and the hut are intertwined in symbiotic harmony.

Finally, it is just a hut. But it's a grand, well-maintained, roomy hut.

If it wasn't on council land I could sell it, just as people sell those beach huts at the coast for as much as a family home.

"Imposing hut to rear of corner plot with coppice behind, and view of Old Hall. Main reception room has storage, bench, windows, one of stained glass (reclaimed, Victorian?).

This room gives way to a storage area with tool racks and shelving, opening at rear, on to a lean-to greenhouse.

Plot stocked with asparagus, blackcurrants, strawberries, raspberries, horseradish, Jerusalem artichokes etc; timber rack supporting loganberries etc.

Tenant, who has relocated, has left period dentist's chair, seed cabinets, collection of objects trouvez, gardening books, weather log books and (bottled gas) ring, plus small cast iron stove. Facility of stand pipe beside path."

I turn the key in the second of the two locks and as I walk in I make a clumping noise on the floorboards.

The wind is getting up, and I can feel it rooting around in the cavity beneath the floor, trying to lift the hut. Yet it is so very still and peaceful inside, apart from the occasional startling slap of the gale hitting the hut side.

My nose is assailed. Sawdust; gas; mildew; damp soil; Jeyes Fluid, paraffin, and a sharp smell that I suspect is rodent urine. And there's the whiff of garlic; the bulbs hang from papery, plaited stems on a nail at the door.

Garlic and death. I dig around in my mind for a connection and recall that it was the ancient Egyptians always ensured that there was garlic in their tombs.

I think how fitting it would be for this hut to have been dad's tomb. For him to have simply been left where he went down, cocooned by his hut with the things he had held precious in his life, and allowed to go on his eternal journey. Somehow more spiritually uplifting than the chipboard confines of the Benton Funeral Service "Option B" coffin.

Weak light permeating through the old stained glass window is throwing pools of red and blue on to the bookshelves.

The sight of Dad's bench makes me stop in my tracks. Envelopes for storing seeds lie scattered and the hardboard surface is covered with seeds, with only one irregular-shaped area cleared, as if by a sliding elbow, or Dad's head.

The hut looks to be unchanged from how it was when Grace and me came last time but now there are old net curtains across the clear windows. These would have enabled Dad to look out but stop others looking in.

And there are far more curiosities on the shelves on top of the old chest of drawers.

When I was a boy, Dad had a shelf devoted to bits of crockery, old buttons, horseshoes – bits that he found as he dug his plot.

By the time I set off for Cambridge, the collection had grown to include stuff from every corner of the allotments – I remember the fragments of porcelain, a musket ball, a flattened snuff box, an oyster shell. They will all still be here somewhere.

It was clear that Dad, the amateur historian, had unwittingly become curator of a collection that told the story of the land that was once part of a thriving country estate.

I suspect he was curious about them in a detached, forensic way. Conversely I (the young aspiring professional) marvelled at the fact that, more than a hundred years ago, not just a nameless labourer but a person, with hopes and fears and passions, had smoked the very clay pipe whose brown-stained bowl lay there on the shelf, full of soil.

In fact, as a teenager, the shelves displaying bits of Willow Pattern pots and shards of china teacups, the copper nails, and a pot egg that would be put under broody hens helped to consolidate my fancy to study history.

I wanted to follow trails that took me into the very presence of people who had gone before, to find out if I could pick up the sound of their voices, conjure them up from their handwriting.

Now the path had led me back to where it all started.

I take the kettle to the tap, fill it, find teabags in an old cigar box, rinse

Dad's cup and, with my tea and my cigarette, sit back in the old dentist's chair and listen to the wind buffeting the side of the shed.

The comforting feeling of security that comes from being shielded from the wildness out there seems to hark back to an ancient instinct to find shelter.

From the chair I can see Dad's journals, notebooks with each year written on the front, but I cannot bring myself to delve, just as I hesitate to open drawers.

I go out to throw away the teabag and rinse the cup and the gusts of wind take my breath away. Bill is riding – trying to ride – along the path from the Bottom End. Every so often the wind brings him to a stop and he falls from the high saddle onto the bowed leg.

As I lock up, and he reaches the hut, he takes another tumble.

"Just popped down to turn a bit over. I always leave it in clods and let Jack Frost get the bad back breaking it down."

"Good idea," I say.

He holds on to his cap and casts a rheumy eye over the haze of young weeds that has started to cover dad's patch.

"You need to be bending your back a bit, by the look of it. Huw was struggling to get on top of the digging at the end."

I say that I certainly need the exercise. Chastened, I make a mental pledge to do some weeding.

He raises his good leg and, with great concentration and effort, gets it over the crossbar.

"Bill…" I say, "isn't that saddle a bit high for you? We could lower it."

"Not at all. Made to measure. Rough enough now but she'll be as meek as a lamb by teatime, you just watch." And he is off, standing on the pedals and moving at snail's pace into the gale.

There is an example there for me, I can see. The fighting spirit. Picking yourself up again when you get blown over, refusing to stay down. But it is an example for later – when I can see a good reason to fight.

As I head for the Top End gate and home I notice that the door of Yeti's shed is partly open. His shed resembles a sentry box and I'm puzzled why in this strong wind the door is not slamming. I decide to secure it anyway but as I approach I see a huge pair of feet – Yeti is inside.

"Getting out of the wind for a minute, Yeti?" I ask.

He is sitting perfectly still on a box and the shed sides are tight to his shoulders.

"No, Cliff, I'm watching for vangals. Harry at the railway side had his sprouts kicked down last night."

As I walk away he draws the door to him as far as it will go, like a shy child on the lav. He doesn't seem to grasp the fact that his herring-box feet are on show.

"I'll learn 'em if I catch 'em!" he shouts, his voice muffled, like a ventriloquist's dummy that keeps protesting after being put back in the suitcase.

"See you, Cliff!" he calls, and then resumes his silent vigil.

Back at what is home but never feels like it, I settle in front of the television just as the regional weather forecast comes on.

I wait to hear of the winds weakening as Bill promised but see instead a TV reporter on a bridge, her hair swept out horizontally like a windsock.

She is shouting a warning, above the gale. We should all batten down the hatches and await tonight's near-hurricane gusts.

FOUR

"Let's not wait until I'm back in harness after the break," says Ken brightly. "Let's have a pint in town, Kyff, and get things going."

The sparkiness of old is still there.

"They've got Golden Slumbers on tap at the Druids. Pure nectar," says my learned friend. "It'll be a change from that Australian piss." His laugh, down the phone, sounds even more insane than I remember it.

"Oh, and sorry to hear about your dad, Kyff," Ken adds, with as much empathy as he is capable of. "I always watched my mouth when I used to call for you. Your old dad could be … well, shall we say, a bit direct?"

So I have sorted out a lawyer. After weeks of inertia I have taken a leap forward. Dr May would approve.

I feel pleased, as I put the phone down, to have an official ally to help unpick the strands that had held my old life together.

Ken Curtis, twinkle-toed centre forward, arch hoaxer, my sixth-form pal, would be a nicely non-stuffy choice for tidying up my "affairs", although he is the last person on earth I'd talk with about the broken bits inside. Unless he's changed, his interest in women stops once he gets up to the neck.

Until I went to university Ken and me had been sporting team mates, fiercely competitive squash opponents and formidable beer swillers. I have no illusions: our friendship was not deep, founded as it was on manly pursuits, bravado and generally considering ourselves wittier and wickeder than your average. Ken stood out, just as Erik did.

When he was a schoolboy, on the football field you could spot him a mile off. Pigeon-toed gait, mop of black hair. Enormous white shorts – when he broke into his quicksilver runs it was as if a line of washing was threading itself through the opposition defence.

But there must be at least a hundred people still out there – my contemporaries, dads and mums now – who best remember Ken for a minor scandal. Low as I am at the moment, I can still summon a grin at the memory.

Ken was a demagogue, clever but not bookish, daringly inventive in his disobedience. He was the first in the class to have facial hair and, if not the first to have spontaneous erections, a pioneer in demonstrating to the uninitiated Nature's amazing hydraulic potential.

Looking back, I can see that he was probably clinically off his head much of the time – a teacher's nightmare because of his razor intellect, outrageous charm and his guile in turning the tables on school staff.

The Ken's Knob affair happened at the end of the third year.

Our school soccer team had run rampant and won three trophies – mainly thanks to Ken's shooting boots – and one day we were asked to bring in our kit for a photo to be taken.

The photographer stood us against the school wall, arranging the defenders at the back and us forwards down on our haunches with the trophies in front of us. We were told to fold our arms.

"Be happy, lads!" said the photographer. "This is going to the Chronicle, so … happy smiles. Right! Let's have another in case someone closed their eyes."

That night, as I walked home, Ken rode past me on his bike and, having spotted me, doubled back. He looked as if he'd been up to something.

"Listen Pugh. Don't tell a single soul," he confided. "But I think everybody'll be able to see my cock on the team photo."

There was no hint of a smile.

"Cripes, Ken."

"Should be just under my right elbow," he said, as if I needed telling where on his body it might be.

I was appalled, thrilled, scared, in awe.

"Your cock? How?" I asked.

"While that bloke was telling them to close up at the back, I flicked open the leg of my shorts a bit, just a little bit."

"Ken!" I gasped.

"Then I lifted my elbow just before the click went. I'm sure you'll be able to see it. But maybe not all of it," he said earnestly.

Chronicle sales must have hit a high that week. Crinkled cuttings were pulled out of pencil cases and school uniform pockets and shown round, knots of pupils falling back squealing with laughter – "Look … it is, it's Ken's knob! Just there!"

More of the team photos had been torn out and left, with the salient feature ringed, on the school notice board, and pinned up in the art room.

Some kids reported that when their parents had come across the photo, they'd pitied Ken, believing the lad was the innocent victim of a random breeze, or the over-generous cut of his shorts.

Colin Latham had told me that he saw his mum pass the paper to his dad and heard her whisper:"Lovely one of Kyff. But surely that isn't what I think it is, Gordon?"

My mum cut the picture out as a keepsake and noticed nothing.

The excitement lasted two or three days, during which Ken kept silent and innocently oblivious ("What photo? Cock? Whose cock?"). He knew no teacher was going to ask:"Curtis, did you deliberately put your penis on show?"

Understandably, back then I wouldn't have pencilled Ken in as a potential solicitor – a showy barrister, maybe, or, more likely, a playboy footballer. But by the look of his advertisement in the phone book it was clear he'd established a big, thriving practice.

I could tell by our phone conversation that he had remained larger than life. Exactly how large surprises me as I sit with a half of bitter in the near-deserted lounge of the Druids, waiting for him.

The door swings open and Ken bowls in, recognisable but in an inflated form. The pale pinched face is full and florid, the Dennis the Menace hair tamed into a black mat now, speckled with grey, the slender waist replaced by a modest paunch.

Those big white shorts would fit him now, I think, as he bounds over to me and shakes my hand.

"Kyff! Bloody hell – Kyff Pugh! Right, let me get you a proper-sized drink," he says, pulling a disapproving face at my half-pint glass and heading for the bar. The hen-like walk is unaltered by the years.

We have lived the best part of half a lifetime since we last met. What we have each experienced in that time would fill a book and yet, with our pints of Golden Slumbers to hand and time spreading out in front of us, waiting to be filled, for a few moments we are dumbstruck.

Ken bustles through the impasse.

"Kyff bloody Pugh! Now, what the hell's happened to you since they transported you to Australia?"

I sketch in the framework of my life since our last meeting, which had been at the barely organised, over-emotional farewell drinking session Grace and me held in the upstairs room of a pub in town when we were leaving for Perth.

By the time I have brought him up to date, leaving the break-up with Grace as only vague outlines, his glass is empty. I fetch more beer and, after taking a long draught, Ken begins to re-trace his life for me.

His path to prosperity had been gradual and steady and rock solid but the diversions seemed to me to have been spectacular. He had married, divorced, fathered a child with his accounts clerk (married), had re-married, separated.

"When I say I'm between women, it's usually misunderstood!" he says with a big, growly laugh, rocking back in his seat. "I wish!"

We now seem to be competing to talk. The beer has washed away any awkwardness and by the time Ken replenishes the supply we are paddling, knee-deep, in nostalgia.

"Bloody hell. So your dad's gone. End of an era," he says. He appeared to be raking round in his mind for memories of Dad.

"Did I ever tell you, Kyff, that once when I called on you when you first came back from uni I touched a nerve, some throwaway remark I'd made about boxing."

A sensitive topic. Some of Dad's pride in Wales was embodied in the sportsmen it produced. The plucky, bloodied, titches from the Valleys, refusing to stay down for the count, gave him the perfect metaphor for his underdog principality.

Boxers, forged out of coal and steel; fabled heroes of *rygbi*, rather than plain rugby, breeding slight but flinty running backs to outwit and outpace the English defence.

"Some little Welsh boxer was in a coma after a major fight," says Ken. "It had been in the news. I just remember this tiny pipe-cleaner of a man, this little scrap of a bloke, with his huge ears."

"It would have been poor little Johnny Owen," I say. In my mind I can see "Merthyr's Matchstick Man", as the papers called him, that skeletal chest of a bird in winter.

"All I said was that this poor mite looked so frail that one good punch would have demolished him. Christ! Your dad really tore a strip off me. I didn't know it but the lad was world class and he'd just died. I was damn glad when you came downstairs, ready for the pub."

Ken is frowning. I can see that he is re-living the tongue-lashing.

He starts on some other anecdote but I retreat into myself, wondering what visitors must have thought of our house, and my parents. It was so quiet; no laughter, no spontaneity, like a small rather shabby institution. It was not like at the Lathams. When I went to play with Colin we'd shout and have what his mum called "daft carryons" leading inevitably to "gigglefits". We would roll on the floor and wrestle until Mrs Latham shouted: "Steady! Don't get too giddy lads!"

Mr Latham was even more relaxed. I never saw him come home miserable.

Once he arrived from work, put down his haversack, breathed in, put his arm out like an operatic tenor and started singing...

"Valencia! Put your head between your knees and whistle up your Barcelona..."

We were in stitches. Then Col's mum shouted "Grub's up!" as she always did, and I knew I had to go back to the silence.

"Did he really hate the English?" Ken asks, after taking a long glug of beer.

"Not only the English. Everybody but the Welsh I think. He didn't discriminate," I say, with only a slight feeling of disloyalty. "He was always reminding people that the Welsh were the original Britons but that they let themselves become enfeebled over centuries."

"Tell you what," Ken says, "if your dad had lived a thousand years ago, he'd have been the one at the front of a pack of equally hairy-arsed Welshmen rampaging about the hills repelling the English. He'd have been the one wielding the bollock-knife, and shouting about Owen Glendower."

I can't deny it. Dad was a bit of a zealot. He'd taken belonging to a ridiculous extent. Belonging to his country, that is, not so much to people; and belonging to an immutable view of the world.

Ken moves on to news of classmates, one dying, two dead, one changed from man to woman.

He ponders aloud over whether poor Robert Sole, who, when lists of pupils were read out by teachers, was always referred to as Sole, R. rather than R. Sole, is still trying to get everyone to call him Bob.

And had the benighted V. D. Jenkins, our owlish religious studies teacher, been hurt by our puerile jokes ("I've got V. D. this afternoon")?

"Have you ever thought," Ken says, "how everything to do with private parts was sexy then – knickers, periods, weeing, even the diseases?"

We recall the catchphrases we adopted, the lingo of a short-lived sub-culture.

"Remember, Kyff, how if anyone smelled a fart in class, the cry would go up ... 'I think it was Kyff wot made that whiff!'?"

We laugh at the silliness, the innocence and pure happiness we enjoyed. No – we didn't just laugh. In the tradition of the characters in our comics, we chortled.

"While we're talking about names," Ken says, "where on earth did Kyff come from anyway? Wales, of course. But why Kyff? Never thought to ask before."

I explain that Mum told me that Dad used to get sent a magazine called Cymru and discovered this famous painter from Anglesey called Kyffin Williams.

"I've since seen a couple of paintings by him. Think he specialised in celebrating craggy-faced old farmers and their clinically depressed sheep, against a backdrop of shit-coloured mountainsides in bad weather."

Mum had wanted me to be called Gareth, or Dylan after Dylan Thomas, but as usual deferred to Dad, who liked the Celtic ring to the name Kyffin.

Aneurin Bevan died just after I was born, so I could so easily have been Nye.

"To Dad, Bevan was God. He used to say he had three reasons – that Nye Bevan created the health service, that he'd resigned on a point of principle and that he'd had the guts to say publicly that all Tories were lower than vermin."

This amuses Ken: "Nye Pugh. Nye Pugh. Sounds like a battle site in Vietnam. But surely Kyff must have been a bit of a bloody millstone?"

"Too true. Kyffin Pugh," I say, irritated. "Kyffin Pugh. It sounds like a sneeze. Or something you'd say when you stubbed your toe: Who left that kyffin pugh there?"

Ken is wheezing with laughter now.

"It was murder in Perth, always having to spell it, explain it," I tell him. "Sir Kyffin Williams RA has a lot to answer for. Actually, in Wales, I'm Kuffin.""Could be a dirty anagram, kuffin. Anyway, your dad's name was a bit of a precedent. Huw Pugh. Hard to get your top set round. Easy to slip into the Huw Poo," Ken says.

"Yes, just ask the vicar who took the funeral," I say.

Ken is up and back with two more pints in what seems an instant as the bell goes for closing time.

"Maybe it's a Welsh thing, this odd way with names. Look at Dylan Thomas and his Organ Morgan, Mrs Willy Nilly, Bessie Bighead…" I say, and then think of Dai Dower, another of Dad's boxing heroes.

I am a little dizzy now. I'd forgotten that I am on the tablets, forgotten that I am supposed to be languishing in the black pit of despair.

To distract myself from the unpleasant headiness I am feeling I ask: "Did you know that Dad liked jazz? Trad. New Orleans. Stuff to tap your feet to?" In fact, Dad's feet never moved but I always wondered whether his toes were secretly shimmying to the music, in his slippers.

"Well, his favourite was a man called Parry, a clarinetist from Bangor."

"Go on," says Ken with a roaring laugh, "tell me he was called Clarence. 'Let's have a big hand for Clarrie Parry!' Or was it Barry Parry? No – wait! Don't tell me. Must have a slash…."

He stands up and squeezes his knees together but makes no move for the toilets.

"No, it wasn't Barry," I say.

"What then – Gary Parry? Larry Parry? Come on Kyff, I'm desperate."

"No," I reply, laughing with a freedom I've not felt for so long, but also a feeling that I am dangerously close to tears.

"No – don't tell me it was … Harry Parry?"

"Yes. Harry Parry," I say.

He whoops triumphantly. "Isn't that what those Jap pilots used to commit?" he says, rushing off to relieve himself. His laughter makes him sound unhinged.

I notice that the place has emptied around us. The barmaid is hovering, her presence giving a broad hint that we have to leave.

I need the toilets now. I find them with difficulty and pass Ken at the door. I am unsteady and have to hold on to a pipe while I pee.

In a moment, Ken would want to arrange a meeting. We would plan the divorce and the division of all wordly goods. The enormity of this prospect hits me as I stand there in the silence, rocking and pissing and laughing and, suddenly, crying.

I lean my head on the cool pipe I'm clinging to, and try to compose myself by thinking hard of other rhyming names.

I splash water into my eyes, blow my nose and go out to meet Ken, who is waiting at the front door of the pub.

He looks at me closely, tilting his head to get the best of the light.

"OK?"

"Fine," I say brightly.

"No worries, as you Aussies say. Golden Slumbers is ambrosia but it can challenge the inner man."

"No – I'm OK."

"Right, you go thataway way, I go thisaway," Ken says. "But let's get together in the office, Monday if it suits you."

"Yes, thanks Ken. I'll ring. It was a good night."

"A cracking night. Haven't laughed like that since Wife Number Two had her car crash."

Ken pulls up his coat lapels and rifles through his pockets for his gloves.

"Just two things you ought to think about before we get stuck in, Kyff," he says.

"First you need to be absolutely sure that you'll not want to go back to the good lady once things are rolling. And eventually you might need to decide whether you want me to play it nice or nasty."

"Well, I certainly won't be going back," I find myself saying, although it sounds to me as if it is someone else speaking. "And I'd definitely want the nice option. I'd like it to be amicable."

"Amicable. It nearly always starts like that. You'd be amazed how good intentions turn shitty. Possessions turn into trophies to be fought for."

"Anyway, we can try to keep it friendly," I say. "It wasn't really her fault."

We shake hands and I walk unsteadily into the bitter night.

Then I hear him shout, "Kyff! One last thing while we tarry – did that Harry Parry ever marry?" and his crazed laugh rings out in the silence of the night.

FIVE

It has been a long night, but we have finally reached the penultimate item on the allotments association annual meeting agenda, "Memorial to Huw Pugh" – the business I'd been invited to witness.

There has been muted support for the idea of a community allotment, a subject left "on the table" in the light of the threat to the allotments. We've debated the vandalism problem and decided that it is not yet time for vigilante patrols.

We've applauded this year's show successes and heard, rather excitedly in Madge's case, of the forthcoming visit of an Italian delegation of gardeners under the town twinning scheme.

We are now well into Manure Day.

Someone doubts that the riding stables, the usual source, can supply manure this year, and someone else gives the name of an alternative. A man on a bar stool says he'll ask a farmer he knows.

Cecil really is a terrible chairman. The longer the meeting goes on the more chaotic it becomes.

Someone suggests, above a babble of voices, ordering a lorry load of mushroom compost this year but this is shouted down.

Old Bill announces solemnly: "No! You want real stuff. Take it from me, nothing feeds like real manure. Starve your land and it'll starve you. Or, as my old Dad said – you can't grow stuff without arseholes."

"Bill! Language!" Madge says, tapping his hand.

Wilf chips in: "You're right Bill, every man jack of 'em."

"But are you all quite sure you can transport manure anyway?" the well-spoken man from the funeral, nicknamed Winco, says loftily. "I do believe the EC has been looking at banning it."

A large woman wearing a leather jacket and a face full of menace shouts: "For God's sake – get on with it! Cecil, let's have some order!"

Cecil is ineffectual, giving everyone as much time as they like to ramble on, and allowing them to return to subjects that had been dealt with long before.

Points for action are lost in the babble of private conversation. Somewhere, someone is saying miserably into his drink: "That last lot was full of plastic and sticks. I want pure muck for my money." Elsewhere someone is rhapsodising over hen droppings.

"Through the chair!" demands the woman in the leather coat.

A bearded man, leaning on the bar, drones on regardless: "It's no good too hot. You want it rotted down. What I do is…"

The only consensus, finally, is that the manure matter will be investigated and that the date of Manure Day has been agreed.

"Right, so what exactly did we decide about the vandals…?" asks Winco, who then reminisces fondly about the use of the birch on the Isle of Man, and laments the disappearance of the tawse strap from Scottish classrooms.

A wavering voice asks: "Who's sending off the seed order this year?"

"Wake up Bertie! We dealt with that stuff a hour ago," shouts the bearded man.

The club committeeman – "You're signed in, sunshine," he had assured me from his border post – interrupts the meeting to say that it is fifteen minutes to last orders.

There is just the Meeting Point item and Dad's memorial to discuss, then we can all be spared further suffering.

Prof stands up and describes his plan for a disused, gravelly corner of the allotments to become a rallying point where gardeners can get information, swap plants or just chat.

It would involve making unofficial (and, probably, prohibited) use of the side of the wall of a disused railway building at the foot of the embankment bordering one side of the allotment.

"Didn't hear that," says Cecil, looking at the wall to distance himself. He seems to play things by the book but perhaps the allotments being under threat has loosened his scruples.

A corrugated plastic canopy would be fixed to the wall that faced the allotments, to provide shelter. The area would be partly shielded by trees on the allotment side and invisible from the line.

A "donor" had already been found for the welded metal framework and another for the roofing sheets, although neither would know of the gift.

So nothing changes. As a boy, I was always intrigued by the source of all those cans of paint, brand new rope, virgin timber, glass for cloches, and copper piping to strengthen bean frames. They were unrecorded bonuses from workplaces.

"I didn't hear a word of any of that," says Cecil, looking at the ceiling.

Prof continues. "In the next couple of months people will need to know what's going on. We need to be able to communicate," he says.

Pat speaks up.

"I'd like to give a bell. It's an old one from a boat. Terry and me picked it up at an auction. It would be ideal for getting people together. We could hang it somewhere with a little plaque with a dedication to Huw."

"That's sweet," says Madge, touching Pat's hand. "Huw would have liked that idea."

At Cecil's prompting I formally approve the memorial plan and thank Pat for her gesture, and someone successfully proposes that a working party be set up to install the bell and create a rallying point.

"It'll be our nerve centre," says Madge.

Cecil is on the point of bringing the meeting to a close, ignoring any other business, but, as people begin folding their agenda sheets and reaching for their coats, Prof stands up and asks for one more minute of their time.

They stand like statues as he declares: "We've talked for a whole evening about the new season at the allotments. Yet, for all we know, anytime now we might be told to move off."

He looks to be fired up.

"Are we in denial or what? Do we value what we've got down there? Do you really mind if that bit of ground you've got your stuff growing on goes under tarmac?

"Do we want a bloody great hangar of a building instead of our bits of fruit trees and our huts? Do you want another few hundred cars in a jam along the road at the Bottom End?"

"What you've each got down there is just a pinch of soil, compared to what ten per cent of the population own. But you have charge of it.

"Just remember too that you've got more rights to that land than some billion-pound conglomerate based in Germany."

A pattering of applause echoes round the emptying hall, backed by a few cries of "hear, hear!"

But it doesn't sound anything like a war cry.

SIX

"Multigravida, Mrs Pugh. That's the word we medics have for ladies like you!"

Mr Kwan was beaming.

"And guess what – sometimes, to add insult to injury, we have the temerity to put the word 'elderly' in front!

"But you'll maybe have remembered that from last time when you were what we call, in our lofty way, primigravida."

He flicked open medical notes and said: "I certainly won't be using that word 'elderly' within your hearing because you appear to be absolutely blooming!"

Mr Kwan was a charmer, and he rejoiced in the fact. Impeccable English (peerless non-Oz enunciation); flawless olive skin; glossy hair combed precisely, each strand a filament of wet liquorice; almond-shaped eyes twinkling behind expensive glasses; the bow tie with the zigzag motif toning with the lilac shirt.

Everything added up to his being a man who enjoyed being on show, having women hanging on his every word.

"Yes, I seem to be very well," said Grace in a tentative voice. Her eyes were eager, cheeks flushed.

When I squeezed her hand supportively, she did not reciprocate. She was too deeply focused.

"Excellent!" said Mr Kwan. He looked at each of us in turn. The smile was fading. It was time to be purposeful.

"Now, let's be frank," he said briskly. "All's absolutely fine so far but as you know only too well there are hazards along the road, a road you've travelled before, Mrs Pugh," he said, unclasping his hands and patting Grace's wad of notes.

"B...u...t..." He seemed to be drawing out the word so he could enjoy the power of imparting better news.

"...we're here to get you and your baby safely to the destination. We have the equipment and the skill to give you the very best chance of a happy outcome."

"About the chances, Mr Kwan..." I said, then immediately sensed Grace resenting my intervention. Her hand moved only millimetres away from mine but it was a telling fraction.

"We've seen various statistics about risk but we wondered..."

"Ah – you'll both find some guidance about risk in the leaflet, Mr Pugh, and of course we have a duty to point things out, talk them through. But ... we must remember that what's true for one patient does not apply for another. Mother Nature often laughs at the figures."

He nudged his spectacles a little higher on his flat nose.

"Occasionally, supremely healthy women are dealt a cruel blow out of nowhere. Unaccountably, twenty-year-old yoga addicts can have more trouble delivering babies than those who, for whatever reason, decide to leave things later in life..." He smiled at Grace and said: "Our elderly ladies."

Actually, we hadn't left things late. Grace was not a career woman who had put child-bearing on the shelf to reach up for and enjoy later. We'd tried early in our marriage, and again after Grace had been given some corrective surgery.

The trying wasn't the problem, though the knowledge that we were always on a mission had tended, over the years, to change what chemistry there had been between us.

"My advice?" said Mr Kwan. "Put aside the depressing stats, and try not to dwell on what you've gone through previously. This is a brand new pregnancy. So travel hopefully!" he pronounced, grinning as he raised a fist.

"Now," he said, reaching for forms "let's organise some tests…"

I knew that Mr Kwan was far from convinced that things would turn out well. But then he couldn't lose. If it went well, he was a hero; if it ended dreadfully, it was expected – after all, it was there in the statistics.

As we left and got to the car I felt an ominous gloom hanging over us, yet dear, desperate Gracie was bright and positive, almost recklessly so in my view.

"I feel so right this time, Kyff," she said firmly.

Sensing from my silence that I was less optimistic, she said: "Kyff, I know you tend to look on the black side but it's not a raffle that you might or might not win. There's care involved and science – and we've got Mr Kwan this time."

I would play along and dare to hope. Sharing my fears would only damp down Grace's brittle optimism, which I knew could shatter like a glass bauble.

As for my hopes, I felt a flutter of excitement whenever I thought of having a baby in the house. It would break the two-way conduit of marriage; it would bind us, give us a joint focus. It had seemed lately that this was why we were together.

It might have been a hormonal thing but Grace suddenly seemed to have swept away all the past distress, convinced that this was the grand finale that would make all the hospital visits and the bleak, barren days worthwhile.

Over the next weeks Grace got down her pregnancy guides from the top bookshelf and re-read every text she could find on preparing for a late birth. She stocked up on recommended foods she had shown no interest in previously.

I skulked about the garden when I needed a smoke, and drank wine alone under the sunshade while Grace sipped her vitamin-rich potions and worked tirelessly at being relaxed.

Three months before the predicted birth date she arranged to have extra, unpaid pre-natal leave and rested several times a day in the new, ludicrously expensive orthopaedic reclining chair we'd installed.

Her Springsteen CDs and the dance music she loved lay forgotten. Now, instead of doing hip-wiggling at the kitchen sink to Latin beats, as she had done in her few lighter moments, she lay back and dozed to meditation CDs, and Mozart for Mellow Moods.

She had decided, dictated rather – and that in an unexpectedly cold tone – that we should buy baby clothes and other paraphernalia only when she neared full term, only then. I suspect she believed that to take anything for granted was to open the door to another tragedy.

When things had gone terribly wrong before, and Grace had been lying around – pale, distant, her hair lank and her eyes puffy, hugging her dressing gown round herself – I had asked if she would like me to "do something with the baby room".

"Just blot it all out," she'd said in a strange detached voice.

Now she declared that there would be no toys or mobiles in this second newly decorated nursery room. Seeing the traces of the old paint and the tiny slips of wallpaper at the wall's edge from three years ago brought back the sense of cruel anticlimax I'd felt at that time.

Grace was blooming and, a week before the birth was due, we visited Mr Kwan and he ushered us out of his clinic with reassuring words and professed excitement. He rubbed his hands with exaggerated glee, plainly for Grace's benefit.

"Not long now Mrs P!" he said.

In the car, Grace let her head drop back, and sighed.

"Just think. This time next week…"

Next morning I was in the university refectory supervising Sharon over a cup of coffee when the call came.

Sharon was near to tears, having gone off at a tangent in a big piece of work, and I was gently hauling her back on track when Miranda from the office click-clacked towards the table, stopping short to mouth a silent "Sorry…" to Sharon, then holding up an imaginary phone to her ear and pointing at me.

"Your wife," she mouthed soundlessly.

I scrawled a few bullet points and handed them to Sharon and said:"It will all be fine. Try not to stray too far from the central theme. But I'm afraid I'll have to cut things short," then couldn't help adding, with an excited note that surprised me:"I think I'm being called for paternity duty."

Sharon, sitting abandoned, surrounded by paper and books, smiled and called after me:"Good luck then."

Grace's voice was even and controlled.

"Kyff. I think my waters have broken."

"I'll be there. Or do you want to get an ambulance?"

"No, I'll wait for you."

I grabbed my case and hurried through the campus to the car park. I held my keys and pass for the barrier in my hand, for a quick getaway. I was composed as I started to move off but grew angry at the cars stacking up ahead of me at the barrier.

There was obviously a problem with the exit machine. A van driver had got out and was hitting it with the palm of his hand. I tried to reverse only to find that three cars were on my tail.

Leaping out, I went to each driver in turn and said I was involved in an emergency, asking them to reverse to let me out. They obliged; one slowly and reluctantly, looking suspicious about my story. It all seemed to take an age.

I knew of another exit at the back of the building, near a goods delivery area, but had forgotten that this also had a security barrier. I parked, then ran into the reception. I held up my identity tag and pleaded with the security man to let me out through the barrier.

He laboriously searched a drawer for some sort of key and seemed in no rush to get out to the barrier and raise it.

When I hit the main road there was more traffic than usual, then a diversion round a trench across the road. I took a set of crooked-leg turns working towards home. The minutes seemed like hours, and I had palpitations by the time I jerked to a halt outside home.

"So sorry Gracie! Bloody traffic!" I shouted through the car window.

She was leaning against the kitchen door, trying to look brave and holding on the door handle. The bag she had packed so carefully, so well in advance, was at her feet.

I will never know whether the look on her face was anxiety or whether it was accusing. But lately I've been thinking: Does Grace blame me for us losing Lizzie?

With a little help from my friends

ONE

"Achtung! Party kviz time! And no-von vill escape!"

It is Cecil's jolly daughter Jane, awash with vodka, yelling above the music.

She has been annoying her parents for weeks with her jokey German. It has become an irritating habit that started when Cecil had mentioned that the hypermarket company trying to build on the allotment site was German-owned.

We are partying, in a geriatric kind of way, at Cecil's – me, Pat, Wilf, Ray and his wife Eileen, and a recently divorced neighbour called Carol – under the attentive care of our host and his wife Barbara.

The button lit up on the old music system is marked MELLOW, perfectly appropriate for Viennese musical lollipops. The DISCO RAVE button shows no sign of wear.

The chatter is bright if a tad earnest; we're all really working at being sociable and engaging and have eased some of the tension by gravitating to the safe haven of the kitchen, well out of the searching light of the living room.

I move to fill a space next to Pat, who is sitting on a low stool, her back arched like a dancer's. She's probably thirty years older than Jane but there's little difference in their body shape. The Christmas lights are on her hair, which is silver-grey and closely cropped.

She has a midnight blue pashmina round her narrow shoulders. Barbara compliments her on her figure, Carol coos with envy. I think, but don't say:"Class. Taste."

Pat just shrugs and smiles awkwardly at the attention and says: "Pilates helps but I think I'm just lucky with my metabolism."

I think of my piggy white thighs and back fat – features I am augmenting at this very moment with mince pies topped with cream.

Pat is an attentive listener, saying very little but not, I suspect, out of shyness. Occasionally her interested look falls away and she appears distant. The raw newness of widowhood I suppose.

Wilf is picking up only fragments of conversation on his stereo hearing aids, his thick glasses turning like searchlights on to each speaker in turn.

I wonder whether I'm the only guest to face the melancholic fact that we are handpicked guests, chosen as neighbours having links with the allotments but mostly because we would otherwise have been on our own this New Year's Eve.

Does this spread, of cold turkey, cheese straws and wedges of pie, and the improvised bar on the sink draining board, all smack of the yuletide soup kitchen manned by volunteers doing their good deed for the year?

My cynicism has been flourishing lately but this fleeting ungrateful thought seems to mark a new low. Maybe it's all part of the depression. But the truth is that the kind (yes, genuinely kind) Hon Sec, Cecil, and the equally kind Barbara have thrown open their doors to those who are less fortunate than themselves.

I suspect that Carol, who is squat, sweet-natured and just back from a tinsel-and-turkey bus tour to Blackpool, might even have been planted by Barbara in the hope that we could give each other solace this Christmas.

I'm grateful for the thought but the rhinestone-bottomed jeans immediately cool any ardour she might raise.

That said, beggars can't be choosers, and I've already learned how easy it would be to become a recluse, and for no-one to care – a state beyond my comprehension a few weeks ago, when I was basking in the affection of people who valued me.

The past three days of being cooped up, not needing to speak, and willing the celebration season to pass have given me a life's lesson.

I now know that for the sake of my sanity I need to be in company. And – hey presto! – here I am, in the warm, being introduced to Drambuie by Cecil and eating warm mince pies, all to the sound of The Skaters' Waltz. Decadence.

Reading had been helping me fritter the lonely hours and take me out my surroundings. Books had been my Christmas present to myself.

I've always derived pleasure from the act of buying books but, as I'd handed over a pile of paperbacks at the till, I'd felt nothing. I'd simply picked up the books rather than selected them, although there had seemed to be an involuntarily tendency towards introspection.

One buy was the entire Pepys' Diary in hardback. I think I was unconsciously drawn to this because of a need to share a life, even one lived 350 years ago. It is also the kind of history I love – history with intimate human feeling: guilt, fear, greed, fragility, lust, compassion.

Another, a paperback, Mindfulness Made Easy, came with a free meditation CD and a cover tag line that must have spoken to me: "Lose your fear, gain the happiness you deserve."

When I got home I threw a big shovelful of smokeless fuel on the fire and, although it was still early evening, changed into pyjamas and put on the CD.

I sat down on the hearthrug and in the firelight settled into the prescribed posture, loosening my shoulders, tucking my tongue behind my top teeth, straightening my back and cupping my hands.

I was prepared to shut out the distractions but there was none. However, mindfulness was elusive, constantly slipping the leash.

When I woke from a profound sleep I was lolling forward with saliva on my chin. The banked-up fire had turned to a pan of glowing ash.

My head was filled with a dream I instantly replayed in glorious, glowing colour.

Grace and me were on the beach reading. The sun made us feel we were under a grill. We were becoming irritable with each other.

We were dehydrating but when we reached for the water bottles, shaded under the bag Grace used for carrying towels, they turned out to be full of sand.

Grace stood up and brushed sand from her thighs and carefully took off her sunglasses, blew on them, shook out a tee-shirt and gently wrapped the glasses in it.

She looked down at me and said:"I'm so thirsty. I want it to snow."

I laughed. This was Perth! But she glowered at me then stared ahead.

"I'm going home," she said.

I said OK, we'd head for the car.

"No", she said. "Real home. Wiltshire. Where there's snow."

When I analysed the dream I took this to be a portent; perhaps she really was planning to come home. Or was it wishful thinking on my part?

Like me, Grace must be in limbo now. There's nothing for her in Perth now, except acquaintances and a job she has no great passion for. Australia was a great adventure but only when we were together; I think we were only brave enough to go there by combining our courage.

I stirred myself and I trudged up to bed and on Christmas morning – a jet-black, stormy, window-rattling English Christmas morning – I woke early but delayed getting out of bed because of the cold.

As I lay there in the dark I could hear the children in the bedroom of the adjoining house squealing with pleasure as they found their presents ("He's been! He's been!").

The muffled sound of their delight as they unwrapped toys and the stark silence of despair, within a few feet of each other.

So this is how the lonely live.

TWO

"Drink up or it'll evaporate, Kyff!" says Cecil, who is at my elbow with the Drambuie bottle. He recharges my glass.

When Prof, the last of the loners, arrives, his thin, floaty hair is dusted with granules of snow – it really is bitter out there.

"Just in time Prof," says Jane, kissing him on the cheek. "Men versus women!" She unfolds the Trivial Pursuit board and squares up the question cards and then herds us to the dining room table.

"The girls might as well start the new millennium as they intend to go on..."

Then she gives Prof's shoulder a nudge and says:"Brainbox is here so maybe I'd better not start boasting yet."

"Moi?" he says, grinning and showing his ochre teeth. "I know nothing, Jane. You're the one with the A-levels."

Cecil smiles and gazes at his daughter as if she is holy.

"And there's Kyff here," Prof says. "He's a pukka prof."

"Not quite, Prof – just a lecturer with a few letters after the Pugh."

Carol looks my way and cocks her head slightly as if she's impressed. Barbara, well-upholstered and exuding home comforts, goes from person to person with a whispered offer of drinks.

Pat is given the dice and while she shakes, and the counter is being moved, I ask Prof whether I'm right in presuming he's a teacher. I doubt it; something about the weird halo of hair and the nicotine stains left on his fingers by thousands of roll-ups.

"Hell no!" he protests. "I was a librarian for years until the council decided that learning, and the enrichment of our lives with ideas and understanding, was frittering money and shut the place down.

"No," he says, "Pat, there, is the teacher." Pat smiles at Prof warmly, as if she, too, looked on him as a favourite uncle.

"The 'Prof' is ironic. It's probably because this" – he says pointing to his unruly head – "is a receptacle packed full with things curious, useless, and odd. I just like swotting up about things. Always have. I've ended up with thousands of answers but none of them to the really important questions."

There's a hitch with the quiz. We fail to realise that Wilf can't hear the questions. When Jane, who is becoming increasingly flushed and loud as the vodka takes hold, asks him to name a Gilbert and Sullivan show he answers: "Motor scooter."

We are all dumbfounded until Prof announces loudly, and as if Wilf is invisible: "He must have heard 'Lambretta' for 'operetta'."

"Sorry, Wilf, we can't give you that," shouts Jane sweetly, as if it were a near miss. Pat kindly finds paper in the quiz game box and, with discreet gestures, suggests I write the questions down if Wilf doesn't hear.

I note that Cecil is strong on stuff that made the headlines in the last thirty years.

Jane is hot on English literature and recent pop music but is not sure which conflict was started by the invasion of Poland or what a square root is.

Pat gives her answers, almost always correct, in a self-effacing way ("Could it be...?"). She is an impressive all-rounder.

Wilf is hit-and-miss but he knows his British geography and his royalty. Cheering marks any correct answer he happens to give, and he chuckles, indicating that at least he can hear the applause (and that he does not notice that he is being patronised).

Prof, meanwhile, lives up to his reputation as a voracious repository of facts, revealing encyclopaedic interests and prodigious reading.

He pretends to struggle in recalling that it was the Hopewell Indians who built mounds in Ohio, and says that he "has an idea" that a bellibone was a sixteenth century term for a beautiful lady. He "seemed to recall" that it was T. S. Eliot who wrote about growing old and wearing his trousers rolled.

I compliment him. He shakes his head and says: "It's all instead of real knowledge."

I do quite well but embarrassingly come a cropper with a history question, failing to recall that Roman Colchester was called Camulodunum.

Led by Jane, everyone makes an exaggerated "Ooooo!" noise at my slip-up.

"Before my time," I protest.

"Are you sure, Kyff?" Pat says, and everyone laughs.

Ray only answers a couple of questions correctly, one of them when his wife, out of habit, finishes his sentence for him. Retrieval of facts seems to be his problem. "But I know the flaming answer!" he keeps protesting. "It's … bloody hell … it's, err, wossname…"

In the end, the men are clear winners.

Prof looks across at me and holds up his plastic wallet of tobacco, raising his eyebrows enquiringly. We go out for a smoke.

As we put our overcoats over our heads he pulls me back into the living room and, as we peer round the door, he announces solemnly: "We are just going outside and may be some time…"

"Titus Oates and wossname," says Ray.

"Tight as newts more like," squeals Jane. "Or maybe twin trolls."

Hoots of laughter follow us as we step into the snow flurries tumbling into the pool of light round the window.

"Of course, Scott and Oates didn't get on," says Prof absently, shielding his roll-up from the snow.

"Oates was a cavalry man and he was appalled at the state of the ponies Scott had lined up. Did you realise the poor bugger was handicapped? Had one leg shorter than the other from a war wound."

"No," I say. "But when I was at college I saw his reindeer-skin sleeping bag, in the Cambridge Polar Museum, the bed he climbed out of to go out and sacrifice himself. So poignant."

The powdery snow is coming thick and fast now; we pull our coats further over our heads so they become tents.

Pat appears at the door wearing coat, scarf and woolly hat. I'm disappointed to hear her saying goodnight to those inside. She is going home.

As Cecil and Barbara show her out I hear her say: "I know you'll understand. The first on my own and it being the millennium makes it worse."

She steps into the dark and, pulling her hat round her face, smiles weakly as she peers at Prof and me – pathetic addicts huddled under coats, getting a nicotine fix.

She offers a little wave and says: "They should have an extra health warning on those cig packets about pneumonia!"

We shake our coats free of snow and go back into the house. Holding court in the centre of the room, wearing a wet cap and sodden anorak is a fat-faced man with a bulbous nose and prominent grey eyebrows.

He is telling some convoluted joke but stops when we arrive.

"It's old Prof – just in time to give me a New Year kiss. But no tongues! Ah, and you must be Kyff!" he says.

"Waggy, our resident comedian," Cyril announces.

Waggy shakes my hand and says: "Once resident, now itinerant. I always have the car engine running when I finish my spot!"

He is taking his whisky in glugs. I notice that he never smiles when he makes a witty comment but smiles constantly at other times.

"To be fair, they were a better bunch than usual tonight. Around Christmas, folks sit back and say 'I've forgotten work, I've got a pint in front of me – now make me laugh.' Strangely enough, it always turns out that the more drink they have, the better my material."

Jane has switched the TV on. She is every inch a young woman but she has her hands clasped and is craning her neck excitedly like a child at the scenes from Trafalgar Square and the world's great cities – some of them already in the twenty-first century.

"Ten seconds!" she shouts, springing to her feet and making us link arms. I hold hands with Cecil and Waggy.

We have an awkward stab at singing Auld Lang Syne. We kiss the women, shake hands, Jane's face goes white and she holds her mouth and rushes off.

"I suppose you call that bringing up the New Year," says Waggy, easing himself onto the settee beside me.

THREE

"I loved your Dad, Kyff,"Waggy confides. "Absolutely loved him, the gruff old bugger."

He takes a mouthful of whisky, appears to chew on it, and then swallows with a faint sigh.

"Nearly made him laugh – once."

Everyone else has fallen silent now the anticlimactic once-in-a-lifetime millennium moment is over.

"In fact I love the Welsh. Great romantics."

He tips down a third of the drink left in his glass and takes a moment to enjoy the warm wave passing down his throat.

"Great romantics. And how the Welsh love sheep. And I mean love," he says, speaking a little louder, ensuring he has the attention of the room.

"No!" he says, silencing the resultant chuckle. "Listen! That business about shepherds is true. It happens all over – Australia, New Zealand, Ireland – wherever you get good-looking sheep showing a leg and shaking their daglocks, and bachelor farmers with their tongues hanging out."

Jane, who is sitting on the carpet, lets out a shrill laugh. She seems to be revived but is a ghastly white.

Waggy drains his glass and says:"Did you know that once there was a big international conference of sheep farmers and they found out when they got talking in the bar that they all had the same wham-bam-thank-you-ma'am technique once they'd chosen their partner, and driven her head first into a corner … All of them baaa the Welsh."

Waggy stills the premature titters by raising his hands.

"No – really. The Welsh delegate was appalled. 'It's obscene, look you!' he said. 'You actually mean with you lot there's no *kissin'* first?'"

When the laughter dies down, Barbara chides Waggy and accuses him of bringing down the tone expected by allotment-holders.

"Well, Babs, we can't all be gentlemen gardeners. People like Winco," Waggy retorts.

"Winco's our posh one, Kyff," says Cecil, as an aside to me.

"Waggy came up with the name. But I don't think he really was a wing commander. A flight sergeant, I think it was."

I remember the funeral and the haughty voice behind me in church, the exaggerated anger over the size of a mustard seed. That must have been Winco.

"Doesn't stop him cultivating the air of an ex-pilot," says Cecil. "I once asked him straight out and he said: 'Actually I flew a desk most of the time.'"

Waggy continues: "On the plot next to Winco, thanks to our Machiavellian Hon Sec here, is his sworn enemy, Yeti. Then, on the other side, Old Bill, with string holding his jacket shut and the arse out of his trousers! Nice mix."

Prof, who is half asleep in a big recliner chair, with Jane sitting propped up against his legs, opens his eyes and says lazily: "Like that old newspaper slogan: All human life is here."

"I've met Yeti," I say, "and Old Bill was around when I was a kid. He seemed antediluvian then, to me as a little lad."

"And I bet he was having to fall off that bloody great bike to stop, even back then, and getting the weather wrong," Prof says languidly.

The conversation peters out.

Waggy had become the focus of our little group but now tiredness and the whisky seem to have damped down his compulsion to entertain. He has a big fleshy face that looks as if it's been around many more years than him. It is puce and heavily lined.

"When are you heading back, Kyff? To Oz I mean," he asks, and I notice Cecil looking expectantly at me for my answer.

"Not sure," I say. "I might not even go back at all."

There's a silence. Barbara looks at Cecil. Waggy looks at them both. Prof, meanwhile, looks to have drifted off.

"Well," says Cecil, "your dad's hut's there for you, and his plot. It would only be right to offer it to you first. You'd be very welcome, Kyff."

"Actually, I'm not much of a gardener," I say defensively. "And I'm not sure of my plans."

"Anyway, think about it if you're not moving on straight away. That hut is the Ritz of allotment sheds. Must be the biggest in Britain. But God only knows how long we'll be there now the council are stepping things up with the supermarket plan."

Prof lifts his head and says, with sudden, surprising anger : "Well, I can tell you now, Cecil, that I'm going to do my best to block the buggers, if only for people like poor little Wilf.

"There he is, living on his tod, half blind, and stone deaf, just growing stuff and minding his own business and they want to tarmac over his world over, and mine.

"He said to me: 'You know, Prof, if this lot goes there'll nothing for me to hang around for,' and I thought: No! We've enough sodding supermarkets and not enough community. Commercial fascism. Bloody bullies."

Cecil looks flustered. "I know you're right Prof but I've a horrible feeling that finally, despite all the fine talk, most of them will eventually back down. You can't give people fighting spirit."

"No, Cecil. But somehow we have to take the buggers on, like Huw was doing. No surrender. If we sit back and let it happen those goggly eyes of Wilf's will haunt me forever."

He looks round for his drink and, failing to find it, suddenly brightens and raises the vaseful of daffodils on the low table in front of him.

"It'll be my New Year's revolution!"

FOUR

I'd just filled the old pot hot water bottle and put on one of Dad's cardigans to sleep in when the phone goes. It's Grace.

"I thought I might just catch you as it's New Year. I didn't wake you?"

"No. Still up. I was out with friends," I say, and am surprised how smug I feel saying it. Out with friends…

"Oh," Grace says, waiting for me to provide more detail. I decline.

"Are you OK? Are you beginning to feel better?"

"I'm OK," I say, which is true but imprecise enough to be open to any interpretation and, if I'm honest, win a bit of sympathy.

"What's the doctor saying?"

I try to sound a bit frailer than I am feeling: "I just have to keep taking the tablets and resting and exercising and he says I ought to be looking forward and making plans."

"And are you?"

"Resting? A bit. Exercising – not much."

"Making plans I mean?"

"No."

"Anyway, I just wanted you to know," she says, "that I'm packing a big container for shipping. They're picking it up next week."

"That's kind of you," I say.

"We never did get round to deciding what you needed but I had a really good think and look round and tried to guess what you'd want."

She had chosen the items with the sort of thoughtfulness she always showed.

"There's your new camera, your address book, your black fountain pen, and cards from three or four students, and your precious cricket yearbook. I've put in the mail I've dealt with, and some you ought to look at."

"Thanks."

"Your thesis is in there, and your file with your CV and certificates. I thought I'd put in some photos but … well, it's not easy, I didn't know how you'd feel."

"I'd rather not see photos thanks."

"There's three or four T-shirts you used to like and the silk shirts from Singapore."

"Thanks."

"By the way, I've told Mum. About us. Finally."

"How did she take it."

"Devastated. Mortified."

"Did you mention … how it happened?"

"No. I couldn't."

"Then I won't."

"Thank you, Kyff."

"She's going to ring you from time to time."

"I'll just say that we'd stop caring for each other."

"But we didn't. It's not true. I never, ever stopped caring. I still care. But she'd believe you."

"Yes."

"I could tell that she was hoping for a consolation prize – me coming back."

"And are you? Coming back?"

"I'm just reviewing things. Being here's not the same."

She sounds vulnerable. Perhaps she's had some wine.

"It used to feel that it was me and you together, discovering, surviving.

152

It's begun to feel like a place that's far, far away from where I should be."
She *has* had some wine.

"I understand."

"I've begun to feel like a foreigner. Imagine, Kyff, after all that time."

"I can believe it. I felt the same when I got back here."

"I think in a way we were home to each other, wherever we were. Home wasn't really a place."

"Cue violins…"

"No, I really believe it, Kyff."

"That's because it's true. *Was* true."

FIVE

The blessed thing about nightmares is that they go away. Within minutes the heart stops racing. A loved one says: "There … it was only a dream."

You have cigarette and pull the curtains aside and see that dawn is breaking, a normal dawn.

Unlike what I think of as waking nightmares – appalling happenings that are imprinted on the memory, horrors you can't wake up from.

That business on the terrace had been a waking nightmare. It will always be there. It will play at random times like a film you can't avoid watching. I know every word of the script, can anticipate every piece of action, right until the last line of dialogue – "Judas."

What happened at the hospital had been the same.

I had been holding Grace's hand, my shoulder going numb on the bed head.

The senior midwife – Irish, big-hearted, orange-haired – oozed reassurance. But something about her urgency, something about a knitting of the brow, and the brisk setting up of monitoring leads and tubes made my legs go weak.

"Now then, husband," she said, pretending to scold me, "we'll need you from under our feet for a while." She pointed to the plastic chair under the window.

"He's done his bit. Now this is women's work, isn't it Grace?"

Grace nodded dutifully. Fear had taken her voice.

The senior midwife began an examination, then held Grace's fingertips and said cheerfully: "I think I'm going to need reinforcements to sort you out, young lady."

She left the room and I took the chance to say: "Hang on in there Gracie. It'll be fine."

"I want it over," Grace replied with quiet desperation.

They were talking in the corridor. I moved to the partly open door and heard the senior midwife whispering with very deliberate calmness: "Go straight away and fetch Dr Stelios."

Two young midwives came in and then a heavily built doctor, arriving slightly out of breath, called out: "Hello there Mrs Pugh – may I see how the land lies?"

He lowered himself to see beneath the tented sheet covering Grace's raised legs and motioned for a steel trolley to be pulled nearer the bedside.

There was talk of contractions, waters, the cord, the heart rate, all of it in reassuring tones for Grace's benefit.

One nurse was staring fixedly at the monitoring machine at the same time obscuring my view of the flickering figures; I didn't want to see them anyway. The other nurse was at the doctor's elbow, the senior midwife at the bed head with her hand on Grace's brow.

"We've got a bit of a rush on now, Mr Pugh," she said with a slow gentleness that did not mask suppressed alarm. "If you want to leave us for a bit, feel free."

They wanted me out.

As I left, Grace lifted her head and asked "Kyff. Is she going to be all right?" and someone, one of the nurses, replied for me.

"Just relax Grace. Relax. We're keeping an eye on baby."

Five, maybe ten, minutes passed. I stood in the corridor restraining the urge to go back into the ward and insist on being with Grace. Then the senior midwife poked her red head out to check where I was.

"Could you come in, Mr Pugh?" she said in a tone pitched precisely to indicate that I should not expect good news.

The doctor and the nurses stood silently round the bed as if they were holding a vigil. Grace's face was turned to the side and her eyes were wide open. She was still, ashen, and for a moment I feared that she was dead.

"Mr Pugh," said the doctor, taking my forearm in his thick fingers and squeezing it, and looking with uncomfortable intensity into my eyes.

"I'm very sorry to have to tell you this but I'm afraid your little daughter did not survive. We are all very sorry."

Lizzie – gone before she'd arrived.

I wanted to see her.

I was led to the bed. And there she was, beside Grace, alongside her legs. A bluish head, a little bigger than a tennis ball, peeping out of swaddling sheets, and, resting on her cheek, a miniature hand with perfect, almost transparent fingers crooked into a dainty fist that might have been bone china.

I stepped towards Grace.

"We'll leave you for a moment," said the doctor, steering everyone out.

I touched Grace's head, the bouncy lock of hair. She did not respond. Perhaps it was the effect of medication but she seemed to be staring without blinking to some far-off horizon, as if she'd escaped to somewhere else.

"Grace…" I said, lowering my head to her face. I put my cheek alongside hers but she didn't move.

I sat, struggling to find words for Grace, but she lay silent and still. I felt angry that, deep in her own grief, she had no word for me. It was not only Grace who had lost Lizzie.

The doctor returned.

"Do you want to sit down?" he asked kindly, leading me to the chair beneath the window.

"Thank you."

"I have explained to your wife…" he said, bringing a chair from across the room and putting it close to mine.

"These tragedies happen when the cord is in the wrong place and the baby is denied what it needs.

"Your little girl was in such a rush to be born after your wife's waters broke that she left us no time to save her. We are all very upset for you."

I offered a thank you and then asked the question that I already had the answer to.

"If we had been nearer the hospital, and we'd got here much more quickly, might the baby have stood a better chance?"

He cocked his head to one side thoughtfully, half closing his eyes, as if debating inwardly how much to say and how exactly to say it, and whether what he said would be a judgement.

"It is best not to dwell on what was unavoidable. No-one can be sure of outcomes in different circumstances. But yes, the figures show that of those in the situations with the cord, the ladies who get attention very quickly tend to have more babies that survive."

I went over to Grace and held her hand but she did not respond. Her eyes were closed now and there were tears on her cheeks.

"Your baby was the unlucky one in ten with this sort of problem who do not make it. Now the priority is your wife," he said, gesturing to Grace. He stood up, briefly gripped my arm and then left.

A nurse knocked on the door and then came in with tea. She did not look at either of us. Another came in and took Grace's hands.

So I was right. I had not got Grace to the hospital quickly enough. I had let our baby die.

I needed desperately for Grace to say this wasn't true but she was still unreachable, staring, her head on her forearm, lying as still as the little swaddled scrap at her side.

SIX

Yes, Penny finally decided, she would pack the silly bloody knickers after all. And the matching black negligee. She fished out from the drawer the classy silk-covered box with *Ytalon* scrawled on the front in lettering made to look like smeared lipstick.

The stuff was from Paris and there was no doubting the quality; Graham would have bought it when he went to the World-in-One international conference. So Graham, so unimaginative.

Penny had first parted the pink tissue paper and glimpsed inside the box on Christmas morning. She had feigned delight, reached over and kissed Graham's cheek.

To be fair, Graham had promised that there would be a cruise ("A proper treat") when things eased up at work. Since his promotions, work had dominated their lives and lately Penny had wondered whether things would ever become easier.

She had thought no more about the gift until the complementary spa trip late in January.

Benjie's gift had been ample compensation. He had bought and wrapped chocolates for her, and given her a glue-encrusted card that he'd made in secret – an offering that made her swallow hard and reach out to pull at his ear lovingly.

The underwear had gone with her on the January trip but had returned unsullied. Unpacking, she had placed the box between jumpers in a wardrobe drawer and it had remained there until this afternoon when she began preparing for another weekend away.

As she slipped the box into her bag it dawned on her that Ytalon, a name that had puzzled her, was possibly the French word for stallion. She smiled at life's little ironies.

Penny couldn't quite bring herself to look forward to this second weekend at The Yews, heavenly as the place was.

Last time, she had hoped that the pampering and the fact that they would have time together would make Graham reachable, focused on her, and that World-in-bloody-One wouldn't even be mentioned.

She hadn't expected a firework display of attention, just for him to be companionable, just be there.

Before dinner, champagne was delivered to the room. She had put the lingerie box under her pillow, having had a really good look at the items while Graham was showering.

The negligee set seemed to her to have been crocheted from silvery, spiders' webs. It occurred to her that they made a fitting symbol for the state of their marriage – the knickers so ludicrously brief as to be impractical and the bra top over-generous in cup size.

The diaphanous top would be even roomier now than in January. She had lost a lot of weight during The Scare, as she had begun to refer to it in retrospect in phone calls to friends.

It was easy to be light-hearted, now that she knew all was well.

Although she had begun to eat heartily again she could still count her ribs in the bathroom mirror, and feel her skirt slipping down annoyingly.

Benign...

Surely the most beautiful word in the world, she thought – not for the first time. During the past week it had been the word she'd cradled in her mind each night as she fell asleep, and the word that made her wake with a smile.

Graham had been reassuring and strong when she had found the lump; he'd said that it would be sorted out, whatever it took, but had then been abducted by work demands while she was left to fret and wait at home.

For a couple of days she had been too afraid to go to the doctors and, when she did, she was not assured by what she heard. Everything would hinge on the biopsy. Her relief on getting the lab result had been marred when Graham forgot to ring, and then had failed to ask for her news as soon as he got home late that night.

"Jesus!" he'd said when she'd told him her news, and told him how hurt she was.

"What's happening to me, Pen? Imagine me not thinking!" he'd shouted, appalled at himself.

He had cuddled her briefly before sinking exhausted onto a kitchen chair, bowing his head and running his fingers through his hair.

"Berlin was firing questions at us all day between meetings so I got no break. But there's absolutely no bloody excuse."

On that first trip, over the candle-lit dinner in the plush dining room of The Yews, she had plied Graham with wine, teased him, and really worked on excavating the good humour that she knew must still be there.

His efforts at reciprocation came over as hard work. He laughed but his eyes showed no joy. He was weighed down.

Her anger flared when he left the table suddenly just as the dessert was arriving because he had forgotten to make an important business call.

"Promise – just this one, Pen," he had said as he dropped his napkin and hurried off. She had stomped off to bed, past a surprised waiter on his way with her crème brûlée.

She had read the signs long ago. Graham's director role at World-in-One UK had taken its toll. But after just couple of months into his new role as Chief Exec he had become hardly recognisable.

He dispensed with small talk, never really relaxed, slept badly and had become pouchy and pasty. He had always been big and rather shambolic; now he had ballooned and moved as if he was wading through chest-high water.

Today he was absolutely off-duty; not to be disturbed; fully shielded by his PA. Yet before he'd even finished his breakfast he was being emailed by the PR people who had to give some response to a TV station's coverage of an anti-World-in-One protest at some sodding allotments.

It had seemed to Penny that Graham was only his old self (and then fleetingly) when he had just received some good figures, or emerged from the garage with a fax about a beneficial turn of events in the business.

He now inevitably drank in the evenings, the few evenings he was home, and fell asleep in the big chair, even when football was on.

Away from home he had flourished. Berlin had loved him; so much they had ensured he was rewarded with the top job.

In his two years he had justified their confidence in him, leading a brilliant expansion initiative, but Penny knew that relations were now not as cordial.

Home for Penny had become a centre for Graham's rest and recuperation, a depot for the replenishment of luggage for foreign trips. At weekends it turned into a monitoring station for business bulletins. Penny provided the memory-jogging service for important dates, like Benjie's birthday, school sports day, Mother's Day, her own birthday.

As Penny zipped up the bag she could hear Eileen, in Benjie's bedroom, telling him about her recent holiday. At certain moments he sounded fascinated, at others he was obviously maintaining a well-mannered silence, a quality she thanked the prep school for instilling. They were sticklers for manners.

"What – actual frogs on sticks Nan?" he was saying.

"Yes," Eileen said, "and insects. You could buy ants' eggs and crispy grasshopper things."

"Ugh!" Benjie exclaimed. "My friend Jamie's mum once made him try Marmite."

"Oh dear, the poor lad."

"Did you try anything horrible Nan?"

"Not horrible but I ate too much sticky rice with mango and coconut milk. Everybody eats it. I felt a bit sick but the Thai people were so kind I didn't want to upset them. You know, Benjie, they greet you in such a lovely way … like this."

Penny could picture Eileen putting her palms together and bowing.

"Anyway, thanks for all the presents, Nan!" said Benjie, who had now heard enough travellers' tales. He bounded down the stairs.

Benjie was loving having Eileen to stay and, for Penny, the visits had become far more bearable.

They seemed to have reached a spirit of compromise. Certain subjects were out of bounds and Eileen had learned to hold her tongue, so poor old Graham was no longer having to soak up the tension generated by two strong, opinionated women.

Eileen and Benjie went downstairs and, as Penny waited and then followed, she could hear Benjie enthusing about the uniform for his new school. She stopped at the foot of the stairs as they talked in the kitchen.

"It's purply Nan, and its got orange edges," Benjie was saying.

"Wow!"

"They've got boarders."

"The uniforms? It's called piping, love."

"No, the school. It's got beds for kids."

"But you won't need a bed Benjie. You'll be what they call a day boy."

"I know. At first I thought I'd be sleeping there but Mum explained."

"Silly boy!"

"I said to Mum that if I did sleep there I'd need to take Raggy, and I'd still want Mum to say goodnight."

"Don't worry. I don't think Mum and Dad would ever want you to go away to any school where you would need to be a boarder."

That was that sort of thing that made Penny's hackles rise.

Penny believed that Eileen had made it clear in little weasel ways that she thought that they had become rather grand since Graham had become such a high-flier, had obviously decided that Benjie would never go to public school.

He probably wouldn't, although Graham had been more pliant on the subject lately and had certainly not discounted the idea. But it was bugger all to do with Eileen.

She suspected that Eileen believed that she had become rabidly aspirational, driving Graham on, when in fact it was Graham who was driven, pathologically driven.

They had managed to stretch to buying this wonderful house because of Graham's whopping bonus but, as Penny had learned, the personal cost was proportional to the almost scandalously high remuneration.

World-in-One had bought Graham's life.

Graham was never very forthcoming but lately she'd noted his impotent rage over obstacles in the way of expansion, things he couldn't change. She had also picked up on the jitteriness at the UK end before the meetings in Berlin – all those phone calls to prepare explanation and justification to the German board.

He went on the defensive whenever she sounded alarms about their relationship; he seemed to be pleading for her to endure things for a just little longer, to build a bigger nest-egg, to establish himself more firmly.

"It'll be different eventually, Pen," he would say. "We'll have time."

Business careers rarely followed an even upward trajectory. She knew that at this moment Graham was buckling under the pressure. She also knew that he could never show her his fear because that would entail association with failure.

Penny was determined that during the weekend away she would reach out to him, tell him she was behind him, that if the job wasn't right he should resign. Even if he did not respond, he would feel secure about her support.

She wondered how his mother would react if his career faltered. Eileen had basked in the glow of his meteoric rise; embarrassingly for Graham, when he became Chief Exec she had framed the Financial Times profile of him.

There was vicarious enjoyment of the perks Graham's job commanded.

"Good lord – The Yews again! Lucky you!" Eileen had exclaimed when Penny had rung to ask if she'd come over to look after Benjie. "A freebie I expect?"

"Just a little extra treat that comes with the job," Penny said.

For some reason – probably because she knew it would impress Eileen, and perhaps make her envious – she had added:"We can take six a year. And I get my treatments free."

"He really did fall on his feet with this job!" Eileen said. If only she knew.

Penny gathered up the bag and went downstairs. Benjie had taken the dog out, probably down to the copse at the end of the long lawn. The stand of old, mixed trees, fronted by a curtain of silver birch, was still an exciting novelty.

When talking to old friends she kept having to remind herself not to talk about "the copse" or "the old stables". It was so easy now to sound grand.

Eileen was at the breakfast bar. There was something about her bony stature that added to the irritation caused by the things she said. She was infuriatingly persistent. Penny thought of her as a droning gnat, circling incessantly, unswattable.

"Cuppa Eileen?" she said.

"Yes, dear. That would be nice," Eileen replied than added hurriedly: "Benjie's been telling me about the new school. So the poor mite thought he'd be sleeping there did he?"

"Yes. But don't worry, Eileen. He won't ever be a boarder if I can help it."

"I really am so relieved, Pen. Sending them away is cruel."

"I agree Eileen. But then, it's only my view. I fear that son of yours seems to be slowly warming to the idea."

"Graham? Surely not!" she said, incredulous.

Yes, your bloody God-like son, Penny thought, straining to maintain a conciliatory smile.

"Yes, he's even got a couple of prospectuses."

"No..." Eileen said, as if there had been some miscommunication.

As Penny filled the kettle and put it on the AGA, she turned her back to Eileen, shut her eyes and silently mouthed, "Touché."

It tasted almost as sweet as "benign".

SEVEN

"Shit!" Graham exclaimed, looking at his watch. They should have left by now. It was an annoyingly long haul deep into rural Sussex, and there would be the usual Friday night traffic. A drag.

He was being driven mad by the clutter around the improvised office he'd rigged up in the garage. Weeks after the house move, he was still head high in stuff sitting where the removal people had left it.

There was so little time he hadn't been able to get anyone in to fit out a proper office in the stables. It was ridiculous – he still had to kneel on his seat to reach the fax, and now the printer was on the blink.

Nowadays there was no hiding place; work was work and home was work; time off was work.

The request today from the PR people had irritated him, given him indigestion, but he couldn't blame them for trying to get the right tone. Benton Hall was going to be a showpiece development for World-in-One. The protesting would die down eventually.

Typical that, when they should have been well on their way to the spa, here he was still rushing out an update for Nigel. It would not make happy reading.

Berlin had noticed the wobble on the shares quoted on the stock exchange after newspaper speculation that the World-in-One's UK figures this year would show they'd slipped to third place in the British supermarket league table.

One article blamed the slowing rate of expansion and, by implication, Graham. Evidently some big shareholders were becoming fidgety.

The buck stopped with him, in his suite of offices in London, and also right here, at the plywood board serving as his desk, in this virtual island surrounded by bikes, storage boxes, tool racks and stacked chairs.

He sat down at the computer and thought hard, his fingers poised over the keyboard. He needed to remind Berlin (and the chairman) that there were factors he could not influence, and he needed to do it now. The spa would have to bloody well wait.

Graham heard Penny shout from the kitchen, asking if he was keeping an eye on the time and was about to shout back when the phone rang again. It was Nigel himself, speaking from the airport.

The chairman seemed unusually cool. A grilling in Berlin would not have been in his weekend plans.

Graham asked: "Shall I follow you over?"

"No," Nigel said decisively. "It's just me. Max has gone into crisis mode."

He indicated where in Graham's report he wanted the emphasis to lie and then suggested the outline of an optimistic note about the second half of the year.

Annoyingly, as Graham stooped to take notes, writing on the plywood as there was no paper within reach, Penny appeared at the garage door, smilingly urging him to hurry up, looking at her watch and doing a little running gesture.

"I'll finesse it at this end," Nigel said brusquely, and rang off.

Graham slammed down the phone down and turned on Penny.

"Look Pen, I'm rushing to clear up a load of bloody important stuff so we can get off. Jesus fucking Christ – give me a break!"

He saw her face crumple with the hurt as she turned and went back to the kitchen.

It was a ninety-minute journey to The Yews and neither spoke.

The new automatic cruised along almost unaided so there was chance to think once he got onto the country roads.

He cleared his head of work worries, not without effort and for a few moments harked back to the days in the flat, with Penny, all the training and then the struggle to afford the study for the Masters in Business Studies. Without being boastful, now he could claim to be a leading expert on supermarkets.

People had a really simplistic view of the field. They wouldn't guess that he had to know about socio-economics, footfall, food technology, consumer law, employment legislation.

Then there was the psychological side, an aspect that had always fascinated him: the stuff about ambience, aromas, the harnessing of emotional responses for profit. He loved the way that commercial ends could be achieved by such an apparently innocuous factor as colour. There was a whole box of selling tools.

He sometimes pictured his octogenarian Aunt Milly in her residential home in Felixstowe spraying her underarms, blissfully unaware that the can shape had been carefully crafted to match the average size and shape of the European penis.

Customers thought they were wise to the tricks of the trade but really most were naïve.

How many who responded on cue to a promotional blitz boasting of generous price cuts noticed that the prices had been raised just three weeks before?

They didn't know that in the early days music-to-shop-to had been given a tempo that matched their heartbeat, compelling them to walk slowly so they saw more, bought more. They did not know that they had been secretly filmed reacting to displays of goods.

They didn't care – why should they? – as they picked up their two-for-one packs of chops, that the farmer who supplied them had barely broken even this year.

He loved the fact that actions had measurable effects. Upselling, shelf talkers, loss leaders, product sampling, loyalty schemes and celebrity endorsement showed up as pleasing little peaks at intervals along a flat line showing sales over time.

That said, he had no illusions about the personal costs. He knew that work had engulfed him. He saw the irony that lay in his situation: he was giving his life to win consumers, and all the time he was being consumed by the job.

The warmth inside the car, the silence and the gentle purr of the new automatic were combining to relax him now. He consciously forced his shoulders to fall and tried to put current worries to the back of his mind.

He was enjoying the chance to look objectively at himself, his career, his marriage. It felt as if he was facing up to a crisis that had crept up on him.

"Do you mind?" he asked Penny as he slid his favourite CD into the player.

"Go ahead," she said almost inaudibly.

The sweet, sad wail of the uilleann pipes had been a sensory oasis on most of his trips to the airport, and on his night-time car journeys home.

It seemed to be the only thing that took him out of himself. The reels were wonderful but it was the slow airs that got him. Plaintive, echoing; he imagined the piper on an Irish hillside at sunset and when he put the mental picture and the music together it soothed him.

It struck him that colleagues would have thought his musical taste eccentric. It was true that there was something of a mismatch.

Here he was, wearing shoes that cost more than the average weekly wage, riding along in a car that cost the company as much as a terraced house, finding solace in the music, he supposed, of Irish peasants.

He took another a furtive glance at Pen through the central mirror, and detected immediately that he was dealing with more than a sulk. He thought he saw tears; maybe the music was doing to her what it did to him?

He turned to his catalogue of successes for comfort, and tried to feel again the glow he'd experienced when Berlin had approved his appointment.

Evidently, they'd been greatly reassured by his knowledge of British planning regulations, council procedures and keenness to create land "banks." He'd also impressed them, he knew, with his knowledge of environmental issues and his mastery of PR activity, enabling a hypermarket to be slipped into a disproportionately small town with hardly a protest letter in the local paper, let alone a placard.

It was worrying that lately the PR spin had been so ineffective. Lately there had been well-mannered but cleverly orchestrated opposition to World-in-One developments in six towns.

Now there was talk of a national campaign and MPs had begun poking their noses in. Worse still, councils seemed to be hardening against the very concept of hypermarkets.

Graham peered again into the driving mirror, to check on Pen without looking directly at her. Her face was a mask. She had nipped a bit of her bottom lip between her teeth, something she did when she was troubled.

He was overcome by a realisation that maybe he had lost his identity somewhere on the long climb to his goal.

They were just a few miles from The Yews now. He decided that he would try to talk with Penny, so that she would really understand how hard it was for him at the moment.

For the first time in his career he had begun to doubt his ability to control outcomes. He sometimes felt that the job was running him, rather than the other way around.

What was that business theory about people being promoted to the point of incompetence? Ah yes: The Peter Principle.

Maybe I've been over-promoted, he said to himself, shamed to be thinking that a possibility.

Eventually he looked over darkened fields and picked out the spa with its welcoming windows, filled with lemony light, and the silhouetted ancient trees standing sentinel around it.

They got out of the car and Graham held out an arm in a clumsy attempt at reconciliation.

"Don't," said Penny, moving away. "I'm going to have something to eat in the room, and then I need to sleep," she said.

She pulled her coat round her shoulders and crunched on the gravel to the entrance. "It's too late for swimming and I missed my massage slot," she said, with no note of recrimination.

"But Pen..." Graham began but he knew that when Penny's patience was exhausted she was implacably stubborn.

"I want to go home tomorrow," she said. "We'll tell your mum I was ill."

They slept, well apart, in the huge bed. They had breakfast in silence.

Then, while Penny went upstairs, Graham took a newspaper to a sunny window seat on the edge of the dining room. He turned to the financial pages first to see whether World-in-One had recovered any ground by the time the stock exchange had stopped trading on the previous afternoon.

The share price had gone down another two per cent late in the day. Immediately he felt queasy, and regretted having had a big breakfast. He strolled to reception to check out and a girl in a white uniform hurried to his side.

"Ah, we've been hunting you down sir!" she said. "A message."

It was from his mother and it said: "Graham – ring Nigel at Berlin office asap."

The queasiness turned to nausea and he hurried to get into the fresh air.

Meanwhile, up in the bedroom, Penny was reaching into her bag for the lingerie. She laid it on the pillow, took a sheet of headed notepaper from the bureau and wrote: *"Thank you all for a short but lovely stay. Perhaps you or another member of staff would like this (unworn, unwanted) gift."*

She placed the note carefully on top of the box, and went down to join Graham.

EIGHT

"Everything OK, Graham?" Eileen asked after they'd had a makeshift lunch and as soon as Benjie had gone out with the dog. The boy seemed a little disappointed that Mum and Dad had returned prematurely, intruding on his time with Eileen.

Penny had immediately gone to bed to back up her claim to have a migraine but also because she needed to think about the future.

"Yeah, Mum. But Penny not being well spoiled things. Shame. We both needed the rest."

With Penny in bed and Eileen around to keep an eye on Benjie, Graham felt free to give in to the growing urge to check on things in the garage. He had still to ring Nigel in Berlin, and there would be faxes and maybe a couple of regional reports had come in. He was surprised to feel a nervous flutter.

As soon as he walked through the door from the kitchen, he could see the phone message light blinking. There were faxes in the tray. The inner tremor seemed to strengthen and rage rose within him.

"Fuck them all!" he shouted. "I'm supposed to be off!"

He lowered himself onto the blanket chest that Penny had not yet found a spot for; on each side were tea chests and cardboard boxes full of clothes and crockery, framed photos and yet more clothes.

He could see, poking out of a part-open drawer, old cardboard files and, as he looked more closely, recognised them as essays from his business degree course.

They were so bulky and the text was dense. Graham was amazed that he had packed so much work into the Masters, and at the professional-sounding language he had summoned up. It was as if they had been written by someone else.

Rifling through, he discarded each file in turn until he came to "Module 3: Dichter and the Unlocking of Desire".

It had focused on a man who, by startling coincidence, had lived in the same street as Freud in Vienna and went on to make millions by applying psychoanalytical theories in business, becoming "the Freud of the Supermarket Age".

The ringing of the phone snapped him out of his reverie.

It was Nigel. He seemed not to want to talk, and parried Graham's questions about his trip and the reaction of the Germans.

"They want us to go over next week. Early flight Wednesday. OK?"

"OK, Nigel."

His heart plummeted. Graham could see, in his mind, the Spree river, the towering Fernsehturm TV tower announcing that the car was nearing the executive enclave in Alexanderplatz.

There, hidden away in his office suite, behind two formidable secretaries, as perfect and as soulless as wax dummies, and the wonderful sculpture of a predatory bird, the silvery Dr Schmidt would be waiting. This little, icy wraith of a man, who had never, ever invited Graham to drop the Dr and call him Max, even when he had been in favour, when (in Nigel's teasing words) he was "Englander Goldenballs".

He could visualise, all too clearly, how it would be on Wednesday, and the image that seemed to sum it all up was that bronze swooping falcon with its talons opening to snatch up its prey.

NINE

Home, March 22, 2000

My dear Kyff,

Got to congratulate that doctor of yours!!! Whatever he's given you certainly makes you sleep!!! Rang twice, on 22nd and 23rd, usual time, but couldn't rouse you - take it you weren't ignoring me? Or staying somewhere else???!

Anyway, nothing too dramatic, and really I wanted to talk rather than write.

Fact is, I'm planning to come home i.e. leaving this "home" to go back to Wiltshire.

I'm sure that it won't feel like home for a very long time. But at least by joining Mum for a time I'll have a bit of support, AND good cooking.

To be truthful, I've felt in desperate need of that lately (I don't expect sympathy). Thanks to me, we both lost three friends at a stroke, though of course in rejecting you I lost something far greater than a friend, something I won't be able to replace.

Quite a sobering thought with all that life in front of me!!!

I think I understand it all a bit better now.

I never got over Lizzie as you know, never will, and I needed to be hauled out of it. You couldn't really help because you were mixed in with everything that seemed to be destroying me - the grief but also feeling like I failed. Does that make any sense?

I know I was an absolute cow, and a confused one.

Erik was clear-headed and so confident and convincing - you know how he comes across. He just seemed so certain that taking a new direction was the answer for me. I knew, within weeks, even before you flew home, that it was all an illusion, an epic mistake and, you know what, that I didn't really even like him.

I know now that it's impossible to shake things off, things like Lizzie. Just as I've found it impossible to see you drift away.

But what's done is done. There's a saying isn't there about making your bed and then having to lie on it?

I'd wondered whether by leaving Perth I'm selling out, and crawling off for a bit of pampering from Mum, or whether it's an attempt to white out the indelible bad bits, esp. Lizzie.

Anyway, with your problems you could do without my whimpering. It's just that on the phone we daren't really say things that matter, dare we? I can hear that my voice upsets you.

So ... on to practical things, things like your books and photos, the old cameras, the tools, your bike and guitar. Then there's your LPs - they weigh a ton but I know you'll want to keep them.

Oh, not to mention that bloody "bargain" outboard motor that you never quite managed to join up to a boat! Hope that won't be a bone of contention to the bitter end.

Ouch! Writing "bitter end" struck a nerve - it stopped me for a moment. "Bitter" is bad enough but "end"...

Anyway, practically everything you owned is still here. It might be two or three months before the house is sold but I need some idea of what you'd like me to ship. I could sell everything else, even the sodding outboard motor (advice needed).

Hope you're getting a bit better every day. And happy birthday when it comes.

Love (am I now allowed to say that again???)

Grace X

P.S. Talking of bitter ends (no tear this time), I'm told your solicitor came out fighting with his very first letter. My lawyer asked me whether his style reflected your feelings. I said that you were not the sort to get revenge via financial stuff.

Where did you find him? Battersea Dogs' Home???

TEN

Up betimes, choleric from supping an excess of Claret. Partook of a Benson and Hedges reefer that made me cough fit to burst, then a sparse breakfast of Corn Flakes, and having released a Volley of Farts hastened by foot to the Allotment Gardens. There, the sun being up giving unseasonal warmth, great numbers of gardeners scurried mightily like ants about their business, most having wheelbarrows and assorted implements, it being Manure Day…

The wonderful Sam Pepys has been dispensing sleep each night for the last week or so. I accompany him on his rounds of business and his drinking and his plotting and when he writes "And so to bed" I drift off.

Buying the diaries has led me back to history. My head is full of the pictures he paints, the characters he introduces. I love the direct freshness of his shared life.

Annoyingly, I've started to talk to myself in 1660s parlance but (God be Praised!) I no longer struggle to get up and confront the morning, even when, as last night, I've polished off a bottle of plonk.

Well, it was my birthday after all, and I needed something to wash down my celebration meal, "Roast Beef Dinner-for-One in foil serving tray".

There could hardly be a sadder product description – or a birthday meal so far removed from what might have been … Molto Pesce rock oysters with lime and chilli dip, followed by aromatic dhufish chowder (Grace's favourite), in good company, at a seafront table giving the best view of the sunset.

No matter. Dr May's medicinal compound, and Sam's company at bedtime, really are working. Now, as a gesture of thanksgiving to the doc I've made a birthday pledge to do some digging each day. It will be good therapy, and it will keep Dad's plot, and in turn my conscience, reasonably clear.

Not only that, now I'm so aware of how life experience ebbs away, I've begun jotting notes about the allotment and my Benton friends.

I know that my stay here is only a stop-off on the journey and one day I'll want to re-live the feeling of peace that I've found here, the acceptance of me, the friendship and humour and, now, the feeling I'm on the mend.

There is something to note every day and, almost every day now, gifts of seedlings, and young plants wrapped in wet newspaper.

Yesterday a man I'd not met before came to the hut from the railway side with a paper bag, peeped in and putting on a formal face, like a butler's, announced: "Your kidneys, sir."

I was thrown for a moment then he beamed and said: "International Kidneys. Also known as Jersey Royals. Had a few to spare. Thought they'd start you off. They've started sprouting."

Cecil says he's saving me some of the Black Russian tomato plants he'd got going on his windowsill.

"They look appalling. Colour of Cherry Blossom Ox Blood shoe polish. But the taste! Perfect marriage of sweet and acid."

It's as if they're all trying to excite me, induct me into the brotherhood of growers.

As Old Bill biked past me at snail's pace yesterday he pointed at Dad's plot, wobbled out of control then called over his shoulder to remind me that now the asparagus was coming I'd to make sure I stopped cutting after the longest day.

I thought I'd seen tips peeping through but they might have been the weeds that started getting a foothold as soon as Dad's hoe was stilled. They've survived the cold and at this moment seem to be limbering up in the sun for a spurt of growth.

Dad's spade – the shaft with its sheen, and blade polished bright by use – beckons me from the back of the hut. But, seeing the sun again, and feeling a suspicion of warmth coming through the windows, I procrastinate by putting the kettle on then perching on the stool and sipping tea and smoking and flipping through some of Dad's booklets.

I lose myself in a little, sun-bleached paperback, Common For All – The Story of the Allotment Movement, and find that I immediately slip into my accustomed historian role, warming particularly to a quotation from 350 years ago, from Gerrard Winstanley, of the Levellers: "If the Earth be not peculiar to any one branch … of mankind, then it is free and common for all, to work together and eate together…"

As it appears, the common land outside will indeed soon belong to one branch – of World-in-One supermarkets.

I lift Dad's spade off its dowel peg and go to the door full of good intentions but there's a welcome diversion. A lorry has arrived at the Top End and, reversing onto the pavement, has tipped a mountain of manure at the gates.

This seems to have prompted a barrow race.

Yeti is barrelling along like a dinosaur, cutting off gardeners from the railway side; Madge, in dungarees and pink wellingtons, makes her way with a stooping walk, pushing a supermarket trolley. It's as if the mound of muck at the gate is a pile of ice cubes that has to be gathered before they melt.

Waggy has arrived and is walking almost in slow motion with his barrow, stopping every so often to catch his breath.

I retreat to the hut and through the window see Winco with his foot on his fork watching the stampede with a look of disdain.

There's a knock on the window and Prof's unruly head appears. He's grinning and pointing a thumb towards the gate.

"Come on, fill your boots, Kyff!" he mouths through the glass.

"I'll give it a miss, Prof," I say, ushering him into the hut. "Not sure I'll be around here long enough to see muck working its miracles."

Just as I'm filling the kettle at the standpipe I hear Cecil, coming back from the Top End, shout: "Well, I'll go to bloody hell!"

He's pointing to the Bottom End where an open-topped wagon is spilling another load of manure, on a roadside spot being indicated by Wilf who has beside him a barrow bigger than himself, and is leaning on an ancient-looking multi-tined fork.

"We've bloody well duplicated!" Cecil shouts to no-one in particular. "We got a double load from the usual bloke, trying to be kind, and on top of that somebody's bloody well doubled up with another muck man!"

I glance along the path and catch Winco looking detached and superior.

As word spreads about the second manure man, some at the Top End spin round and head to the Bottom End. It all looks like a bit of operatic choreography.

Prof and me are on our second fag and third tea when we hear raised voices and see that the lorry has disappeared and a Land Rover has arrived alongside the manure pile; the driver unhitches a towing trailer and deposits his load, almost blocking the entry to the allotments.

"Would you believe it?!" says Prof. "Winco's ordered mushroom compost. His own private supply." There is a despairing shake of the head.

He is rolling another cigarette, and thinking. I wait to hear what esoteric gem he will pull from the treasure box of his mind but decide to interrupt his thoughts with my own teaser, freshly drawn from the little book about allotments.

"Right Prof. A test: church, sixteen, feet. What's the connection?"

"Well," he says, without hesitation. "It's the length of a rod. Allotments were measured in rods. They used to say that a rod was the combined length of the left feet of the first sixteen men coming out of church on a Sunday morning. Sixteenth century idea."

He smiles that beguiling but awful brown-toothed smile and lights up as if his spindly roll-up was his reward.

"You know Kyff, it's heaven in here. In the hut. Tranquil. Shut off. Like being in a nest. It's as if you're plugging into some stream of goodness, getting your spiritual batteries charged up."

"My sanctuary Prof," I say without thought, and then acknowledge to myself that is exactly how I've come to think of it. In fact I've almost come to believe that the wooden walls really do emit something beneficial and strengthening. Taff's spirit, Grace would say.

"I used to dream about living in a log cabin when I'd watched a cowboy film," I tell him. "There's something more than just the sheltering thing about wood. It makes a deep connection with me, like a bonfire does. I was always finding excuses to work with wood back in Oz."

I think of Erik and me, hand sanding side by side and talking, bringing out the tramline grain on a silvery white panel of Paulownia, and of the nights I curled up and nursed my anger in the summerhouse back in Perth, listening to the cracks and creaks from the wood as it cooled.

Sunlight cuts down at an angle through the window, turning Prof's flyway hair into a golden aura and throwing kaleidoscope colours from the stained glass window onto the floor planks.

"Wood's in our DNA. More than 400,000 years ago people were huddling under wood," Prof says.

It's 2000 and here I am, not exactly huddling, but feeling I'm in my timber lair, away from harm, getting strong.

The pace of the barrow-pushers has slowed now but the manure mountains are still shoulder high. We stroll along the path to the Top End with a parade of barrows passing in both directions.

Waggy says: "They'll have to clear that lot by nightfall or the gates'll never close, and then some unassuming bugger will come a cropper in the dark on his way home from the pub. I can see the Chron headlines now: **'Dung death: I'll sue says widow.'**"

Yeti passes us with a huge wet, and slightly steaming, load. He's steaming too, his hair plastered down with sweat. It's not occurred to him to shed his weighty woollen overgarment.

Instead of swinging left and unloading on his own patch, he turns right and, two plots on, upends the barrow beside a glum-looking man sitting on a bench covered with a plastic sack.

Prof anticipates my question.

"Les. He gardens by proxy. Spends most of his time looking helpless and getting other people to do the work. Today he's using Yeti as a pack animal."

We step off the path to let Yeti and his barrow pass.

As we approach, Prof says, out of the side of his mouth: "Every single conversation with Les includes the words 'crumbling back'. Every one. Today will be no exception. If he does, you owe me a Benson's."

Les makes a laboured effort at standing up as Prof says: "Les – meet Huw's son Kyff. Over from Australia for a bit. Just keeping his Dad's plot in decent order for the moment."

"Nice to meet you," says Les. "Sorry I can't get up," he says weakly, easing himself into a new position on his sack. He's a weedy man with a voice that brims with self-pity.

"Your dad was a great character. Eighty-odd wasn't he, and far fitter than me and I'm only half that."

Prof has inclined his head, waiting for the predicted words.

"It's really frustrating for me having my problem. I just have to stand and watch. You feel as if you've lost your manhood."

I sympathise.

"Oh, don't feel sorry for me, lad. There's people far worse off. And this sun makes the pain almost bearable."

Ray arrives with barrowload, his long back bowed with effort, and his black fringe falling over his face.

"Thought you'd like a bit of muck," he says, slowly straightening himself up. "Poor devil's stuck, aren't you Les? With your wossname."

Crumbling Back nods gravely.

I could see Prof is needled by the interruption. He has been hanging on every word. I decide to put Prof out of his misery, creating a conversational hole into which the words "crumbling back" will fall nicely.

"Your problem – does anything give you a bit of relief?"

"Nothing."

"Is it chest trouble?"

"No. Wish it was. I could cope with that."

"What is it then?"

"You know, don't you Prof?"

"I did but I might have forgotten…" Prof says.

There's a long silence.

"Can't the doctors help with it?" I ask.

"No chance. It's gone too far."

There's another hiatus. I can feel that Prof is seeing his chance slipping away.

"Well, nice to meet you," I say.

"And you, Kyff."

We turn to go but Les calls: "Thing is, they say that if I move suddenly the whole of my invertebrates could collapse like a pack of cards."

Prof lingers, and Les shouts after us: "There's a medical term for what I've got but I can't ever remember it. It's got 'itis' in it somewhere, or 'osis'"

Prof calls back: "Don't bother your head with medical terms. What is it you call it again, Les?"

"Me? Oh, I just call it… Crumbling Back."

I flick open my cigarette packet and hold it out to Prof, who is wreathed in a nicotine-tinted grin.

"Fact is, Waggy," Prof is saying, "what's going on here is very much what nearly happened to cities around the turn of the century."

Prof and Waggy and Cecil are at the Top End at the start of another unexpected day of pristine sunshine and they make a gap for me – a stray cell blending with the nucleus.

The scene from the Bottom End gate could inspire a pastoral suite for strings, or a watercolour. Everything is greening up and there's optimism in the air, a whiff of spring, and a rustic pong.

Cecil confesses that he had trouble sleeping last night, bothered by dreams of manure-related accidents caused by it. He had been out late borrowing red lights to stop traffic – cyclists especially – from hitting the fringes of the muck mounds.

"Yep, London once nearly disappeared under horse droppings," Prof announces.

We know that he is warming up for a fact-shedding diatribe but as he pauses and gets out his tobacco there's no hardship standing here, bathed in sunlight, while the barrows roll past unrelentingly.

"Look at it. They've dug it in, they've spread it, they've topped up their compost heaps, now they're making hillocks of it, and there's still more to barrow in. Just like in London, when they had thousands of buses, thousands of cabs, all pulled by horses.

"They were running out of space for the droppings when they were saved."

Cecil is intrigued.

"How, Prof?"

"Invention of the car," he replies. "A resolution of mixed benefit."

Prof is just relating the consequences of the fly infestations in New York, caused by horse traffic, when his voice trails away as he looks round and notices we've moved off.

Sometimes you have to get away before you find yourself crushed by an avalanche of knowledge.

ELEVEN

It is obvious from Cecil's face that he is either ill or in shock. Even from a plot's length away I can see that beneath the year-round tan is a pallor. His jaw is thrust forward; he is a man hurrying for help.

He steps out along the path from the Top End and then marches down the side of Dad's plot where I am thinning a line of carrots. He is carrying his tweed jacket over his arm and panting in the heat. A wad of hair is stuck to his forehead.

"Trouble, Kyff," he says, gasping and shaking his head. "Yeti's been lifted."

"Arrested?"

"Yes. Arrested. The bloody great chump!"

"Why?"

"Assault. They're actually talking of attempted manslaughter if the lad takes a turn for the worst. Kyff – it's an intensive care job."

Yeti under arrest?

I picture him, a huge globe of goodwill enveloped in one of his enormous cardigans, sitting in a police interview room, probably wanting his mum.

"Cecil," I say – calmly, to try to ease his anxiety. "Listen Cecil. It was nothing. I was here. I saw some of it happening as I walked to the Top

End. It looked to me as if Yeti had just caught a vandal and was holding him down to give him a talking to, showing who was boss."

"Well, it's turned out to be a damn sight more serious than that."

I lead him into the hut and put the kettle on.

"Take the big chair Cecil. Relax a minute. You'll be having a heart attack." He sits rigidly upright.

"I've been down at the cop shop three hours. They've still got him there. What a bloody day!"

Poor Cecil, and poor old Yeti.

Ironically, here it has been a blissful afternoon. Blazing sunshine, a huge cloudless sky, and peace; just the sound of birds and the occasional rattle of a train rattling along the embankment taking holidaymakers to the coast.

There has been butterflies on the lavender and dragonflies straying over from the pond in the Old Hall grounds; people have been wending their way along plot-side paths and going home with flowers and salad stuff and fists full of broad beans and carrier bags filled with new potatoes.

I've been pulling up crowded seedlings and lazily going back and forth with the watering can to lettuces and cucumbers. I've found a patch of alpine strawberries that are now bejewelled with tiny fruit.

And all the while this terrible drama has been unfolding.

Up in town, Yeti was being grilled by police and Cecil was in a nearby room fretting and, evidently, half a mile away, in a hospital ward, a young mischief-maker was being nursed back from the brink of death.

Perhaps I could have prevented it all but the incident hadn't struck me as potentially serious.

As I locked the hut last night, I heard a bit of cursing from three teenagers swishing long sticks and heading up from the Bottom End towards Yeti's little sentry box of a shed. They looked more bored than threatening.

As I walked on, I heard Yeti shout and turned to see him drop his rake and break into a surprisingly nimble run, gaining pace as he went, like an enraged hippo. Winco was struggling along in his wake.

The lads were strolling, veering off the path towards Dad's shed, probably to get over the fence into the grounds of the Old Hall, but scattered when they saw Yeti.

One shouted "Fat bastard!" before he lost his footing in the long grass beneath the trees near the fence and Yeti flopped down on him.

I stood on the bottom rail of the Top End gate for a better view and saw that Yeti was face down on his victim's chest, across him at a right angle. It struck me as odd that Yeti had reached behind his back and clasped his hands together. It was obvious he would not need my help.

I relate this to Cecil as he sits, tense and upright, in the old dentist's chair and sips his tea. Rivulets of sweat are running down the sides of his face.

"The lads had been slashing the tops off plants but what really got to Yeti was seeing them going near your dad's hut. It was a territorial thing."

"But Cecil," I say, "how did he hurt this lad?"

"Hurt him? He near killed him – in fact he's not out of the woods yet. It turns out that, medically speaking, twenty-odd stone on top of a spindly kid's chest isn't a healthy combination.

"The paramedics said the lad could have been brain damaged because the poor bugger couldn't breathe. I think that what Yeti thought was the lad struggling to escape was him trying to get a breath of air."

(Ah, that feeling.)

"Ironic isn't it?" says Cecil thoughtfully. "You get a great lump like Yeti and you teach him a way of controlling his temper tantrums. But by strange chance what you teach him turns him into a murderer – well, it might come to that."

Cecil is calmer now, getting things off his chest.

"He says that on the scheme that he's on they've taught him that every time he gets so angry he wants to chuck somebody through the window he has to stop and count very slowly to ten. One-and-two-and … that sort of thing.

"That's what he did when he lay on this lad. But while he counted, the kid was suffocating."

"The poor little sod," I find myself saying.

"But what's worse," Cecil adds, "was that after counting to ten, the lad started writhing and moaning. Probably the death rattle. Yeti took this to be resistance, and this made him angry, so he thought he'd better count to ten again."

Cecil is more composed now. He lies back in the dentist's chair and takes in a long, drawn-out breath.

I mention the curious business of Yeti's clasped hands.

"That? Well, he says that when he gets what he calls a paddy he's supposed to put his hands behind his back while he's counting, so he's not tempted to hit anybody. Coping strategy taught on the Scheme."

Cecil gets up, revived now and keen to catch up with developments.

"Is that boy really at risk?" I ask, fearing the reply.

"Breathing problems. That's all we know so far."

He promises to call on me later that night then leaves, jacket over his arm, the evening sun hitting the back of his shirt, marching off towards the Top End gates.

I go home with a heavy heart. I eat something, read in the bath and, just as I'm ready to go to bed, I hear at tap on the door and then see Cecil's face at the window.

I open it and he says: "Sorry I'm so late. Just come from Yeti's mother's."

I unlock the door and let him in, and sit him down because he is agitated.

"What a place! Wall-to-wall cats. Balls of wool everywhere! There she was, happily knitting away. Clickety click. She didn't miss a stitch when I said Yeti was in a serious trouble.

"'Oh, he'll have had another paddy I shouldn't wonder,' she said, as casual as you please. She was more worried that he'd missed his dinner than that he might be going to the clink. 'It'll warm through,' she said.

"She held up what looked like something you'd line in a dog basket with and said: 'This is for him. He likes red.' I was tempted to say she ought to start knitting something with arrows on."

We sit opposite each other and Cecil goes through developments step by step.

The latest report from the hospital is good. Two cracked ribs, a punctured lung, no mental impairment.

Yeti is likely to be charged, with what is uncertain but he should be home tonight.

"The solicitor I got says that everything will hinge on intent," says Cecil, "you know, what Yeti was trying to do after he saw these boys causing damage. Was he trying to steam-roller the life out of the lad, or just restrain him until someone came?"

Cecil suddenly looks downcast.

"And that's where we've got a problem. Winco's made a statement claiming he heard Yeti say: 'I'll learn you to spoil people's things.' In other words, Yeti was threatening to make the lad suffer. To be honest, I can hear Yeti saying it."

I think for a moment of poor gentle, daft, loyal Yeti trying to cope with solicitors and their questions.

"But, Cecil, Yeti didn't say that," I say.

"But were you near enough to hear, Kyff?"

"Yes," I say, looking meaningfully at Cecil so that he got my drift. "And what I heard Yeti actually say as I walked along the path was: 'Why do you spoil people's things?' He didn't say anything threatening."

"Are you sure, Kyff?" Cecil asks.

"Certain. You must be shattered but could you run me to the police station so I can make a statement saying what I heard?"

Cecil looks worried rather than relieved.

"Don't get into hot water yourself, Kyff."

"I won't. Yeti wasn't threatening. He wouldn't have had his hands behind his back if he'd wanted to be violent now, would he?"

"Yes he would!" says Cecil, with his first smile of the day.

TWELVE

We've gathered in one of our customary clusters on the path and the warm, sleepy, enveloping morning has been enlivened by a missing person alert.

"Crumbling Back" – Les – seems to have gone to ground.

There have been no sightings for more than a week. We – Cecil, me, Wilf and Yeti – chuckle over Waggy's claim that he's sent Cecil a sick note saying that this time he really does have a bad back, but it's a bit of a mystery.

He is normally around every day, either morning or evening, at this time of year, getting help with his watering cans, or supervising transplanting.

I'd heard that when Les's back trouble had first been diagnosed, the doctor had told him a bit of light work on the land would be therapeutic but he turned it into a prescription requiring him to watch others working several times a day.

"Where the hell can he be?" Wilf bellows at me, cocking a thumb towards the empty hut, while twiddling with one of his hearing aids.

"Snowboarding holiday probably," says Cecil with a straight face. "Or bungee jumping."

"Just a little bit of a situation. He's lying low for a while, Wilf," Prof says, shaping the words like mill girls used to have to do to be understood.

"Come on, Prof, I need to know what's gone off," says Cecil, trying to establish authority with his official voice, and failing.

"It'll all come out soon enough. I'm not tittle-tattling," Prof replies defiantly.

So, a mystery.

Earlier, Prof had ambled up from the Top End in his "going out" clothes, hair gathered in by an elastic band, with library books under his arm.

He had been heading for the Bottom End gate and home but he had been pulled in by the mysterious chemistry that forces us to form a human clump.

He joins today's nomadic little party.

Just before Prof was gathered in, Cecil silently materialised, and then Wilf slid up beside him. Now Waggy, with his rocking walk, is being reeled in from the Bottom End.

I've never noticed Waggy's walk before. It's a gait that any comedian would have chosen, big floppy feet turned out acutely – ten-to-two feet they used to be called – causing him to tilt back and forth slightly as he walks.

While we wait for him to join us, Cecil delights in pointing to two vacant plots that are now being worked. There's a young couple padding about in knee-high grass in the middle plots and nearby two young women, nurses, Cecil says, are digging for all they're worth.

"Got to carry on as if we're staying," says Cecil. "That couple are a bit dreamy, students, or some sort of hippies. But it takes all sorts…"

Meandering, we find ourselves following wafts of scent to Winco's plot. It is fronted with an eight-foot-high frame of canes covered by clouds of sweet peas, planted to form blocks of pastel colour, each perfect butterfly of a flower on a long stem. Show quality to my untrained eye.

"That really is a fabulous sight," I say, and mean it. Winco smiles a little too smugly.

The Hon Sec concurs: "That really is a cracking display!"

"Not bad is it?" says Winco, a shade too humbly. "My seed comes from a tiny nursery hardly anybody's heard of. Sorry, can't reveal the name."

His neighbour, Yeti, today sports another home-knit from his mum's leisure collection. It is scarlet and comes nearly down to his knees but has been buttoned up to follow his global contours. From a distance he must look like a hot air balloon.

He cannot bring himself to agree about the sweet peas.

"That smell from 'em makes me want to puke," Yeti says huffily. The spade dangling on the end of a beefy arm and his grumpy expression give him the air of a red giant who is out to break toys.

"Maybe the scent's too delicate for your nose, Yeti," Winco replies sourly.

Yeti appears to be thinking of a riposte. We wait. When it arrives it's disappointingly mundane: "You, you're posh you are."

"Now then, Yeti," says Cecil, grasping part of a bicep and leading Yeti away. "No need for that." The last thing Cecil wants is a full-blown Yeti paddy, especially while he's still on bail.

The leaden sky starts to shed its rain. It comes in large spots with big distances between them.

"What's that bonny one?" says Prof, cutting in. "Cambridge Blue? Blue Ballerina?"

"No," says Winco, enjoying the chance to put someone right, especially someone who is never – or hardly ever – wrong.

"New one. Limited issue." He corrects his posture slightly as he says it, as if the Commanding Officer were approaching.

"I wouldn't tell you my source even if you tortured me. But it's called Per Ardua Ad Astra."

"The RAF motto!" says Prof.

"Bang on," says Winco.

"Mmmm…" says Prof mischievously. "A woman … a place … some tint off an artist's palette maybe. But a sweet pea named in honour of airmen? Young deluded lads trained in bombing and missile launching?"

"Well, for twenty-three years I was proud to be one of those misguided lads,"Winco counters, almost standing to attention. He has a lean, clean-shaven profile, and it strikes me that he would have looked impressive in uniform, relaxing in the mess after flying his desk.

"You know," says Prof ruminatively, "I can just see Bomber Harris, in an old black-and-white film, holding a bunch of Per Arduas, looking to the heavens and muttering 'Through adversity to the stars...' while Dresden burns behind him."

It was a little sideswipe for Yeti.

"Only pulling your pisser!" laughs Prof playfully. "I don't mean to mock your sacrifice. You must have seen a bit of action."

"Well..."Winco says, tailing off and leaving things nicely ambiguous.

"Seriously, did you get into some hot spots Winco?"

"Well, not so much in terms of shit and bullets. But the RAF's a team job, a case of all pulling together."

"So you didn't fire a shot in anger? Didn't strafe the Argies?"

"Not really. Actually, I was admin."

"Admin?"

"Yes, in charge of inventories for the married quarters."

"Counting the cutlery, checking for holes in the walls and wonky wardrobes?"

"Not personally."

Waggy spares Winco more pain by interrupting to remark brightly that, in gardening books, sweet peas are sometimes called "gross feeders". He gives Yeti a meaningful sidelong stare.

"Why are you looking at me?"Yeti asks in his hurt voice.

"No reason, Yeti. No reason,"Waggy says, beaming and poking Yeti's globe of a belly.

"What?" asks Yeti, puzzled, then looks at Waggy as if he's soft in the head and says:"Waggy, you're daft, you."

Prof, whose hair has turned to rats' tails in the rain, looks through steamed up glasses and chips in: "You're right there, Yeti. Now get under cover before that cardy gets waterlogged and drags you down to the ground."

The big spots have made way for sustained rain so we head for the

Nerve Centre and sit under the corrugated roof.

Waggy puts a mug of tea in my hand, the folding seats come out and for a moment we sit silently and listen to the droplets from the tree boughs landing on the roof. The biscuit box is passed round.

The two nurses who have a plot beneath the railway embankment are trudging towards us. Their anoraks are sopping and their waterproof trousers make them walk stiff-legged.

They are undeterred. Their faces are pink and shiny and they are as bright-eyed as puppies. They're so jolly and full of life and I wish their plot was nearer mine.

Waggy makes another brew. The girls wrap their dripping fingers round the hot mugs and Prof gives them a run-down on the fight to save the plots. They keenly pledge support.

Another gardener, driven off by the rain, takes shelter with us. He holds a pointed cabbage and a plant pot full of baby new potatoes.

"You've seen today's paper, have you Cecil? Bloody wastrel."

"Newspaper?" says Cecil anxiously.

"Hang on." The man slowly, painfully slowly, puts his vegetables on the floor and then undoes several layers of clothing and reaches into a pocket. He opens his wallet and draws out a neatly folded newspaper cutting.

Cecil reads it with a great deliberateness, making little gasping noises. Then he passes it round, and we each read it, re-read it. As the cutting circulates, there is a sucking in of air, contemptuous swearing, tuts of amazement.

Under the heading **BAD BACK CHEAT CLAIMED £7,000** there's a grainy photograph. It is of Crumbling Back helping to carry a coffin.

And under the picture is the line: **'Invalid' was veg-growing pall-bearer.**

At the foot of the article is an even grainier telephoto shot of Crumbling Back behind his shed tipping up a brimming barrowload of manure.

There is shocked silence, broken by Cecil.

"I see he's going to be sentenced next month and he's been told to bring his pyjamas."

"What hurts is that he maintains he only emptied that barrow because no-one on the allotment ever helped him…"

"Well, bugger me!" exclaims Waggy, springing up. "The lazy bugger used to sit and watch me do his weeding – me with my chest!"

"The lying wossname!" splutters Ray, blinking in wonderment at the scale of the deceit. "He had me like one of those wossname ants."

"Worker ants," says Winco, his aquiline face reddening. "I'd throw away the damned key."

Prof shakes his head, incredulous.

"It's only last week that he got me to heel in his winter cabbages, and there he was, right as rain, secretly carting coffins about. Capitalism personified. But you have to give him some credit for conforming to society's mores and feathering his nest while mugs like us fetched and carried…"

"Credit?" snaps Winco. "Credit? Give him a bull-whipping more like!" Winco appears to have reached the boundary beyond which lies cardiac arrest. A big vein is throbbing in his neck and his eyes are standing out.

"No, there's no excuse. He let us all down," Cecil murmurs. "And the damned defence lawyers are as bad getting him to say that, yes, he worked for undertakers but he only did the lighter ones."

"Do they think we're all bloody daft?" he says, exasperated.

"But we *were* all daft weren't we?" asks Yeti.

Out of the shadows
back in the sun

ONE

Up betimes and much troubled by a great noise and going straight way to the window discover that it is thundering exceedingly and the rain falling unabated. Breakfasted and passing the front door to go up the stairs find that a missive has arrived from Terra Australis Incognita (which is curious because it is a land that is yet to be discovered). Praise be that God has fit me for a change in my fortune, a blessing which I do not want spoiled by Air Mail intimations that rudely waken tender sentiments that were lying peacefully abed...

The soft spot I've developed for Sam Pepys seems to be turning into an obsession. I've even begun to think in his language. But each night he sends me to sleep content.

The letter is indeed from Grace. It is full of what Sam would have described as "pretty stories" (just gossip about the people I once knew) and "much discourse" (about practical matters).

Inconsequential stuff but my heart feels as if it's twisting inside me as soon as I see the handwriting.

It is decorative, cursive and childishly large; the dot of each "i" is made into a tiny circle and it transports me to her side.

She is obviously desperate to tell me that she has sold the outboard motor ("I think I got fifty more dollars than you paid for it!!!"). She is proud of herself.

She tells me she's bringing with her, in her luggage, stuff she will not trust with shippers – my two best cameras, some letters, old photos, medals.

I suppose I'll have to collect it, or have it delivered. Or she might bring it.

....

Yeti is out and about today. His victim is recovering and Cecil believes that it's only when it's clear that the boy won't relapse that the police will decide what charge to bring.

Cecil had told me that Yeti didn't seem unduly worried, and certainly wasn't contrite.

When I call to him he waves and I go over to where he is picking runner beans and shake his hand, or rather he shakes mine.

I tell him it's good to see him back and try to explain that we're all around to help, and that we'll be seeing how things turn out.

"They've told me I haven't got to say anything, Cliff," he says. "But it served him right."

....

"Isn't it always the way!" Prof splutters. "You finally work out a solution to a problem and find that the problem's disappearing."

He's surrounded by tools. We are under the corrugated roof at the Nerve Centre sheltering from a haze of fine, cold rain that confirms that autumn is here.

I've noticed lately that Prof has been spending a lot of time on his knees next to the concrete box-cum-bench that someone had installed to provide somewhere secure for tea-making gear and gas bottles.

The box, abutting a wall of the railway building, has a timber top so it can serve as a bench, and there is a hasp and padlock to make it vandal-proof.

Within a week, youngsters – hiding when the gates were locked – had started to use the Nerve Centre as an out-of-hours HQ.

The walls of the building had been covered in graffiti, initials carved in the bench top. Strawberry hulls, pea-pods, plum stones and empty cider bottles were evidence of nocturnal depravity.

Prof is drawing deeply on the roll-up held between fingers that are as spindly and white as his fragile fag.

"It's taken me a while but I've developed the ideal deterrent to persuade our nightly guests to move on. Shame that we're going to be moved on before I've perfected what is, in effect, a musical cattle prod."

He doesn't wait for me to ask him to explain.

"It's like this, Kyff. They arrive and, naturally, they sit down. When they do, they get a very unpleasant sensation. Look…"

He takes me to the concrete box. He lifts the lid and points to springs on the underside of the bench, electrical contacts and a tape player and speaker that had been rigged up and fixed in place.

"Here's how it works. The last person to use the box switches the thing on before locking up for the night. The unwelcome overnight guest sits on the bench. The bench lid is depressed against the force of the springs.

"An electrical contact is made and – voila! – the tape player lets them have a burst of the most nerve-jangling avant garde music known to man. Stockhausen first, String Quartet With Four Helicopters, then a really brutal bit of Bartok."

I avert my eyes as, in his delight, he reveals those teeth, a veritable Monument Valley of brown outcrops.

"But that's not all, Kyff. When they realise they can't talk to each other because of the racket, they want to kick the thing into silence. But the 'off' switch is inside the concrete box…"

His smile this time turns to a laugh and then a chesty cough.

"The tape loop repeats itself but only three times. They don't know that and they'll have scuttled off long before it stops rolling!"

He insists I play guinea pig so I sit down and recoil at the discordant blast from beneath me.

"Brilliant Prof! If that doesn't work nothing will," I say when I can hear myself talk.

Then we both remember that soon there won't be any nuisances to deal with, no crops to defend.

....

Sitting in the dentist's chair. Resting up.

I'd volunteered this morning to help the nurses clear the last third of their plot and, of course, showed off by going at it like a machine.

Now I'm drowsy. The only noise is from the buzzing of a bluebottle that I can't be bothered to deal with. I need a coffee but can't stir myself to make it.

So I sit here and think about Dad and my childhood, and find that a tiny incident that I have never recalled before has just come into my head.

Mrs Powell had told us to bring a saucer to school. She gave us all some cotton wool and we queued up at the sink to wet it, then she doled out cress seeds.

She let us take the cress home and told us to keep the cotton wool wet.

A few days later – it must have been on a Sunday when Mum always did salad for tea – we'd just started to eat when Dad said something about fancying some cress. Mum said there wasn't any.

Then Dad said that he thought he'd noticed me growing some on the windowsill and he asked me if it was all right with me if he had a bit.

He had asked for it to make me feel good.

....

Carol, the woman from Cecil's party, walks through, towards the Bottom End – the second time in two days. Funny, I've never noticed her before. She looks across to the hut. I get my head down and unroll the chicken wire I'd just rolled up until she walks on.

Waggy is going by on the path, carrying a plastic bottle of evil-looking comfrey juice (a gift from Wilf no doubt).

Carol stops him at the end of my plot with a tinny "Waggy!" She releases one of her blood-curdling laughs but Waggy's face does not change.

"I didn't know who you were when you were at that party last

Christmas. But I do now! You used to be in all the clubs."

"Some time ago."

"My dad loved you!" she says.

"I loved him too, duck, but I was married at the time. We could give it a go now, tell him."

"Waggy ... he passed away."

"Well, is your mum still free?"

"She's passed as well."

"Dammit – missed out again!"

I call him over for a cup of coffee and as we chat I steer the conversation round to the subject of humour and hurt. Humour always seems to create a victim, and what I'd just heard seemed a bit callous.

"Maybe, Kyff," he says. "But it's all cruel in the end – life.

"You work all hours, thousands of times you get on your hind legs and risk looking a prat. Then you lose your little bit of fame, the fags bugger up your breathing, your liver mutinies, and your wife goes on the blink.

"You even have to really scrimp for the first time. Then, guess what? Some bloody great corporation wants to snatch the spot of land where you grow your flowers. Who's the victim there, Kyff?"

I hand him his coffee and, as he lights up, he looks so beaten down that I wish I hadn't struck a serious note with him.

"What's worst for me is losing the chance to make a hall full of people laugh. Just think of that power – the power to make grown adults roll in their seats, cry into their hankies, even experience early onset incontinence," he says, betraying a hint of a smile.

"And don't doubt that I had that power, Kyff. I'll have you know that in my two best years when I did seaside shows I had standing ovulations right down the east coast..."

I talk about luck, how, just when you feel you have the measure of life, something can come along and send you reeling.

"I've tried to make my own luck. Had to. I was one of those people who were dealt a bad hand from the start. I never work in a white tuxedo because I know I'd get black scurf. That's how lucky I am."

He looks deep in thought.

"Another thing. Now the wife's circulation trouble is stopping her walking."

"Sorry to hear that Waggy," I say.

"I've just had a real upper-and-downer with her."

I listen intently, and make empathetic noises.

"She suddenly threw a slipper at me and shouted: 'That's for years of unsatisfactory sex.' I threw it back at her and said 'And that's for knowing the difference!'"

His face remains straight as he takes a slurp of coffee.

"Waggy – great joke but not being able to walk is no joke. Why does there always have to be a victim, and why does everything have to have a punchline, even the bad news?"

"Especially the bad news, Kyff. The really bad news calls for a bloody great belly laugh. What else can you do? You can weep or you can laugh in the face of it all!"

He shakes his big, purply face with its deep folds and creases.

"Well, Kyff – what do you suggest instead?"

I have no answer. Waggy is looking increasingly maudlin.

"All those laughs. Gone! But there was a time when a blast of laughter, and I mean a blast, would sometimes hit you like a train, and it was maybe just for some little fill-in line.

"Other times you'd go out with what you thought was hilarious stuff and think you'd strayed into a bloody monastery. Oh – that terrible silence! You'd want to curl up. The sweat would be running down your chest under your shirt."

He seems to be thinking about this. I offer a cigarette and, as he takes it, he looks at me intently and says: "I know you must be thinking, 'Yawn, yawn. Here we go, another sad clown, another tortured face behind the laughing mask.'"

"No, Waggy, It's your way of coping. But it must be hard work. I can't remember a single chat with you that hasn't been turned into a string of jokes."

"But the jokes disappear, Kyff," he says in an anguished voice. "They just float away. I keep having to replace them."

He seems to become aware that he is taking himself too seriously and his voice becomes lighter.

"It's just a shame that Madge didn't come up with some mix that preserved all my stuff, and the laughter. If they were all just there in Kilner jars," he says, pointing to one of Dad's shelves, "all my set-ups and delayed drops, all my punchlines, and my voices, and my put-downs for smart-arsed hecklers, all labelled and ready to replay any time, I'd be as happy as a pig in you know what.

"I'd remember what I'd achieved. The laughs would be my trophies. Thing is, Kyff, after a lifetime there's nothing to show."

I struggle to find the right reply. Platitudes would not pass muster with Waggy.

"I know, I understand perfectly, Waggy," I say, looking round at Dad's cupboards, his shelves and seeds; his drawers and his journals and his local history books.

"Dad felt the same. Maybe we all do."

....

We've been getting lots of support in the Chronicle over our fight and a petition Cecil organised is growing day by day.

So when the bell went this afternoon, I expected Cecil to be getting us together with some news about the future.

As it turned out, it was to spread the word that, having considered the evidence, the police had decided not to prosecute Yeti but had given him an informal warning about taking the law into his own hands.

There is only a small bunch of us but a cheer goes up and the nurses whoop with delight.

Winco is silent. He senses that there is bad feeling about his readiness to give evidence that probably would have put Yeti in jail.

"Well," he says piously. "Justice has been exercised. That's all I ever wanted."

No-one responds.

It had been a "Scheme day" for Yeti but as we chat happily about the outcome we see him ambling up – a broad grin spread across the globe of his face, the poop deck of hips and buttocks giving a shudder as each big foot is plonked onto the path.

We all shake his hand and the nurses hug him, making him blush.

Waggy teases him, and says that it must have been the weight of his cardy that had really done the damage to the vandal's chest. He wants Yeti to promise that he'll not act like that again, to think hard and do things differently.

"I will do things different, Waggy," he says. "If there's any more vangals I'll squash them proper. That'll learn 'em to spoil people's things."

TWO

I've enjoyed a happy few days and I know why I've felt so content. It's because they've been spent with Pat. We have become friends. Confidences have been exchanged.

Cecil asked me to do a local radio interview about the fight to save the allotments and I persuaded Pat to come along – ostensibly in support but in reality because it feels good to have her at my side.

She called to pick me up – morning-fresh, shiny-eyed, cheerful. Whatever the time of day she always looks as if she has just stepped out of the shower.

There's a wholesomeness about her. No make-up, her cropped hair proudly grey; gentle manner; straightforward, thoughtful. It all combines to draw me to her and it seemed that we were on our way to becoming kindred spirits.

We dropped in at the Chronicle office and gave a young reporter a joint bulletin about our latest initiatives to save the allotments.

At the radio studio, we were handed paper cups of water and in reception heard a radio trailer saying that in a few moments listeners would be hearing from allotment holders who are "digging for victory" (oh dear!), and then they played the totally inappropriate English Country Garden.

The interviewer, Haleema, was sweet and courteous but too young to begin to understand the birthright we're losing.

"But you could always buy your lettuces at the new supermarket," she responded, on air, when I tried to explain that the idea of a bit of earth being something that belongs to everybody has been around since Saxon times.

I ploughed on with my message: that allotment gardening isn't just growing things; it's a place for exercise, rest and recuperation, friendship and pride in producing wonderful fresh food. It's lungs for cities and havens for wildlife. It's heritage.

"You can understand the council's point of view," she countered. "After all, you're on what is now premium land and all you're doing is growing things for a hobby."

Pat protested that residents have a right to feel strongly about the extra 450 cars that would pass their houses each day, going to and from the supermarket.

She stressed the threat to local shops and then glowed pink with indignation when the leader of the council phoned in to join the debate, saying that the gardeners should remember that the use of the land was always just a loan that could be called in at any time.

"And councillors should remember that they are only temporary incumbents until the next elections," Pat said, interrupting.

Later, we sat in a coffee house and I told her: "I was really proud of you today."

"And me of you. I think we did quite a good job even though we were flogging a dead horse."

She seemed suddenly to have sunk into melancholy. I tried to cheer her up by saying that at least we've bothered to try to protect the irreplaceable – a patch of green for the future.

I suggested seeing a film, having a meal, but she said she really had to get back.

When she stopped the car I thanked her for the lift and for the support, and told her to keep her pecker up. As I said this I found that I had a hand on hers as she gripped the steering wheel.

"You know, all things considered, I think you're quite a bellibone."

"A what?" she asked, making a quizzical face.

"A bellibone. Remember? The quiz answer? Cecil's party?"

"My memory! I haven't the foggiest!"

"It's an old word for a beautiful lady."

Years ago, when I did a bit of judo at Benton Church Hall, the teacher pulled me out to demonstrate the sweeping ankle throw. He shook me off balance and as I transferred my weight my foot was swept away. I was a goner, though he took care to ease me onto the mat. It came to me, later, that this was the perfect metaphor to describe the next moment in the car.

The comparison with a bellibone did not have the desired effect. In fact, it fell as flat as I had done in the judo class. I had strayed too far.

Pat looked pointedly at my hand on hers, turned to me and said, softly but firmly, "Please don't misunderstand, Kyff."

That night, before I rustling up my solitary supper, I looked up Ken's office number. I was ready to put the house up for sale. It was time.

THREE

They say first impressions count.

So what was that poor, well-spoken, best-bib-and-tucker chap from the Town Twinning Committee to think when he dropped in to check that Benton Hall Allotments was appropriately set up to receive his party of Italian gardeners?

Maybe the weather – oppressive thundery heat being held down by a wash of grey – is to blame but there is an air of giddy expectancy round Dad's hut where a few of us have gathered in readiness for the guests. But ready we aren't.

Alas, the twinning man arrives early, silently and unnoticed from the Top End. Reaching Dad's plot he stands stock still and beholds a tableau that might have depicted leisure hour outside some institution.

As I shake hands with the visitor, Prof appears from inside Dad's hut, where he is brewing tea and where Cecil has been giving him a haircut in the dentist's chair. One half of his head is near bald, shoulder-length frizzy hair cascades down the other.

As he looks round the door and smiles that smile, the twinning man's mouth falls open.

Meanwhile, Yeti – who has been digging – has shed his orange knitted top, rolled it up to form a pillow and is reclining on his back on the grass path, giving off steam and looking for all the world like a sumo wrestler between bouts.

Nearby, sitting on a box, Wilf is holding a large, malformed carrot.

"Isn't nature wonderful?" he is saying to no-one in particular. The multi-forked carrot has a striking resemblance to a naked couple interlocked. Wilf says he is sure this will please the visitors, "them being Italian".

Opposite, towards the railway, the young hippy couple are meditating serenely with cupped hands on their carpeted patch.

As I talk with the twinning man, Waggy – oblivious to the visitor – is relieving himself flamboyantly against the hut side and is then joined by Wilf, who lives in dread of "being caught short".

Waggy, I notice, is even more purple than usual today, and even louder than usual. He has been at the bottle. I can hear his jokes only too well – and so can the anxious-looking officer charged with strengthening harmony between European partners.

I cringe as he loudly shares with us the origin of the word innuendo ("It's Italian for suppository ... Get it Wilf? WILF! In your endo!").

He is saying that, although it is true that the Italians had invented the toilet seat, we should remind our visitors that it was a visiting Englishman who had suggested putting a hole in it.

"Well, I'll gather the party together," the official says grimly. "I do hope the afternoon is beneficial on all sides."

Prof, framed by the hut door, smiles his ghastly smile, his pinhead eyes twinkling. Brushing back half his hair with one hand, he waves farewell with the other.

....

Cyril's appeal yesterday after rallying us at the Nerve Centre has yielded a good crop of volunteers to welcome those members of the Italian delegation who have an interest in gardening. Giving them a barbecue had been Madge's idea.

Later, they'll attend an evening of English traditional music and dance in the Town Hall.

Finally we are shaping up. A burly chap from the railway side arrives at the Nerve Centre with half an oil drum and a sack of charcoal.

Pat helps me create a table using an old door, and Madge goes to and fro bringing paper plates, food, her homemade wine, Union Jack napkins and even posies from her garden.

Suddenly, Cecil slaps his forehead and says: "Hell fire! What if they bring a gift for us! It's the kind of thing they do over there. They're always handing out pennants and things."

Ray, who is dropping bottles of beer into a plastic barrel filled with water, looks round and asks: "Why don't we just give them a wossname?"

"Yes, why not?" I say, and suggest that we could also present a few packets of Dad's seeds of old English varieties of vegetables.

"OK Kyff, you get the seeds and I'll get the wossname," says Ray, striding off. "I'll get large, shall I?"

"Yes, large," I reply.

The sun has broken through by the time Ray arrives back carrying a Wilkie's cake box containing a huge pork pie, and the visitors are coming up from the Bottom End gate.

As they come near, we can see that they are immaculately dressed, almost entirely in black, and all six, along with a black-haired girl I take to be their interpreter, are walking in an almost processional way.

Waggy is already into the beer and is part-way through a poem about a girl from Brindisi whose virtue was easy when Madge puts her fingers to her lips and he slurs into silence.

Cecil – wearing his full set of badges and his tweed jacket despite the heat –just extends his hand in greeting when the air shakes with a deafening cacophony. Schoenberg at ninety decibels.

Yeti, who has just lowered himself onto the Nerve Centre bench, springs up and runs squealing past the startled guests.

While we shield our ears, Prof grapples furiously with the lid of the security bench. As the screaming of violins hits an agitating climax, he finds the switch and, blessedly, restores the silence.

"Grazie per la musica," says the unruffled party leader, a leathery grandfatherly figure with slicks of white hair above each ear.

There is much hand-shaking and incomprehensible talk and then

Cecil leads us and the Italians on a tour of the allotments.

We descend on Wilf, in his polytunnel, feeding a large, warty pumpkin. He has not heard us approach and springs back, startled as the black-clad group materialises before him.

"This man is a world champion. *Champione.* He grows very big vegetables," Cecil shouts at the translator, whose perplexed smile indicates that her English is far from good. It's clear she got the job because the leader is her dad.

"Ah – si! Immenso!" proclaims the leader finally.

The translator considers a moment and then says: "Papa say yes, very immense."

Wilf then draws out of his capacious apron pocket the erotic carrot, as if to invite comment. He has misjudged his audience.

"Amico – Mio Dio! Non si fanno questo!" shouts the leader in protest.

After an interval the translator says quite disapprovingly: "Papa say friend, my God it is a naughty thing," and then crosses herself.

Winco is figuratively standing by his bed for inspection as we pass and he fawningly explains the intricacies of his gardening year, none of which is understood by the visitors who can only mutter "eccelente" and "grazie".

When we reach Dad's hut, the Italians poke their heads round the door and make approving noises, pointing to the *"museo"* exhibits and Dad's wind and water meters and then venture into the hut while I wait outside.

The leader gestures to ask if it is all right to sit in the dentist's chair. He leans back and I can hear him making approving comments.

"Papa say this is place of peace. He is saying it must be … *'la casa del uno speciale'* … it mean 'the home of a special person'.

I surprise myself by leaning into the hut and agreeing.

"Si – molto speciale," I say.

The leader shows an interest in the leeks growing on the nurses' plot. Prof, who is unrecognisably sleek now with his haircut complete, bypasses the translator and says: *"Essi sono i porro. Nero il prefererito."*

"Ah. Si!"

"Leeks. Nero's favourite," Prof says as an aside to us, as humbly as he can manage. The man's knowledge knows no bounds.

We wend our way back to the Nerve Centre where Ray and his wife have been tending the barbecue. Madge begins to hand out plates and busy herself with cutlery.

Ray raises a thumb and calls to the translator: "Will you ask if everybody's ready for wossname?"

Her face goes blank while she searches her mental glossary for "wossname", fails to find an equivalent, and takes it to be a colloquialism for food.

Beer and Madge's wine seem to loosen tongues momentarily but each conversation peters out so we are grateful for the sausages, grilled sweetcorn, new potatoes and Madge's pies. We all have an excuse to stop trying to talk to one another.

Well, not all. Old Bill, wearing a jacket that might have been fashionable forty years ago, has cornered one of the Italian gardeners – a suave figure with prominent gold teeth – and is trying unsuccessfully to get him to understand that "in England we say 'A cherry year a merry year, a plum year a dumb year'", even though we don't.

The young couple are sitting side by side on upturned buckets. They each have a jam jar filled with sprouted beans. I am suddenly envious of the air of tranquillity around them.

Food and drink taken, the uncomfortable silence returns. Only Waggy refuses to be mute and, with gesticulations, keeps attempting a sort of physical Esperanto to cut through the impasse.

The translator excuses his behaviour by saying: *"Papa. Comediante."*

"Tell him I used to be called The Walking Joke Book," demands Waggy, slurping beer from a can.

There is an awkward silence and then the translator ventures, *"Lo sono stato chiamato a piedi ...* joke book."

"Ah," the unsmiling leader replies, no doubt intrigued by the idea of a book that walks.

"Twelve gags a minute, tell him," says Waggy. "Hecklers blown out of the water. Not a dry seat in the house."

The translator pretends not to have heard.

"Right!" shouts Waggy. "Titian. Venice painter? Me say poem…"

"No, Waggy," says Madge, taking hold of his wrist. "Please. Leave it."

"Here, special for you, Italiano poem…" He raises his beer can and declaims…

"While Titian was mixing rose madder
His model posed nude on a ladder…"
("Leave it Waggy!")
"Her position, to Titian, suggested coition
So he nipped up the ladder and 'ad 'er
– Boom, boom!"

There are a couple of desultory "bravos" but no laughter. Perhaps the visitors believe they have heard an English translation of a classic lay from ancient Rome.

With much hand-waving Cecil tries to explain to the party that the allotments are doomed (to which the leader says "Eccelente!"). Then, to fill the void, Cecil begins showing him tomatoes…

"…no-one knows why this one is called Atkin's Stuffing but I think the name Brandywine – this one – is self-evident…"

The twinning official arrives just as we've all settled for simply sitting there trying not to look at each other.

Cecil breaks the silence by tapping a wine glass and says that he hopes they will accept a small gift of historically important seeds to grow in Italy, and some traditional English food.

Ray parades the pork pie for approval and receives a round of applause.

The Italian responds at snail's pace so his mono-lingual daughter can give some clue as to what he is saying which is, in effect, that he hopes the English gardeners will enjoy a taste of Italy, some *lardo di Colonnata*, presented in a small box made from Carrara marble.

He holds the box aloft and is still holding it when the regular teatime freight train going west rumbles distantly.

The interpreter begins to say, "It is special lardo. Piggy's back with no meat in. Blanco wearing rosmarino dress…" but is drowned out by the train, which takes a full minute to pass, during which the leader trembles as he keeps the box held high, obviously judging that it would be discourteous to lower it.

"…is for put on bread," she says, as the rattling subsides.

The leader lets down the marble box with a clunk and concludes by expressing the heartfelt wish that the plan of the allotment holders to build their own supermarket selling vegetables will flourish.

Cecil sees the party to their minibus and we gather round the curious gift and peer in as if regarding a religious relic.

It is clearly piggy's back, about two pounds of it. It is very blanco – and glistening sickeningly now in the sun. And there's the rosemary garnish.

A rare delicacy for lard-lovers. But there are no takers, not even Yeti, who judging by his expression was clearly expecting something that would fill a corner.

"Not touching that stuff," he says glumly. "I only eat food."

FOUR

Waking this morning out of my sleep on a sudden because of a mighty thud and on going down see that a package of leaflets protesting about that most vile threat to the allotments has been delivered by Pat who had so promised. Hastening to the window, I catch her looking most comely in her purple fleece, trackie bottoms and milk-white trainers and desire to be in her company if only she would tarry but she hastens away on foot, probably to her Pilates class...

Poor old Sam was in trouble last night. Money worries, work worries, his supper disappointing, his wife abrasive, and his ire raised by the presence of *"her mayd who is a lazy slut"*. But he usually has a way of finding consolation even if it's by sticking his hand up his servant's skirt.

OK if you have no conscience and a suitably intimidated servant girl to abuse.

Reading of Sam's goatishness and seeing the two girls walking to work from the Bottom End past the hut through a fine morning drizzle remind me forcefully of the lack of a woman in my life.

Pat is a delight, and our chats remind me of the joy of intimacy with a woman. We've already reached a depth of friendship that sometimes takes years to achieve. But she is grieving, and fiercely loyal to her husband's memory. That will be a waiting game.

Meanwhile I'm resigned to getting my kicks by kneeling on the wet path to tease out couch grass that has taken hold on one edge of Dad's plot.

The damp soil opens and spreads for my searching fingers. There's a perverse pleasure in clearing the tentacles of grass, tracking back to the very root.

Old Bill appeared yet again as an itinerant prophet of doom, riding past my back, his pedals creaking.

"Ooh – couch grass? You've got that for life, Kyff boy," he says.

For the first time I am aware of his rich, rural accent. I don't remember noticing as a boy that he spoke differently, and it has just registered with me that he's not from these parts.

Ray knows Bill best and once told me that he had come to join a racehorse trainer in the area at fourteen with hopes of being a jockey but had his leg shattered in a fall before he could ride.

I stand up and watch him head for the Top End, sitting on that giant boneshaker and then falling heavily onto his bowed leg on reaching the gate, and suddenly I realise why he keeps his saddle so ridiculously high: it gives him a view he would have had from a horse.

....

The bell goes this afternoon and the half-dozen of us who are on the allotments stroll to the Nerve Centre where Cecil has already got the gas bottle hatch open and the kettle on the ring.

We gather under the canopy out of the swathes of fine rain and, as Cecil spoons coffee granules into assorted mugs, he says: "Just wanted you to know that I got a letter today from the council saying they were going to push ahead.

"They're letting every allotment holder know about the offer of a move to Low Drove and that everybody would get a little shed, and it would be little. Just enough for tools."

"Could be worse," says Winco, a comment that draws a look of contempt from Prof.

"They say if we don't like it we can always appeal to the Attorney General."

"Where? What?" asks Wilf, who had perched on an upturned bin as near to Cecil as he could. "Did you say Low Drove?"

"Shingle and sand," says Waggy.

"You're right, Waggy," Cecil says. "I've been down for a butcher's and its all subsoil and stones. Poor access. Exposed site. No proper path. It's a moonscape."

"Maybe we could convert to quarrying?" Waggy offers.

Prof has remained unusually silent, rolling a cigarette very slowly and deliberately with those thin, bony fingers, his eyes black dots through misted-over glasses.

"Let's be clear," he says.

"The council want to take land that's been allotments for four generations, land that was bequeathed to people in the town, and hand it to a supermarket company.

"They want us to leave behind soft fruit, fruit trees, the huts we've built and the land we've enriched and in return they want to give us a sandy, barren site and a pissing little box for our buckets and spades.

"We need to consider the offer fully," says Winco, looking slightly nervously towards Prof, whose face has hardened.

"No, Winco. Geen. Jo. Voch. Enna. Ne. Jok. Nope. No – in any language. As they're German: nein."

"But the council are following procedure, offering alternative plots within three quarters of a mile of us, as they must do by statute," Winco insists.

"No, Winco – the rule says 'suitable' alternative plots. They're offering us a bloody beach and the cynical sods know that the land is useless."

Ray looks glum. "You know, it really makes you want to throw in the wossname," he says.

"Trowel," says Waggy, but the quip was lost on us.

Cecil asks us to pencil in a meeting so we can arrange for leaflet distribution, get some more publicity in the Chronicle, consolidate for a last-ditch fight. But he has the look of a David who has challenged a Goliath and then forgotten to bring his slingshot.

Prof, on the other hand, has a new posture, defiance showing in his body language.

"Don't get downhearted shipmates! Courage mes amies!" he says with a laugh, bending down to give Wilf an affectionate squeeze.

"A crumb of comfort. This morning, in the financial paper, there's news that all is not well with World-in-One. They're losing ground, if you'll forgive the pun," he says, gleefully rubbing his hands together with exaggerated glee.

"They've slipped down to third biggest in the rankings and the UK shareholders are nervy. So the Germans are getting rid of the British boss. Graham somebody. Some young whizz kid made good.

"And how about this for an irony. They've put him on garden leave. Serves the bugger right for trying to concrete us over."

....

An amusing little playlet is acted out as I help Cecil do a quick survey of the plots before we sit down to draft the final appeal to the Attorney General.

We wave to the new young couple who moved onto a plot last week and Cecil decides to go over and welcome them.

They look like woodland creatures, in their knitted caps with ear-flaps and long-sleeved jumpers in military colours. The girl, broad and strong, wears calf-length working boots and a long tie-dye skirt and her emaciated partner wears thick knitted socks and sandals.

They are both out of breath, having just unrolled a large carpet alongside one that already covers a quarter of their plot.

"Welcome!" Cecil says. "I see you're already tackling the weeds. It's a long job using carpets to kill them but not everyone agrees with spraying."

She replies firmly: "Absolutely no sprays for me."

"That's fine," says Cecil.

"I'm a Jain," says the girl.

"Well – another Jane!" says Cecil. "My daughter's a Jane."

"Really? When did she convert? There's so few of us."

"Convert? No, she's always been a Jane."

"Is her mum Indian?"

"No, she's from Kidderminster."

"I thought with your daughter being a Jain perhaps it was a family thing."

"No, we just liked the name."

"Ah – I get it! She's a Jane, a J.A.N.E., not a follower of Jainism."

"Not that she's mentioned."

"Ah. Well, Jains try not to kill any living thing, not even insects. Not easy, I know, on an allotment."

The insipient old fogey in me tells me that one day soon they will see the folly of their quest but I am touched by their conviction, and their search for another way to look at the world.

I can see that Cecil is already patronising them with a slightly mocking smile.

The intolerance I had begun to feel about my students in Perth has gone; I've rediscovered my sense of protectiveness over the naïve and idealistic.

"You see," the girl is saying, "we've got a bit of a moral quandary. We're Jains but we also believe in self-sufficiency and so me and Ben are having a go at growing stuff but not killing things along the way. Except the plants we'll be killing to eat."

"I think the plants will understand," says Cecil blithely.

"The really big challenge will be worms," says the young man. Ben is pitifully thin and, with his patchy beard and tumbling hair, Christ-like. Passion shines out of him.

The girl who isn't called Jane rakes back her tumbling ringlets with her fingers and says with breathless enthusiasm: "We're going for no-dig cultivation but there's bound to be casualties."

The pair seem to be in that age band where exotic and wonderful spiritual experimentation seems not only permissible but a matter of duty.

"Oh – and we're planning to get bees," the girl says excitedly. "Yes, I know, strictly speaking as Jains we shouldn't be stealing their honey. That's almost as bad as eating eggs, which after all are chickens' babies. We wouldn't stoop to that."

Ben nods on cue.

"Or commandeering cows' milk," he mumbles into his jumper. "Absolutely criminal when we've got soya milk."

"Oh," says Cecil, once more smiling indulgently.

"We've checked that hives are allowed, by the way."

"Yes," replies Cecil, rather guardedly. "But there's quite a skill involved with beekeeping…"

"Point taken," says Ben timidly. "But we plan not to be too, you know, conventional. We're going for the old, traditional top bar hive, and everything will be natural. I think we can kind of get on their waveband, share their vibe, be at one with them."

"Right!" Cecil says suddenly: "Well, we'll leave you to it, Ben, Jane. Sorry – of course you're not a Jane."

"No. I'm Farida now. Indian. Means turquoise. It's the colour of my aura."

When we reach Dad's hut we look across the plots. Farida and Ben are again sitting straight-backed, hands cupped, deep in blissful meditation on their carpets.

....…

Bill drops in – literally, falling on to his bowed leg – as he reaches Dad's plot where I'm enjoying a therapeutic session pulling weeds from the soil, which has been softened by overnight rain.

I winkle out a dandelion and this sets Bill off telling me about the childhood names people used to have for different weeds and wildflowers. I make the mistake of showing too much interest.

Propped up by his bike, he is settled, droning away while I stand, desperate for a cigarette and a coffee. He's just moved from bedstraw to creeping jenny when I break in.

"Sorry Bill but I must get on. You know what they say: 'Don't break bread until the hay's spread.'"

"Dead right, Kyff boy. Dad lived by that. Never a truer word."

I immediately feel mortified that I've got the dear man to enthuse over an age-old saying that I'd made up on the spot as we chatted.

Could Waggy's cruel wisecrackery be catching?

FIVE

Round The Houses
from the Chronicle's man in Westminster

Only rarely is a Member from our region chosen to step into the ring with the Prime Minister, aka Baby Face.

But it happened yesterday and to his credit the feisty Brian Tusk did his very best to land a glove or two on a man who is renowned for boxing clever.

Ironic that both combatants came out of a Red corner but this did not persuade Tusk the Tank to pull his punches. Going into the bout, Baby Face was euphoric, having just mauled the Leader of the Opposition; the Speaker had to step in and stop that one on humanitarian grounds.

Having tasted blood, the Members were becoming restless as Tusk the Tank rose and showed his muscles in this, the final bout before lunch.

The members were also becoming peckish, and for this Tusk had himself to blame. Reddened by the fire within him, he tried to find a weak spot by charging in with a rhapsody about pies.

"Prime Minister," he began, "in my constituency there's a butcher's called Wilkie's, where for more than fifty years they have been making the best pies in the land…"

"Yummy, yummy," chorused a trio in the benches opposite, rubbing their bellies with circular movements.

"…and we have a third-generation baker who…"

"Any candlestick makers?" quipped a Member from the second row, prompting a whinnying call from a matronly backbencher to "Grow up!"

"Order! Order!" the Speaker bawled from his big chair.

Baby Face was untroubled. He'd been greased up so well by his seconds that even well-aimed jabs were sliding off like fish from a wet slab.

The Tank simply couldn't find the target and was not only losing on points, he was losing his audience. Minds, led by bellies, had begun transmigrating to the Members' Dining Room.

There, a bit of underdone animal and a bowl of spotted dick, washed down with a drop of claret, would stiffen resolve to Make Things Better For Hard-Working Families.

But there was a fight to finish.

The Tank took a deep breath and went in again, flailing and leading with his chin.

"In fact, Prime Minister," he declared, "we have a real community. What is more we have some of the most famous old allotments in the land…"

The Speaker, hinting at disqualification, interjected: "Will the Honorable Member please get to the point! Even newer Members should be aware that there's a reason that this is called Parliamentary Questions…

"…allotments that are historically important and unique and which are about to be paved over by a retail conglomerate with approval of the local council."

The hungry mob on one side of the ring bawled: "Question! Question!"

"…so will the Prime Minister order an inquiry into the way in which major supermarkets spread their tentacles, ruining local traders, damaging the environment by flying in goods produced by cheap labour ...

(Cries of "Yah Boo!")

...and how they are winning planning permission, sometimes applied for under false names, on the promise of creating jobs which turn out to be poorly paid, and which result in other job losses..."

"Market forces!" cried a dapper young MP for Somewhere Salubrious, stroking back his blond mane with a pale hand decorated, on the little finger, with a rather large gold ring. "The market at work!"

Tusk was still chasing shadows when Baby Face backed away into his corner, opening his gloves in a gesture of conciliation.

"Look. Look..." he said, with seductive sincerity paired with an insincere smile.

But the Tank was in again with his haymakers.

"...destroying communities and forcing suppliers into the red by driving down the prices they are offered..."

Speaker: "Order! The Member shall be seated. The Prime Minister will reply."

And he did – for what it was worth.

"Look, look ... business has to be allowed to flourish," said Baby Face. "But not at any price. However, as my honourable friend must know, many councils are benefiting from reciprocal arrangements with supermarket companies, and whenever allotments are lost, replacement land is offered elsewhere.

"Furthermore, my honourable friend will know that we have this month introduced minimum wage legislation to protect retail staff."

End of contest. Poor Tusk, bloodied but unbowed, was seen to crush his order paper.

Baby Face was unmarked. His new cosmetic dentistry was dazzlingly intact. Tusk, MP, is a new boy. He will learn that raw passion can come across as gauche, embarrassing even, in the chamber, where the team is the thing, and where the oil of pragmatism usually lies thick enough to sink any bobbing point of principle.

The anticlimax over, Members trickled from the chamber sniffing the air, eventually picking up the aroma of *filet jus* (none of the Bisto of boyhood here) and following their noses.

Meanwhile, back in Tusk territory, the Benton Allotment Holders were out and about as usual, not so much digging for Britain as entrenching an ancient right for their community and its future.

But they would be wise to keep an eye cocked for that giant supermarket trolley rolling relentlessly towards them, like a tank (a proper tank) to crush their sheds and mangle their mange touts.

Or is that manges touts? Maybe one of the Socialist brothers in the House of Commons dining room would know...

SIX

I'm tempted to find an excuse when the news editor of the Chronicle rings to ask if they can send a reporter and a photographer for a "reaction piece" now that the allotments look certain to disappear.

"I gather that for you these allotments have been a family thing?" he says. He doesn't know half.

A couple of hours later Cecil greets the pair and brings them to the hut where we sit and have tea.

Finally the reporter, a sleek twenty-something with slicked hair and darting eyes, and the plump old-hand of a photographer, who has settled in the old dentist's chair, steers the conversation round to business.

They seem interested enough in my arguments and fascinated with the hut and all Dad's paraphernalia but the reporter clearly has an agenda.

"Now the decision's been taken, are you going to fight on?" he says. "Do people feel strongly enough to try to block the bulldozers?"

I know he already has a headline in mind: **Gardeners dig in for battle.**

I bluster and try to stress the special quality of the site; its historic importance, the beauty of the place.

The photographer rocks forward a couple of times and finally lurches from the chair and suggests that, as we talk, he takes a couple of pictures.

"We want to show that history," he says, huffing and puffing over the equipment slung round his neck.

"What about if…" he says, "we put you there, with some of your Dad's bits of stuff in the background." He steers me to the shelves and then props open the shed door. "Better. Nice bit of available light," he says.

"Do you mind?" he says, rearranging the bric-a-brac on the shelves, raising some of the bigger hunks of metal, including a couple of horseshoes and a rusted old sickle, so that the shelf alongside me looks overloaded with historical remnants.

"Could you look out of the door as if you're taking a final look?" he asks, clicking away. "A bit sadder if you can."

He then poses me with my elbows on some of Dad's journals, looking out of the window. "Now…" he says "…you're thinking of those who've gone before."

My embarrassing ordeal is over. It is no consolation to think that it is all in a good cause because we all know that the cause is lost.

SEVEN

Ken rings to tell me that "the papers" are ready.

"I've got it all tidied up without too much legal GBH. Give it another couple of months and you'll be free, boyo!"

Free? As if Grace had kept me manacled. As if I'd ever wanted anything other than to be with her – until that evening on the patio with the strange silence, the unopened beers, Erik bringing back my tools and taking away my wife.

What would I be free of, from?

I still carry too much regret for this final separation to give any sense of release, or relief. But there has been a profound change in me. Perhaps I've begun to let Grace go.

Over the last few weeks Grace has given plenty of half-hints that perhaps we could forget that crazy time, not only pick up where we had left off but also be stronger together because we'd survived all that, and Lizzie.

Maybe I want to punish her, even if, in not responding, I punish myself. I'm not proud to have felt satisfaction after putting down the phone knowing that she was sitting there, desolate and scared, at the phone table in a kitchen half a world away.

But my strongest theory is that I am using her betrayal to help me over a barrier to a new and independent life. I am strong, stronger than at any time in my life. I want to test myself against life.

My life in Perth was happy I suppose but it was life with a high fence round it – a barricade against the hazards of life, against illness, against loneliness. Lizzie led us out of the barricade and once she left us, we hurried back in again and grabbed our shared security blanket.

Now I know that there is no sure-fire place of safety – no magic shield against illness, lightning strikes, loss of love – no matter who you are.

I met Grace in 1980. One night in December, at the end of term, when we were due to go to Wiltshire for me to meet her parents, I called at her room.

She was ashen, in shock.

"Have you heard about John?" she said.

"John who?" I asked. Two friends were called John.

"Lennon," she said. "Dead."

I remember saying: "Poor John. How could they?"

So the multi-millionaire peace-making dreamer turned out to be as vulnerable as anyone. And, at this very moment, George Harrison is nursing his wounds after some knife-wielding madman's uninvited visit to his bedroom.

There is no hiding place in life, I'm realising. Life is dangerous, even if you stay in bed where an eiderdown can turn into engulfing water.

The Queen's not safe. She, too, had a mad bedroom guest. She can't even count on her power as a ruler – as I left Perth, they'd announced that in the referendum half a million Western Australians said in effect: "Move over Sheila, and let's have a president."

I suppose back in Perth I liked to believe it was possible – if you lay low and didn't go looking for too much adventure – that sickness, poverty, calamity and loneliness would stay away from your door.

Like the broad beans we used to sing about in the Harvest Festival children's song, once I *"nestled in a blankety bed".*

I was deluded. Now the pod has been popped I've ventured out and I'm chancing it, and that means never going back. Not to Australia. Not to Grace. Not into a capsule.

Now my hands are calloused, my face is tanned, my waist has reappeared. And I do believe that my lardy legs have been slightly reshaped, slightly.

Each day I see people who greet me with pleasure. I've pitched in with them for a common purpose. And gradually I'm forming a clearer picture of Dad and what made him Huw.

Weeks of hoeing and weeding and tending plants, and tramping the streets pushing protest leaflets through doors, has given me plenty of time to think and the physical work seems to have mended me.

Once I would have given anything to have Grace beside me in our bed or lying reading, propped up on her elbows, on our favourite grassy bank overlooking the ocean.

Now I can picture her, but it is with affectionate remembrance and without that desperate need to be within reach and to be assured of her.

I can say that with certainty, having spent this rainswept morning going through the old black-and-white prints that I took when I first started work and treated myself to a Pentax camera. The fact that I asked for them to be sent on showed that I am healing. That I am well enough to look back.

Grace on a swing. Grace in hilarious hot pants. Grace in her dressing gown with wet hair, that springy tuft standing proud, her eyes, comically slightly crossed, turned up towards it – these were photographs that a couple of months ago would have plunged me back into longing. Today they are just pictures.

I had developed and printed them in the bathroom at the flat when we were first married and had never lost the memory of Grace's face (they seemed all to be of Grace) resolving on the paper as I submerged my hands and teased out the detail that lay within the developing print.

Ken had used the word "dissolved" over our marriage and in a sense the chemistry that made the image of a joyous Grace emerge from beneath the eddying of the developer was now working in reverse.

Now she was fading from me – the pin-sharp image of shared days in Perth growing fuzzier with my move to England and now slipping into pale fogginess and, no doubt, finally to spotless white. Like the marriage, she really was dissolving.

....

"You might even imagine that you'll see the person you have lost," Dr May had warned.

That is the first thing I think of two days later when I look up from tying in Dad's lolloping autumn-fruiting raspberry canes, which were being dragged down by the berries.

Pristine sunshine banishes the rainclouds and, peering towards the Top End, I spot a woman whose walk is exactly the same as Grace's, the back arched a little, head up straight.

She is talking to Cecil at the gate – maybe asking whether people could walk through the allotments. It couldn't be her but for a moment…

Cascades of raindrops fall on my wrists as I work, nipping off short lengths of soft string with Dad's ancient bone-handled penknife.

As I turn to go to the hut, I am stopped in my tracks.

Wilf is taking the path to the Bottom End and I can see, as he walks away from me, that he is in his best suit.

He is carrying in his arms a white box, big enough, I realise, to accommodate a giant leek. Show season is just starting.

But what makes me freeze and lean slowly back against the shed is the fleeting notion that I've encountered this scene before, or something like it.

I sit with my coffee and draw deeply on my cigarette, trying to gather the right synapses to bring together the incident that is deep inside.

When it comes to me, I feel a deep churning.

Lizzie's coffin was like that. It was white. And I had cradled it in exactly the way that little Wilf, with his laboured, swaying walk, is doing now.

EIGHT

There's a tap on the hut door and then I hear Grace's voice.

"Kyff?"

I know it can't possibly be but it is true.

Grace is here. I am transfixed. I can only grip the door frame and hope that my legs won't buckle under me.

She is flushed beneath that burnished paste-egg complexion, and looking paralysed by the moment. Her eyes are filling with tears.

She comes towards me and for a moment neither of us know whether to kiss, or hug, or keep our distance.

In the end we reach out and hold each other's fingertips, squeezing until it is painful, as if a prison warder has said: "You can now touch for one more time but it has to be through the grille and only for five seconds."

Then we let go and put space between us.

She sits on the edge of the old dentist's chair with tears streaming onto the cornflowers of her blue cotton dress. I have my back to her, holding on to the bench, weak-kneed and speechless.

"I shouldn't have…" she says.

Then: "It's just that I wanted to make absolutely sure that you got your special stuff, and we were heading north and Mum said it would be easy to divert."

"It's OK," I say. But it isn't. I am quaking, disorientated. Just by being there, Grace – more composed now and looking at me searchingly – has thrown everything into turmoil.

"Kind of you."

"There's two boxes. They're at the house behind the dustbin. Grandad's medals, your Grandpa's navy things, the old watches, the old diary from when you were little. There's certificates, official papers and things.

"I've put in some of the old letters from me. Just in case you still wanted to keep them."

"Thanks."

"The other box is full of your LPs."

Yes, I want to say, LPs full of songs that describe moments like this. When you feel near-nausea because of love, even damaged love, when – and I can see it in your face – there is agony inside.

"I'm sorry. I didn't ask how you are," I say, making coffee.

"Getting on with it." There is no self-pity in her voice, just a note of resignation.

"I needn't ask about you – you've shed ten years. You look terrific."

"Found a lot a peace here," I say, hoping I don't come over as self-satisfied. "Physical work, fresh air and friends; people I'd never have guessed I had anything in common with. And there's the spirit of this place," I say, gesturing to the hut walls.

"Taff's spirit."

Grace's eyes follow me everywhere, as if she is trying to catch up the time we've been apart.

"Well done on selling the house," I say, "and especially the outboard motor."

She smiles and shakes her head.

"No, it was your handiwork that sold the house. The couple had three kids and they all loved the summerhouse. The poor parents never stood a chance. They saw it as the perfect den for sleepovers."

She puts the coffee mug to her lips.

"I can recommend it for overnighting," I say.

She lowers the mug and looks down. No smile.

"I know, Kyff. It was a terrible time," she says.

"No worries – now it's history," I find myself saying, and believing it.

"But, as you know better than anybody, history doesn't go away does it, Kyff?"

"True, Grace. But it gets buried over time so you only come across it if you go looking for it. I'll be trying not to look back and you should try not to, Grace."

We could fill the rest of our lives with things we need to say, things we have discovered while apart, things that we have never said before but should have said. But what would lie at the end of that path?

My head told me that the process of catching up would be like taking stitches out of a surgical wound that has not quite healed.

For one moment, my heart says: "Send your mum home, Grace. Let's try again."

Instead I say: "Better not keep Mum waiting too long."

"She's OK. We've got time."

"I'll walk with you to the Top End."

I can see Mary in the side road opposite the gates. She spots me, winds down the window and waves vigorously. She is beaming. I don't like to think of not seeing Mary again.

Grace and me stand on the pavement wondering how to say goodbye, which moment to choose to go, watching for breaks in the traffic so she can cross safely.

There is a gap coming up, and I reach down, squeeze her hand and say: "Go now, Grace."

I don't notice the walk back to Dad's hut. I am deeply preoccupied with the realisation that this really is the day Grace and I said the final goodbye.

However much I have dwelt on Grace's betrayal, however great the distance in miles and the time I have put between us, we can't wipe out the years that we were Kyff and Grace, that rather nice and reserved couple in the Northern Suburbs, and - so nearly - Kyff and Grace, Lizzie's Mum and Dad.

We could have, should have, been on the patio, still under the sunshade each evening, eating something nice, drinking something cold, and being quietly content with one another.

Instead, we are individuals coming home to roost - one emigrant returning to her childhood home, and the other, at forty, with no job and no plans, imprisoned in the house that as a teenager he couldn't wait to leave.

I lock the hut, and as soon as I reach home, carry into the house the box that represents much of my life so far. In the hall, near the front door, is an envelope. It says "Kyff" on the front and the writing is unmistakably Grace's.

After reading it I fold the paper carefully and hold it between my palms for several moments as if to keep it safe.

NINE

Darling Kyff

Not sure I'll find you this morning. Either way I've faced the fact that we'll probably never meet again after today. You'll make sure of that (no blame there!).

We both know that this is not really what you want but the hurt I caused won't go away.

Having managed to face losing me - even though you never really lost me for a moment - I know you daren't backtrack.

You'd never be able to let yourself trust, even though I would die rather than let you down again in any way.

I won't say goodbye because as you know I can't bring myself to say the word to you, or even write it.

But I thank you for your love and your kind fussing, and for being my partner on the great adventure.

When I'm up against it, I'll picture us eating baked beans from the tin in my college room or reading in the sun on our grassy corner overlooking the beach. But most of all I'll think of the caring, especially over Lizzie.

I'll specially remember your little acts of love, e.g.   waking sometimes and finding that you'd covered me up. Not to mention going out for the eggs for my Sunday soldiers!

Love always,

Grace X

P.S. Remember what I said about sorting the washing.

TEN

Madge is always desperately curious about my marital state. I can tell that by the number of times she raises it, and the studied casualness of her questions.

Something makes me stubbornly resistant. I reveal nothing, not out of a wish to be secretive but because I am never sure that I can talk about Grace without showing emotion.

Yesterday's visit has sent Madge into a spasm of feverish curiosity.

She is standing on a box, pinning up more – even more – bunting across the front of her shed, when she turns and sees me heading for the Top End gate.

She almost falls in her hurry to get along the side of her plot and ask: "Kyff – did the lady find you eventually?"

"Yes thanks."

"I'm so glad! I think she came on spec, just hoping to catch you."

"Yes."

"Would have been a shame if she'd travelled a long way and missed you but she said she was just passing."

"Yes."

"Lovely woman isn't she? So bonny! Looks as if she'd just come back from somewhere nice."

As she says this Madge raises an eyebrow expectantly - it appears to be forming a physical question mark.

"Yes."

"We had quite a chat but she didn't say whether she was a friend, or whatever."

"No."

"Anyway, she certainly knew your dad!"

"She did."

I know that meek and gentle Madge would really like to take my lapels, and beat me black and blue just to hear me spit out the words (along with a few broken teeth): "OK Madge. I'll come clean. She's my ex-wife."

But she merely says: "Anyway, it was nice to meet her. Whoever she was."

Grace had certainly made an impression.

When I next see Cecil he says: "Glad you were around when that woman friend dropped in. She came to me asking after you. I knew you wouldn't mind me steering her your way."

Of course not, I tell him but don't say who she is.

"We had a bit of a chat, mainly about your dad. What a smashing lass! I think you can tell a lot from people's faces, and she looked as sound as a pound."

In our closed little world, inconsequential events punctuating each life become public property and gain substance.

Waggy walks through with shopping as I sit reading, on the bench outside the hut, and calls: "Hey, lover boy - did you lure her back by promising to show her your seeds?" And within a couple of days Prof is saying: "Is it true you've been bringing women back, defiling the sacred hut? Shame!"

Prof has come over from his plot ostensibly to give me some young leeks but really he is as interested in my visitor as Madge.

"Don't deny it. It was the wife. The person you never mention," he says.

I don't reply and lead him into the hut. He would want coffee with his fag. I take the stool, he settles back in the dentist's chair.

"A nice big smile will tell me that I am right," he insists. I laugh, of course, but divert his curiosity by pointing out that I am not the only one who keeps marital matters private.

"There's no secret," he says. "I met Mary at the Fabian Society when she was young and hungry to know everything about the world.

"Several years and two baby boys later, she stopped coming with me on protest marches. Should have seen the signs. Couldn't get her really discussing things of an evening. The fire had gone out.

"I'd rabbit on about some incredibly interesting discoveries and she'd just yell things like: 'For God's sake! Can't I just sit here quietly and enjoy this bit of mince!'

"She'd lost all sense of wonderment. Her mind had stopped being boggled by things I found absolutely mind-boggling.

"When eventually she left me with the lads and went to do charity work overseas she told me that being at home had been like living in a reference library."

"Oh, Prof," I say. "Sorry things turned out like that."

"And you?"

"Well, with me it was a bit messier. I thought we were doing fine but then it all suddenly seemed to change. We just decided that we'd be happier living apart."

Oh, did we? And are we?

"Me and Mary had more fights than Mohammed Ali and made up every time until the last big bust-up.

"I remember I was telling her something about space. I think it was quantum mechanics, and how it related to gravity. She'd never really grasped it. Funny, she always struggled to get her head round the concept of light years.

"Anyway, she was reading her magazine and then, well, she reared up, threw her wedding ring at me and said 'That's it!' She never came back and we never found the ring. Think it got a soft landing in the dog's food."

I wonder whether, with his sons having left home, campaigning and political agitation have become replacements for family life.

"You know what I admire about you, Prof?" I say, putting my hand over his tobacco pouch as he reaches to prepare a roll-up and giving him a Benson's.

"My looks?" he says, showing me more with his smile than I want to see.

"No. Seriously – you stick to principles. You remember what's right. We'd never have fought like we have for the allotments if you hadn't been around making sure we didn't just lie down and take it."

"I'm no working class hero, Kyff. And I've often been tempted to give in, buckle down."

He was enjoying the Benson's, the firm feel between his fingers, as a change from his thin, scraggy roll-ups.

"Most people as they get older move from left to right, just as they go from sweet wine to dry, and from principled to pragmatic, and from being thin to being fat.

"Your eighteen-year-old anarchist is behind a bank counter at twenty-five. Your union firebrand is a grey-haired eminence at sixty, hoping for a peerage. The world is full of gamekeepers who once were poachers."

He tilts the chair back and looks up at the ceiling, deep in contemplation.

"People don't like the discomfort of feeling the current buffeting against them all the time. It's human. People mellow. Lose conviction. Lose hope. Go with the flow. But the wrongs remain.

"Whenever I waver, or wonder whether to bother getting up to go to some rally, I think of certain people who would think I was letting the side down – people like your Dad. He never wavered once he'd worked out what was right and what was wrong."

It starts to rain hard now, and the wind is lashing droplets across the windows. I get up and give Prof a mug of coffee, and another Benson's.

ELEVEN

Two good things (one of them not just good – intriguing!) have come out of the Chronicle report.

The article, incidentally, is dominated by my physog, my eyes cast nostalgically into the middle distance, as the chunky photographer had instructed. Above it is the headline:

THEY'RE BURYING OUR BIRTHRIGHT
says son of allotment guru

The first good outcome is that, at a time when everyone is down in the mouth knowing that the allotments are going, the report has given them a laugh at my expense.

Waggy was unrelenting. Whenever I passed over the next couple of days he would make some crack delivered in what was a very convincing Welsh accent.

Ray tried to join in. He was spaying cabbages when he spotted and me and shouted:"Are you signing wossnames today, Kyff?"

The nurses were out, rosy-cheeked and beautiful with their rude health and limitless energy, one digging, one raking.

"We shall not be moved, Kyff!" one shouted, waving to me.

So the interview had been worth it, just for that uplift, that moment of camaraderie, something that will soon disappear from our lives.

And the something intriguing? That came yesterday.

It was a call from the County Archivist who said that he'd seen the picture of me in the hut. He'd had an eye-glass on the copy of the photograph he'd got from the Chron because one of the items on the shelf looked interesting.

"Please don't get excited," he said. "Most of the trails we follow lead nowhere. But I want to check because I understand that before World War One the Benton family handed over a couple of other interesting oldish items.

"These were probably imported by family members on their travels and didn't indicate any occupancy going way back but we always like to check.

"Could be that what's in the picture is from the Far East – it's the roundish metal disc with a criss-cross pattern on. May I drop in for an unofficial peep?"

"Of course," I replied.

Dad would have been in his element.

....

Old Bill seems to have turned in on himself since we got the news that we are being moved off. Yet force of habit seems to be compelling him to carry on tending his plot.

I stroll over to him as he uses a great, broad fork to spear clods of manure from his heap and scatter it on his patch. He looks up, wipes his nose on his sleeve and looks at me with doleful eyes.

"A bad job, eh, Kyff."

"A bad job, Bill."

Once more he rams the fork into the manure pile and I realise that he is venting his anger.

I am fascinated by the fork, which has lots of tines and is recessed to hold large loads. It is nearly as big as Bill.

"That's some tool, Bill," I say, and he stops and shows me the shaft, which has the letters WW, in a Victorian script, burned into it.

"Used by my dad and his dad before him, and maybe even his dad."

I run my hand down the glossy shaft, slightly indented by flesh on wood over generations, and ask Bill what the tool is called.

"Don't rightly know it's got a name," he says. "Our lot have always just called it the old shit-shifter."

For a second I imagine the fork hanging on a barn wall as an exhibit in an agricultural museum, and Bill's name for it spelled out tastefully in raised italics on the descriptive card beneath.

Before I head back to the hut I say to Bill: "Sorry that we couldn't save the place for you and the others."

"You did your best boy," he replies, giving the manure pile another thrust as if he was bayoneting an enemy.

I start to head home so that I can take a call from a commercial radio station but with the allotments in their end-of-season glory I can't help simply standing and staring.

Madge appears at the path alongside her patch, which this evening looks as if it might have been planted as an offering to a sun god.

Apart from growing pickling onions, shallots, red cabbage and currants, Madge dedicates all her efforts to flowers. She is always hungry for colour – in her dress, in her make-up, in her allotment, and round her shed. This is the climax of her year.

Her outdoor chrysanths in russet, yellow and bronze fill almost half the plot, and golden and scarlet dahlias fill most of the remainder.

Perhaps as a gesture of denial that we will be leaving she has just repainted her hut frontage, and her garish display of toys, flags and bric-a-brac have been washed and reinstalled.

Cut flowers hang upside down, turning papery, and plaits of garlic decorate the door. Tonight in the calm of an Indian summer her plywood man barely has the energy to turn his wheel.

Throughout the fight to save the allotments she had kept on the edge of things, hoping for good news, trusting in what she saw as the inherent goodness and fairness in all concerned.

She has found it impossible to confront the reality of the situation.

When I spoke to her weeks before she called the council plan "not very nice". She meant that it was devastating.

"Well, Kyff, what's the latest, love?" she says.

I hurriedly search my mind for the words that might sweeten the pill.

"A bit bleak, Madge, I'm sorry to say."

"Don't worry. Something will happen."

"Possibly," I say. "But…"

"No, surely," she says, looking as if she is trying to draw on courage that isn't there.

"Surely they'll not be allowed to do it. I mean surely they can't destroy all this." She holds out her arms in a gesture that seems to be presenting her patch for the admiration of the world.

She looks up into my face and then adds: "Can they Kyff? Will they be allowed to do it?"

It is a question that I avoid, answering instead with a squeeze of her shoulders before I walk on to my radio interview - and another ten minutes of flogging a dead horse.

……………………………………

I am the teatime guest on Join Jazzer, and the radio host is professing interest in allotment life, having just played Lonnie Donegan's *Diggin' My Potatoes*.

"But just think, Kyff - all that hard work, the cost of your seeds and your rent and then vandals pop over the fence and mess it all up!"

Jazzer talks at bewildering pace.

"Come on - aren't the council doing you a favour by shutting you down?"

Jazzer (showbusiness for James) sounds as if he's on amphetamines. He has an annoying cackle of a laugh and a fake curiosity that doesn't quite extend to listening to answers and trying to understand them.

I'd seen his picture in reception. Face to face he is plumper and more primped but disappointingly unglamorous in the bare studio with the knees of his jeans in rags and a rather camp, flustered manner.

I try to explain that, although they were originally introduced to help feed the rural poor, allotments are much more than an inexpensive source of ultra-fresh food.

I try to get over points about the satisfaction involved, the changing seasons, the sense of community. His eyes suggest I'm being a little too worthy for his audience and I'm sure he's about to break in, and he does.

"But be honest, Kyff, after a year of hard work, all you've got is a load of cabbages, a few spuds, pneumonia and a bad back."

He cackles once more in self-congratulation.

I rise to the bait.

"But, Jazzer, you and your listeners spend a lifetime tuning in to music. Imagine – sitting there, getting fat, eating pap, listening to mere sounds. What have people got at the end of listening to your programme for a year?"

He decides it's time to play another track.

TWELVE

The County Archivist turns out to be a brisk, lively middle-aged man who appears to want to be somewhere else soon.

He has brought an assistant from the city museum ("our Roman man"), who has a billiard-ball head, a disconcerting stare and no conversation. His fishy eyes start roaming round the hut before he's through the door.

I'd washed mugs particularly thoroughly and even put out biscuits but evidently there was no time for tea in the hurtling world of antiquity.

"You might be right, Jim," says our Roman man absently, picking up the encrusted metal disc. "Could be a hedgehog or a tortoise with legs and head broken off. The breakage would be deliberate if it's votive…"

His voice tails off. His eyes alight on Dad's scrap metal shelf. He kneels down and holds up a piece of old lead piping, whitened with age and scored over the years by plough shares and spades.

"There was a very old hall here once," I venture, "Before the existing hall. Maybe…"

"Yes, we know about the old hall," says the Roman man flatly.

I consider myself rebuked.

Questing fingers delve and filmy eyes peer. We watch the Roman

man in silence, the County Archivist shifting from one foot to the other.

Finally, the bald globe rises like a surfacing buoy.

"All done Alex?" asks the Archivist. "Good – we'll take these if you don't mind, just the pipe and the mystery object, and we'll be in touch," he says, stepping out of the hut.

"Do let us know if you hear of anything else that's been found."

"I don't think there will be anything," I reply. "The hut's been the collection point for anything and everything that's been dug up over the years."

I add, "Dad was a bit of a local historian," but manage to stop myself adding: "And I happen to be a proper historian."

What if the stuff turns out to be Roman, bits that have been under my very nose every day and not even sparked the notion that they might be ancient? I am sure that Dad is already looking down and smiling smugly.

....

I spend two days away from the allotment to let things sink in. I have the feeling of approaching the tape in a race and seeing those alongside you accelerate. I know the race is lost.

Cecil rings to say that the new MP is still rooting for us and hoping that the Secretary of State will grant a reprieve.

"The poor young chap's an idealist, a real ball of energy. But he knows it's hopeless."

He starts to say goodbye and then adds: "By the way, the stuff I took for you to the village show did pretty well. Your runner beans got a second and you got a third for the beetroot with foliage. Madge dominated the cake section again."

That image of Wilf carrying his long white box flashes through my mind.

"Any news of Wilf at the nationals?"

"Heartbreaking. It was a winning size but it burst overnight. Wilf blames the humidity in the marquee. Poor old lad – that was his last time."

When I next stroll through the Top End gates I see that it is business as usual. There's activity everywhere. It's as if they have heard good news that hasn't yet reached me.

I walk via the railway end path. Someone is sowing overwintering beans, another composting lettuce that have gone to seed, tying onions into bunches. A more realistic old chap is preparing to abandon ship, gathering bamboos and tools.

The Jain couple are also out, admiring their new beehive and covering the last bit of plot with old carpets they've brought on a barrow. Yeti and Waggy are deep in conversation with them as I arrive.

They are so immersed that I barely get a greeting so I stand and listen. Bees are coming and going and Yeti asks if either Farida or Ben has been stung.

"No way," says Ben. "They pick up vibes. If you're cool, the bees are cool."

"But this business about every living thing having feelings defeats me…" says Waggy. "So you'd honestly feel bad about pulling up a parsnip would you?"

Farida puts on her intense look.

"Root crops especially are capable of feeling. That's why when we've killed the weeds, or rather allowed them to die, under the carpets, we'll be growing leafy things."

"Oh, so that's what NSPCC means! National Society for the Prevention of Cruelty to Carrots!" says Waggy but Farida and Ben are not amused, maybe hurt at being mocked. For a moment I despise Waggy and his wounding ways.

"Why don't things squeal then if it hurts?" says Yeti in that sleepy way of his.

"They can't tell us," says Farida. "Just as fish can't tell us they feel pain."

"But that's because their mouths are always full of water," says Yeti, who seems now to have become a target for the encircling bees. He wafts them with his dinner plate hands.

"Stay cool!" says Ben. "It's your cardigan. Scientists say they love purple."

Waggy seems to be framing a mischievous question about whether there's an insect heaven when Bill pulls up behind us and announces: "Watch it – they's swarming."

"No, just going about their business!" says Ben.

"Take it from me, they's swarming. The foragers are all of a dither and they'll be setting off in a minute on a sortie."

Farida and Ben smile equably, armed with new-found knowledge.

Bill says: "They used to say that a swarm in June was worth a silver spoon, and a swarm in July was not worth a fly. It's even later because of the weather so the swarm won't be up to much. But they's definitely swarming."

Yeti has begun to thrash about. The bees love his cardigan.

"Not so rough!" says Ben.

Farida has also become a target and she moves to Ben's side.

"I'm skidaddling," says Bill, riding off. "Remember, when they sting they send out a message saying 'Come on boys, get stuck in' to the rest of them. It's all done by chemicals."

Waggy, Yeti and me turn as one but after a few paces there's a piercing scream from Farida, whose blonde curls are infested with bees. Ben is bravely trying to pick them off one by one, flicking them away gently until he's stung on the hand.

"Cripes!" he shouts and by thrashing around attracts more bees to him.

"Get them off!" Farida screams and again Ben goes into the fray, only to retreat with another sting.

"One got me!" she shouts, holding her ear and beginning to run across the carpeted plot. A ribbon of bees follows her and she squeals and grasps her neck as she's stung again.

We look on, helpless, then see the two nurses, cardigans over their heads, running to the rescue, holding a sheet of polythene.

They swat Farida smartly round the head several times and then pull her away. Ben is behind a compost heap clasping his hand and looks on appalled as Farida is swaddled in polythene. I can hear her making little noises as the nurses lift the polythene to tend to her.

There will be much merriment around the allotments about the cowering dreamers dealt a painful blow by hard reality.

Those knocked about by life can hardly wait to see idealists come a cropper. The bee episode will be more proof that you have to have your feet on the ground not your head in the clouds.

Waggy will be in his element but I'll like him less for the sourness in the mocking jokes that I know he'll be treating us to by tomorrow.

THIRTEEN

"You're last out, Kyff," I hear Cecil shout. "I'll leave the Top End open."

I look round the door of the hut as Cecil heads off down the path, a bunch of cornflowers in one hand, pink asters in the other, and a marrow under the arm of his tweedy jacket.

I wave and shout "OK" from the door and without turning he tilts the marrow in acknowledgement and shouts: "Night!"

It's a clear and tranquil evening and, to my surprise, my mood matches it perfectly. I'm enjoying the feeling that I fit in, here on Dad's patch. I've been gathered in by Cecil and the rest of the Good Shepherds.

They talk easily with me. I've been accepted as if I were one of them, and not just a stranger come to clear up his dad's belongings. I suffer Waggy's tendency to boorishness and endure Prof's more extreme rants but we get on.

In Perth, I had never felt deprived of camaraderie. Erik had seemed to fill that need with the flights of fancy, the irreverence, the things I couldn't share with Grace.

And of course there were things. How could she be expected to appreciate a perfectly executed cover drive for four, or the throaty roar of a high-powered motorbike?

Of course, I'm the same man now. But being drawn into a life centred on aimless gossip, tending plants, sharing jokes and enjoying the vagaries of the English weather has revealed to me an aspect of myself I never knew was there.

Lately, I've begun to eat what I've grown. Now I stop to notice how, between visits to the plot, pea pods bulge, lettuces heart up, parsnips thicken, seeds burst into life. I especially notice (proudly) how, after a week of sun, my Gardener's Delight tomatoes have changed to rich red.

There was such satisfaction in seeing how the crop of plums on Dad's Cambridge Gage threatened to snap off the boughs, and in how a picking party gathered spontaneously.

We shared the crop – with much hilarity, juice running down our chins – after setting aside a boxful for Madge's pies and crumbles.

Now I'm no longer tormented, I've begun to think more analytically about what was at the heart of the differences that Dad and me never resolved.

The job of clearing the hut is still to be faced, and it's a more urgent matter now that the allotments are going. I've come up with excuses for not doing the job but the real reason is that sorting out Dad's stuff will feel like desecration.

When the hut goes, along with everything inside it, I'll have lost Dad, in a way, before I've got to know him. I've been putting that prospect to one side.

When I fill his dented aluminium kettle, or turn on his cobwebby old radio, I always feel that he is looking over my shoulder, with that indescribable expression he always wore – a knowing look, as if he was reading my thoughts and motives, and not approving.

Yet each time I go into the hut I come away feeling I have been soothed. I'm not alone in this. People calling for tea and a smoke seem to go away more content.

The hut has come to represent an inviolable place, "a sanctuary" Prof calls it. And it does resemble a retreat. Maybe it's the way the old stained glass window throws pools of blue and yellow onto the floorboards, investing the place with a near-spiritual dimension, but not a churchy one.

Then there's the silence. Tonight it's total, as if the world's sound system has been turned off.

Outside there's a picture that cries out to be painted. But not by me.

Grace, not unfairly, always said I had the drawing skills of a three-year-old but she conceded that words came readily to me. At school, my expressive strength was writing but my pen could run away with me.

My English teacher Bogey Ansell noted: "Kyff tends not only to gild the lily but then to go back and add an extra coat."

Just before my English exam he had sent my homework book skimming across the desk to me – "Waxing lyrical again, Pugh."

It was exactly the sort of thing Dad said.

I never quite grew used to having my finer feelings trampled underfoot in this way but I didn't have to suffer many more insults from Mr Ansell who, a couple of months later, began to turn jaundiced and thin, and then disappeared.

And now Dad is gone too.

I wonder how Col, my childhood friend, now remembers his dad (long dead now I suppose)? Fondly, warmly, admiringly? Mr Latham deserved that sort of remembrance. He had been the polar opposite of my Dad – outgoing, playful, physical.

Once he had come bustling in putting on an American accent.

"OK, youse guys – who's big enough to get into da ring wid Marciano?"

He then crouched like a boxer and kept tapping us gently on our faces. We laughed ourselves breathless.

Another time he came home and didn't speak. He just stood there, very serious, and did a little cough for attention and then said in the sort of voice people had on the wireless:

Mary had a little lamb
She also had a bear
I often saw her little lamb
But never saw her bare

We rolled on the carpet among Col's cars, laughing until we cried.

"Go to the lav, Col!" his mum shouted from the stove. "You'll have an accident."

While I waited for Col I saw Mr Latham go up behind Mrs Latham and squeeze her chest.

"James!" she said.

She announced "Grub's up!" then gave me my coat and squeezed my arm as she always did.

The kitchen window was open as I got outside and I heard Mrs Latham say: "James. You're really going to have to stop being so rude when Kyff's here. What would his Dad say! You know what they're like..."

FOURTEEN

The autumn sun is baking the plots, runner bean wigwams throwing long bluish shadows onto plots with their arrow-straight lines of winter cabbages, clumps of kale, the last of the lettuce, and rows of onions that have been eased from their anchorage in the earth and now lie drying to a crisp.

The light plays on the deep red veins of beetroot leaves and highlights the island of mauve michaelmas daisies alongside Winco's hut. Madge's yellow-and-gold late-season extravaganza is startlingly bright, as if illuminated by stage lighting.

Waggy's plot is beginning to look neglected. When he tries to chop spreading weeds I notice he stops often to lean on the shaft of the rake. But he still feels the exhilaration of having brought plants to fruition.

Yesterday, he called me over. "Kyff boy – have a gander at these," he said.

In the miniature glasshouse of discarded windows nailed together onto the side of his hut are two lines of chrysanthemums, huge mop-haired things, with white flowers that look like exploding stars. They are so perfect that they seem artificial.

"Irregular incurve the big ones, and spiders. Shame I've stopped showing," he said with a note of regret. "But then it won't be long before we can all stop bothering."

When I'd flown in for the funeral, little had been growing here, just overwintering stuff – pillars of sprouts, stands of kale, iced-in parsnips.

Since then Old Bill's plot has produced a continuous stream of perfect veg and has now been dug over, the weed-free soil left in clumps. Winco, I notice, has followed suit, using his top-of-the-range stainless steel spade, oiled before and after as if it were a classic shotgun.

Opposite me, on Pat's plot, where she had worked so hard and eagerly in spring to carry on Terry's work, the crops had flourished – helped, no doubt, by Terry's chemical contribution – but had been allowed to go to seed.

Now waving swathes of sweetcorn, leaves and tassles bleached almost white by the sun, stand untouched, their cobs baked hard. The late raspberries are turning to pulp on the canes, summer cabbages stand half-eaten by caterpillars and lettuce have turned into spindly towers.

Some weeks ago Pat had told me, without a trace of self-pity, that there no longer seemed to be any point in harvesting anything, yet once her life had been punctuated by treats from the garden.

Evidently, they always shared the first new potatoes with mint; the first broad beans with gammon; the first home-grown salad; the first young carrots pulled up by their tops; the first sweet baby beetroots of the summer.

"But of course, Terry's first love was the sweet peas," she said. "He couldn't wait each year to the first sniff of scent. Every day for weeks in summer we'd have a couple of sweet peas in a specimen vase on the breakfast table."

And there we both were, tenuously united by loss, both there on the allotments on behalf of someone else, both charged with carrying on for someone who had gone, and to safeguard what they had loved.

Terry, I feel, would have been proud of Pat's efforts but I suspect that Dad is looking down shaking his head ruefully at my mine.

There's a chill inside the hut now the sun has fallen behind the hall.
I go outside and lean with my back against the hut, letting the last of

the glow hit me full in the face.

I think of another time, another moment in the sun.

I'm about eight. It is really baking hot, so hot that when I look along the allotment path everything is wavy. I've got new shorts on and Mum has warned me not to get tar on them.

I've got my fishing net with me to catch butterflies around Dad's plot. I'm after dragonflies as well. They come over from the pond near the Old Hall and I marvel at their shiny bodies.

Dad's got his jacket off and his sleeves rolled up and he's raking, hitting the hard lumps of soil with the back of the rake. I can hear him breathing.

When I lick my arm it tastes salty.

Mum's given me a bottle of water with lemon crystals in. It's gone a bit warm but I drink it all down and it tastes good.

I sit on the side of the path and watch some ants but become bored. I ask Dad for a job to do. He tells me I can collect the lollipop sticks he puts at the ends of the rows of vegetables.

The pencilled names have faded. As I hand the flat sticks to him I ask: "Dad – if you could invent a new sort of vegetable and they let you choose the name what sort would it be?"

He keeps hitting the lumps of soil while he is thinking.

"We could do with a new outdoor cucumber. Longer, thinner skin but keeping the old-fashioned flavour."

"So what would you call it?"

"Well, people who breed a new plant often name it after somebody in the family. So I suppose it could be called Kyff. Kyff goes with cucumber doesn't it?"

FIFTEEN

Dad's haunting me. I went to sleep thinking about him and woke restless. Now, sitting here in the hut with his journals and his tools, I sense that he's here, benign and protective.

People talk of laying ghosts. Maybe that's what I have to do; maybe that's what he wants me to do.

I go home and dig out a woolly jumper. I gather the camper's lamp, more fags, some matches, my teabags and my carton of long-life milk and return to the hut.

The old dentist's chair, tilted back a few degrees, is perfect for tea-drinking, fag-smoking, ruminating and enjoying melodic music above the hiss of the gas lamp.

Now darkness had fallen it's easy to imagine that I am anywhere I care to be – in a snow-covered log cabin in Calgary, snugly enclosed by fir trees above a loch in the Highlands of Scotland, or tucked away out of the rain, looking out over peat bogs in Donegal.

Even with the overlaying fug of my cigarette smoke I can still smell creosote, wood shavings, mould, oil.

I drain my cup, stub out my cigarette, switch to the high stool and really study what is here, what Dad surrounded himself with. I realise that over the months I haven't exactly been averting my eyes in here but I've been reluctant to delve.

When you really look, the orderliness of the place is striking – the drawers under the bench, others in the old cabinet sitting on the timber bench, each labelled. I flip through the rows of seed packets, each identified…

"Tomato Cherokee Purple – grow on for seed"

"Tomato Bloody Butcher – trials in Sussex"

"Jaune Obtuse de Doubs – F. yellow carrot"

I'm familiar with the bench-top library, clamped together by bricks used as book ends – booklets about old vegetable varieties, books about the allotment movement – but I haven't really taken stock of everything in the drawers beneath the bench.

Sixty spades on sixty plots over half a lifetime has produced quite a collection. According to Cecil, Dad was notably good-natured to anyone who bothered him by bringing bits of a clay pipe, a horse's tooth or yet another piece of fine china.

There's a shelf and then three deep drawers under the bench. On the shelf is the perfect bird's skull, the horseshoes and the beads that I remember but also a corroded army button, a bullet case, and a 1933 penny, the dated side highlighted, probably by Dad's spit and an abrasive thumb.

I open the top drawer of three under the bench, struggling to draw it out. It's full of encrusted metal, bits of misshapen lead, a horse's bit, fragments from old machinery. Dad was frugal. Perhaps this was his scrap metal hoard set aside for a rainy day.

In the second drawer there are piles of exercise books, Dad's weather journals, each marked with the relevant year.

On the wall behind my back are small hand tools resting on nails and screws designed to hold them snugly. There's an oily sheen on the tired-looking secateurs, a patina on the handles of trowels and the long knife Dad used for cutting asparagus.

I take a dozen or so of the weather journals from the drawer, light the gas lamp, sit back in the dentist's chair and flip through them.

When I read that two years ago, on 20th February, the temperature at 6 pm was minus 7C, a near record, and that snow was forecast and the wind was light, I picture Dad in his old black duffel coat, woollen hat and scarf, switching on the camper's light and filling in the log, fingerless gloves steering the pencil.

Just when I was growing bored with the repetitive entries, I bring out some of earlier journals, ones I must have seen him filling in when I was a boy.

I'm part-way down the pile when loose papers fall out of one of the books. They are newspaper cuttings, yellowed and mounted on paper.

One shows a photograph of me at thirteen receiving a fountain pen for winning an essay competition set by Booth's Bookshop. The other is a sports report from the Chronicle headed **Pugh seals Final for Grammar**. I'm amazed and moved that Dad saved the cuttings.

Opening the book I see, beneath the space where they had been stuck, in Dad's handwriting: *"Y chwareuwr gorau ar y cae. Rhedeg fel 'sgyfarnog. 'Na golled I rygbi."*

Rygbi is the only word I recognised. Rugby. So even in my moment of glory the old boy was wishing I'd played rugby instead…

As I leaf through the journal I find dated pages with no entries. I had no idea that Dad had ever missed filling in his weather log. When the entries resume, above them is another sentence in Welsh:

"Ma' G bant eto. Ma' Megan yn helpu nes gawn ni newyddion."

A mention of Megan. But what was Dad saying? I put a seed packet in as a marker so I could have it translated.

A few entries later there's a note saying:

"Gorfod ffonio i M I ddod. K mor dda, chwarae teg."

M again. Presumably Megan. Again I mark the page, and later I come across two more pages where there is an entry in Welsh. In every one the letter M appears.

Surely not Dad and Megan?

Impossible. Ludicrous.

But then it might explain the coldness between Dad and Mum – or could the coldness have been the reason behind the need for incestuous hanky panky in the hut?

Why resort to Welsh (just as Sam P hid behind shorthand) if the messages were mundane?

Strewth.

"Your Da was fab'lous," Megan had said at the funeral, with surprising enthusiasm I recall.

Just when, after turning page after page of weather records I feel sure that I've found all Dad's asides, I come across an envelope tucked into pages for late summer in the year I left school.

At the top of the page is *"Mae e' mewn a wedi haeddu hyn. Crwt go lew."*

In the envelope is the letter telling me that I'd been accepted for Cambridge – and a card that had come out of the box that had contained my school leaver's merit medal: "Awarded to Kyff Pugh to acknowledge his contribution to the school and the consideration shown to his fellows."

It was signed by the head, above the school motto *"Non sidi sed omnibus* – Not for oneself but for all."

The trawl through the books has become compulsive. I need to see them all. Dawn is breaking but I don't feel tired. I just switch off the camping light, make more tea and set to work again.

There are no more non-weather entries for four years. Then, suddenly, between two entries for early December I come across: *"Gadawodd K a G Dydd Sul. Teimlodd fel y ffarwel olaf. 'Mae'n amhosib I gysuro G.'"*

K and G – Kyff and Grace. G, my mum. It must be about us going to Australia; we went just before Christmas that year.

These are the jottings of a man who had no-one to talk to.

I find paper and write out all the entries he wrote in Welsh. My first thought is to send them to Megan, who has passable Welsh, but then I fear what the messages might turn out to say.

As I walk home to bed, I see a father arriving with his boy, right over on the railway side. The lad is full of life, leaping round, and talking excitedly with his dad.

If only…

I fall into bed and wake at teatime. As I eat my toast I suddenly remember Ceri Thomas, a teacher who lived next door to Uncle Glyn. A Welsh speaker. It's possible she never moved away.

I decide to write and say I've found an old diary of Dad's with bits of Welsh in it and I'm curious to find out what they say, apologising over involving her in something so embarrassingly private.

I know Dad's mysterious scribbles will help me to understand him but I can't say I'm not scared about what I might discover.

SIXTEEN

In the dream, Dad was a life-size doll. He was standing upright among slot machines at a funfair. He looked perfectly human, every pore visible, every sooty hair of the Pugh monobrow standing out black and clear against his waxy complexion.

He had been varnished. Even more bizarrely he also had drawers set in his body, each with a tasselled pull cord.

I only become afraid as I wake. In the dream it all seemed so normal. I was just curious, especially about the drawers. Above the sound of the steam organ a fairground hand was shouting: "Roll up, have a go at opening the drawers!"

I pulled at each in turn, finding them empty, leaving the one at Dad's heart until last. No matter how much I pulled, it wouldn't open.

As I wake I make the connection – with the drawer of the cabinet in the hut, the one that is locked.

I'd not been curious to know what might be in there but, thinking about it now, why had Dad chosen to lock a single drawer of the seed cabinet?

Why bother unless, inside, there is something deeply personal or valuable? Something, I guess, he didn't want to be found while he was alive. An explanation? Pornography? Love letters? A confession?

It is barely light but I feel restless and I know I won't settle until I've been to the hut.

Throwing on some clothes, I gather some of Dad's old, and universally oily, tools into a carrier bag and set off to the hut and get to work eagerly.

The hacksaw blade I feed into the crack on top of the locked drawer makes no impression on the tongue of the lock.

I am sweating and panting with the effort of sawing when I decide instead to prise off the cabinet side with a chisel. It eases away and the whole carcass of the cabinet loosens, allowing me to knock away the frame holding the drawer.

Inside is an old metal cash box. There are slots for every old denomination of coin, from farthings up.

It had been well made. As I pick it up I can feel that there is something rattling inside, but it doesn't sound like coins.

I am frustrated now and try to hold the box between my feet while I hammer the chisel that I have forced under the point where the lock is holding the lid in place.

Hurrying home with the box I clamp it in Dad's vice and then, having thought strategically about the best way of opening the box, immediately abandon intelligence in favour of brute force.

Chiselling a jagged hole in the box side I stopped for a second to peer inside but could only see paper. I managed to drive a big screwdriver into the lock until finally it snapped away.

I hurry to the kitchen and take out the contents…

The sole of a leather sandal; a round piece of broken-off, decorative pottery with a face on it; a piece of terracotta tile with lines incised; a blackened finger ring and a bigger ring, perhaps a bangle. I know at once that they are Roman.

I smooth the sheet of lined paper, which I can see had been torn from one of the exercise books Dad used for his journals.

At the top, in pencilled capitals, it says simply "KYFF". Beneath is a rough plan of part of the allotments – Yeti's and Winco's. The location of each of the finds is marked with a dot and a description: "Bronze bangle found here … decorated spout from flagon (?) found here…"

At the bottom of the page, Dad had written: "Footnote – old lead piping and glass beads (see top shelf) both from railway side, no precise location. Also, what could be brooch fastener – found at path edge, opposite my hut. All poss. Roman."

It is when I am packing the relics away to take to the County Archivist that I notice Dad had written a date, faintly, in pencil, beside his footnote – 10th August 1999. Just months before he died.

So had Dad known he was going to die soon?

If he had, had he reasoned that when it happened I would come home, find the box, and report the stuff to the archaeologists?

He would have known that, if I did, there would have to be a dig. But had he hoped to time it all to hold up the supermarket work?

I'm sure the answer to all the questions is "Yes".

SEVENTEEN

The letter is from Wales. As I open it I find a photograph of a smiling couple sitting in identical seats in front of identical teacups, with spectacles that nearly match.

Behind them is a bungalow, and alongside them a very clean and shiny car.

When I read the first line of the letter I realise that it is from Ceri.

She had been thrilled to receive my letter, which had been dropped round by the people who now lived in the Capel Terrace house.

First, she said, she wanted to give me an assurance about confidentiality *("We've enough skeletons in our cupboard to supply a medical school!")*.

I skim through her personal news, memories of Dad and Mum *("so quiet, they were like church mice!")*, and her apology for her translation being in colloquial South Walian.

I can't wait to see what Dad's secret notes have revealed.

"OK, Kyff, here goes..." I wonder whether it is wise to read on.

"Right, the first bit, about football. The line says... 'Best player on the field. What a loss to rugby.'"

Relief. Just fatherly pride never passed on.

"Now, all the references to M, presumably Megan, who is mentioned

using her name in one of the entries, and I suppose the Megan I used to know, are all about being asked to help while G is away. For instance there's 'G away again. Megan helping till we get news.'"

"Another one says:'Had to go out and ring M to come. K as good as gold.'"

Now the message you said you found on a page with a university letter tucked in says, 'He's in, and he's earned it' and then, in effect, 'He's a lad and a half' (like the Irish say 'a broth of a boy')."

"There's quite a sad one – sorry! It's the message with K and G in it. It says:'K and G left on Sunday. Felt like the final goodbye. G beside herself."

The letter ends:

I hope this helps, Kyff. And I hope you don't mind me saying, but I think that your Dad must have been such a lonely man to have to scribble down little worried messages like that.

He always seemed like a bit of a closed book to me but then I only met him a few times, and I was quite young. Hope all this helps.

Hwyl fawr, Ceri XXX
*   P.S. Never forget you're Welsh!*

....

I sit holding the letter and thinking back.

I'm about five. I'm sitting in front of the fire on the rug Mum made with bits of wool and a little metal pricker thing. The rug smells new and it feels nice under my legs.

Dad's in his chair reading his paper. Mum throws me my dressing gown and then takes things off the clotheshorse and puts them in a suitcase on the table.

She says:"Right, our Kyff. Back before you know it."

She shuts the case and says to Dad:"Make sure he has some butter puffs with his milk."

The only sounds come from coal burning and the crinkly noise from Dad's newspaper.

I don't think Dad has ever put me to bed. He won't know the routine. What's going to happen when it's time for a goodnight kiss, and to get tucked in? Does he know that Mum always says "Sleep tight and don't let the bugs bite?"

I needn't have worried.

"I'll get your drink," he says, in the voice he uses when he's trying to be kind. "You're a big lad now so you can get yourself to bed."

I take my cricket bat up and lay it right at the top of my pillow ready for tomorrow. Then I go to sleep worrying what I'll do if one time Mum doesn't come back.

I must have blotted out the times Mum went away but, this morning, that single memory is as clear as day.

EIGHTEEN

Phil Harwood often wondered how on earth he had ended up working on the local paper.

His friends seem to have flourished in "proper" jobs. Reporting wasn't a pukka job in his book, not a profession like accountancy or law. Actually, often it felt like being an outlaw the community tolerated but didn't trust.

Journalists in the provinces were on the edge of things, civic observers, instead of being in the centre shaping the big debates, like the nationals. And of course for the most part it was far less exciting than the public imagined.

Today was different.

Today the things he did like about the job – the chance to show initiative, see through smokescreens, reveal something of worth – were coming together. When they did he had a feeling of power and that gave him a buzz.

He had that feeling now. He was at his computer, surrounded by cuttings from the morgue. They were spilling out of manila envelopes marked "Pugh, Huw – Benton allotments" and "Pugh, Huw – weather records".

He was staring into the distance as he always did when he was composing his intro. No more than a dozen words, he used to be told by journalistic greybeards.

Old Hedley, long dead, used to liken the intro to the taste of the outside of the roast beef your mum was going to dish up – a morsel that set your mouth watering for the full meal.

It was a quiet news day otherwise so his piece would make the lead story. He had thirty-five minutes to rattle it out but was waiting for a return call, for a quote from a bloke called Cecil, an official at the allotments. He was having to be fetched to the phone.

As Phil said later, just a single glance – and that when he was barely awake – had got him the story.

He had been driving to work past the allotments, where a couple of weeks before he'd interviewed that Pugh chap who'd come back from Australia, and, through the morning mist, he could see people in luminous jackets using what looked like surveyors' gear. There was tape pegged up, which seemed to be running diagonally across one of the allotments.

Surely World-in-One weren't starting work before the Secretary of State's decision? Surely even they wouldn't have the brass neck.

Most likely someone had dug up some old bones.

At the office, he drew a blank with the police, the World-in-One press people and the council, and so he drove again to the allotments and walked in from the Top End.

There, a huge man carrying a spade and watching progress from the path proved monosyllabic, and the old chap with him turned out to be stone deaf.

Then, among the luminous jackets measuring and pointing, he spotted someone familiar. It was not so much the person he recognised, as the huge shiny head that glinted in his memory.

"Museum," he said to himself. "The spooky bloke from the museum."

The bald man directed him to the County Archivist who was grudging with details.

He was playing it down. Someone had offered two or three interesting bits to look at, and then an allotment holder had shown a mixed bag of found items that suggested – "only suggested mind" – that there might have been, just might have been, some Roman presence at the site, "albeit fleeting".

"We'd appreciate it if you'd keep things low key. You know what people are like. They'll be over us like a rash, craning their necks and getting in the way. This is only a quick exploratory trench and probably won't come to anything."

Phil knew that something far more interesting, on a bigger scale and taking much more time, was involved here, and, unwittingly, Cecil when he phoned in obliged with detail that would put flesh on the bones of his piece.

It was the oldest trick in the book. Profess knowledge, present it, and get the truth.

"Thanks so much for ringing, Cecil," Phil said. "Exciting times I hear from the County Archivist." *(i.e. He's talked to me, so you can.)*

"Had you any idea that Huw Pugh had gathered the collection of Roman relics?"

"Well, I knew he kept everything that was dug up but he never commented on what he'd got. Maybe he didn't know what they were." *(No denial that there's a collection, or that Pugh was the collector. And of course he knew what he'd got – he was an amateur historian!)*

"It's obviously going to take months and with winter coming you might find that you're able to hang on to the allotments for a good while longer."

"Perhaps." *(Yes, or he would have said no.)*

"I think you'll find what will happen *(showing helpfulness)* is that the Archivist's people will get an order that gives them as much time as is reasonable to do a thorough job."

"Yes, I gather that's what's been done." *(Oh has it? So it will be a long job. Thanks Cecil.)*

"Just one thing I need to confirm *(get you to cough up)* … I wasn't sure whether the box with the relics in was kept locked? *(The mention of the box is bait)*. It's just that someone's told me Huw kept it hidden away…"

"Not really hidden away. Just in the hut. But it was locked and this

Roman bangle and things were all in there with the plan." *(Bangle. The Roman bangle. And things. And a plan! So old Pugh had kept a note of where the bits were found. People love the idea of maps and buried treasure.)*

"Well thanks so much Cecil for confirming some of the details for me *(spilling the beans)*. We like to get things right.

"Just one other thought – strange isn't it, that someone who loved the place so much has in a way managed to arrange a reprieve from beyond the grave."

There's a pause.

"Well, yes, now you say it, it has probably worked out the way he would have wanted."

Phil now had twenty minutes before the stuff had to be launched, with a touch of a button, to the chief sub, who already had his page grid and a photo in place on his screen.

Phil strode over and gave a thirty-second summary of what would be coming and the chief sub said:"Right – so it's something like *'Huw's hoard halts supermart plan'* then *'Secret cache of Roman finds'*"

"Right."

"Nice one Phil."

NINETEEN

Home Sweet Home, March 26 2001

**Spring is sprung, the grass is riz,
I wonder where Kyff's new home is?**

Dear Kyff

Can you help with the above?

I tried Interpol and rang a few of the surviving Bletchley code-breakers but even they couldn't come up with your address so this will reach you via the Post Office re-direction system. Madge tells me it worked for her.

But first I must reiterate my commiserations about your move to what you can't deny is a fat-arsed, affluent, true-blue corner of the country. As Waggy says, we're all sorry that you've ended up in a place where, word has it, both the beer and the women tend to be on the flat side.

But the deed is done. Just don't come crawling back begging for a roll-up and a bag of organic veg. Or for that matter a handful of tesserae. We've been knee-deep in Roman finds since the dig proper started in the new year - did Madge say?

They found a ditch and then the Roman level and one morning we heard great rejoicing when a young lass called over the top banana to look at some mosaic bits, a couple of them coloured (even you would have recognised what they were!).

It's fascinating, Kyff - Roman history unfolding before our eyes. Luckily, the focus seems to be moving towards the hall grounds.

We're very friendly with the diggers, a bond forged with the help of a couple of Madge's lemon drizzle cakes, so we hear before the archive office of any exciting titbit they turn up. Last week it was a sandal decoration and a bit of a lamp (wonderful - still encrusted from the flame).

If ever you feel willing to let us have your phone number, which I have no doubt is secreted in tattoo form in your armpit, I'll give you chapter and verse. But life goes on very much as before, albeit round the edges of the plastic barrier tape.

Perhaps you heard of Winco's stroke? It happened when we were trying to demolish Pat's shed for her. She was worried because the floor had rotted. She sends her love by the way.

A bunch of us set about it and Yeti had got an old fence post under it using a bin as a fulcrum, rocking it to loosen the joints. Winco had a leg under, hooking out some bamboos and old cloche frames when the post broke and he copped it.

He seemed to faint with the shock and then came round. The stroke happened when Yeti tried to help him. I think Winco feared Yeti was going to give him the kiss of life. Maybe Yeti's lips were pursed ready and it was too much to take!

Poor old Wilf's been in the wars too. Knees seem to have gone. Not surprising after years manhandling those bloody great vegetables.

We've boarded his path so he can come down in his buggy and he's already got some hideous great Triffids spreading tentacles everywhere.

Old Bill went just before you left didn't he? Just when we'd begun to think he was invincible.

Yeti cried like a baby when he heard but he cheered up a bit when I said that Bill wouldn't have felt anything, that he'd just fallen gently off his bike into Jim Weston's lavender bushes.

He seemed to like the idea of the soft landing and he said, "At least he didn't hurt himself."

We've hung Bill's bike up under the eaves at the Nerve Centre.

Did you know Waggy secretly lowered his saddle? The dear old lad never caught on. Just told us that he felt as if his legs had started growing again.

Of course our spiritual friends departed before Christmas. I saw Ben in town recently and he was a model of capitalist ambition, gelled and suited and working in a call centre.

I liked him much better when he was seeking the Gentle Way but the rent man doesn't understand that.

So you're happy in the new job? Mature students must be a joy to teach because they want to learn. One day, I suppose I'll do something legit but meanwhile I'll keep being irritating. I'm a bit of a misfit as you know.

Well, it must nearly be time for your lunchtime drinkie-poos at some scenic watering hole with a glimpse of the sea and a blackboard of bistro specials. Bet it's G and Ts now and then a round of golf...??

I must be off anyway, to carry on the working class struggle.

Don't ever think you're not missed.
Radically yours, brother

– Prof

P.S. Please deny the rumour that you have bought a boat. What next – polo??

TWENTY

"What've you got Steve?"

"Cheese and onion. You?"

"Tuna."

"Swap one?"

"Not likely. Then we'd both be stinking the cab out."

Andy and Steve had always seen off their lunch long before lunchtime. Moving furniture is hard work, even with the lifting gear, and there are some very early starts, many long drives.

Today was light, and local.

They were perched on boxes in a corner of the garage, the only place where there was a bit of leg room.

Andy opened his flask of coffee and cast an expert eye round the cavernous garage, head-high in boxes that (according to the lady of the house) they hadn't got round to opening after moving in.

"Should be twenty-one in here, and two big crates - they're there," Andy said. "The board they used as a desk and the office stuff stay until the main move. Then there's the stables. Mainly tools but a pretty big sit-on mower. I've got the keys."

He passed a cup of coffee to Steve who asked:"What's the story here, Andy? Just moved in, now moving out?"

"They didn't give much away when I did the estimate. I just know that the new place is rented, a lovely big pad but rented," said Andy.

"This gaff must be worth nearly a million," Steve said, casting his eyes round the garage and towards the mature trees surrounding the entrance to the drive.

"And the rest. Just look at the grounds," said Andy. "I've got no idea what the bloke does but I don't think she works. Can't think he's a big boss with a desk like that. Maybe it's family money."

"Even that can run out. Somebody at the office said this bloke was a big boss with a World-in-One but they'd off-loaded him. If it's him, he'd have got a nice fat cheque for failing, so he should be able to settle up with us."

"Anyway, can't be as bad as the Brighton woman," Andy said, laughing through a mouthful of sandwich.

"Remember the bailiffs hammering on the door while we loaded? And her shouting in that posh voice from the top window: 'Eym awfully sorry but my cheque book is in one of those there crates. Do bear with me.'"

Their laughter echoed round the garage.

"Somehow I don't think this pair have hit hard times. They looked too chirpy."

Andy squeezed the lid onto his plastic lunch box and stood up. "Well, better crack on," he said.

As Steve flipped the levers to open the back of the lorry he asked: "What's the wife like? She gave you some soup didn't she when you costed the job up?"

"A cracker. And kind. Thought I'd get cold looking round so she brought me a mug of soup. When she rang the office to fix up for today she said 'Is that Andy? Penny here.' It was 'Penny'. No edge."

"Did you see him, the husband? Was he posh?" Steve asked.

"While I was finishing he came back from a bike ride with the little lad, who never stopped talking. They were wet through but laughing about it. No, he wasn't a bit posh. Just pleasant. Happy. Didn't look like a man who was fretting over his mortgage."

"Looks can deceive. Bet any money they're splitting up and dividing the spoils," said Steve. "Look how many jobs we do where that's happening."

"Not in this case," said Andy. "Not a chance. You should have seen the way they looked at each other. No, they're a real lovey-dovey couple. Looked like they'd just won the lottery."

TWENTY ONE

At the end of the interview, Grace was fairly confident the job was in the bag but the university's Administrator was guarded. Encouraging, but disclosing nothing.

"Well, thank you for coming Grace. That's all as far as I'm concerned," she said, closing a file.

Her desk reflected the near-pathological tidy-mindedness that led her to the job and made her so good at it; a place for everything, everything in its place.

There was one area of doubt in Grace's mind. Not about the job itself – she could honestly say, and did, that she was up to it. Establishing provenance and preserving material were familiar territory, and she'd had wide experience in the area of appraisal.

Not only that, Perth had given her a glowing reference.

The niggle was that probing about her long-term plans, her stability.

"So … Australia. Then a stay with mum in Wiltshire, and now another move. It's been pretty hectic lately, Grace! Do you think you might want to settle if you joined us here?"

Grace had tried to make her assurance sound convincing but how was she to know what the future held? A year before she would never have foreseen all that pain, losing Kyff, coming home.

The Administrator took Grace's elbow and led her to the door.

"It's a rabbit warren of a place so let me guide you back to the reception. Really, it's a massive campus, and we have every facility you can think of: two gyms, three eating places, a bank – and of course a crèche."

It might have been her imagination but Grace fancied that her reaction at the mention of the crèche had been slyly observed.

"That's one thing I won't be needing," Grace said with a laugh. "A crèche!"

Did the Administrator look reassured at this?

The interview questions had not included queries about Grace having a partner, although the Administrator, struck by Grace's beauty, was sure she would not be alone.

And of course there were no questions that would tease out the possibility that Grace might be making a late bid for a baby; delve there and you could end up in a tribunal.

The clues on the application suggested she'd be about thirty-nine or forty, so there was still the possibility and the department really did need some continuity now with the university expansion. So the comment about the crèche was noted with pleasure.

They had reached the massive glass doors of the main entrance.

"So, as I say Grace, you'll receive a phone call telling you that on this occasion you've been unsuccessful, or one offering you the post. In either case a formal letter will follow."

As they shook hands Grace looked admiringly towards the reception area. Minimalist, low desks, high tech. Airy, tranquil.

She left feeling that the farewell had been particularly warm.

On the drive back to the new flat she had felt embarrassed that, as the automatic door opened, she had said so firmly:"All very impressive! Yes, I certainly think I could certainly settle here."

A bit presumptuous perhaps? But she wanted the job and she had wanted to show that she did.

Grace didn't know it but it was precisely what the Administrator had wanted to hear.

TWENTY TWO

Home, September 17, 2001

Dear Kyff,

Many thanks for the invite to the nuptials and abject apologies for having to say we can't bloody well make it (RSVP card enclosed). Trust our Jane to have her graduation on the same day!

Barbara's furious about the clash. Still, Benton will be well represented from what I hear. Better warn the caterers that Yeti's planning to be there.

By the way, Waggy asked me to say that it's about time you made it legal! You should see his new act by the way. Comes on holding a whisky bottle and goes into a drunken routine haranguing the audience. He says he needs no rehearsals and he can be as nasty as he likes!

There's another apology from me. I tried to get you when you were between addresses. Maybe you'd already moved to Jill's (By the way, she sounds smashing.)

Anyway, I had to take an executive decision about your Dad's hut and I hope you agree I did right. I've let Yeti move in.

What happened was that the diggers took another lump off him after they found a few more bits of tile to add to what the Chron now calls Huw's Hoard. He was looking lost so I gave him the keys knowing you wouldn't mind and that your dad would have approved.

It was as if I'd given him Buckingham Palace! He's entertaining everybody to cups of tea and lording it up. He idolised your Dad so he's keeping the plot immaculate. The lady from his scheme was down the other day to help him start keeping weather records.

Another happy man is Wilf. He's got some monsters this year so we're taking him and his buggy and his leeks and his dirty great pumpkin to Harrogate. He can't be sure of course until the weigh-in but we've had the tape measure around it and it's in with a chance.

We're borrowing a forklift and everyone's chipped in for the truck.

A serious note. Barbara and me and Jane of course just want you to know that we're delighted with the way things are turning out for you, Kyff.

Some might say that you're brave to take on Jill's girl but for the lass to tell you that things feel good when you're around is a massive compliment. We all know you'll make a cracking dad.

Talking about dads, and about being brave, we thought it was real plucky of Megan to get in touch and tell you everything. Poor lass. So hard for her to know for all those years things that you didn't.

What a double shock for you, Kyff, what with your mum's health problem, but it must have helped you understand things better.

For what it's worth, Barbara and me think you're quite right to find out about your proper dad. They say it's easier now, and everybody has a right to know where they come from.

Good luck with that and may the sun shine on the big day.

Fondest, and big kisses from the girls
                    – Cecil.

TWENTY THREE

"Hello?"

"Sorry. Were you having a cat nap Kyff?"

"No - just finishing a bit of marking. Then Lucy called for a drink."

"Is she any better?"

"A bit cooler and the rash is no worse but she's devastated about the wedding. When I asked her how she was she just opened her diary where she'd scrawled 'Life is crap!' I told her that she'd be fine by Saturday and that you'd cover any leftover spots with make-up."

"Poor kid. Tell her I'll be home in an hour. Just one new diabetic and a pair of ulcerated legs to go."

"Lucy'll be fine. She's loving all the pampering. We both had a laugh when she said that in the wedding photos she'd look like one of those damnation dogs."

"She'd have got it wrong on purpose. She's quite witty for a nine year old, don't you think?"

"She's so funny. Her caution about me has just melted away. I can say anything to her now."

"She adores you."

"When I gave her the drink I tucked her in and told her that in the newspaper the wedding report would say that the bridesmaid wore a yellow dress, matching headdress and red spots."

"Was she upset?"

"No. Didn't reply but I did notice a raised finger come up out of the side of the duvet."

"Little madam! "

"Perhaps it was her way of saying I appreciate the comment and the way it was expressed."

"The little minx"

"Don't worry Jill – it's just spirit. Teasing that's an expression of something else."

"It's a sort of love. She thinks you're great. And she's not the only one."

"Ditto."

"I keep wanting to say thanks Kyff"

"What for?"

"For the way you are with Lucy, and the consideration, the understanding. The love you show me."

"Well, remember, after the accident, you pulled me back from the brink..."

"Brink? Hardly! You presented with a teeny two-centimetre long sub-cutaneous cranial laceration that had been stitched at A and E. I just told you to be a brave boy, took out the stitches and reassured you that you didn't qualify for a scan."

"Don't be modest nurse, you made me better."

"Self interest. I'd got plans for you. I was glad that shelf came down on you. I knew you were something special even though you were damaged goods."

"I'll just get off and polish my halo. I can wear it again now my head's better. And it is better, in more ways than one."

"I'm so glad Kyff."

"Oh Kyff, before you go, did the florist ring again?"

"Yep - she wanted to tell you that she can't lay her hands on lily of the valley but that she has options."

"Think I might just survive that crisis. Just as long as I get my man..."

"You sound like a bloody Mountie. Got the handcuffs ready?"

"They're already packed for next week."

"Promises, promises. Anyway. Got to go. Her highness is yelling for an iced lolly."

"Be home soon."

"I love the sound of that, Jill."

"What?"

"Just the sound of 'Be home soon.'"

TWENTY FOUR

I'd kept the Roman hairpin wrapped in tissue in the wicker box with a photo I'd taken of the allotment squad, and some stuff from dad's shelves; the pot egg, two barely damaged clay pipe bowls, two or three old coins, a horse shoe and the fish knife with the Benton Hall coat of arms inscribed on it.

Of course I should have declared the pin, and I still get pangs of guilt over having it. But when I saw that Dad had not logged it on his map I started to think about the moral issues surrounding possession.

I took the pin home and held it lovingly. A simple pin, as long as my little finger; probably bronze under the crustiness, square in section and tapering down to a point. The pea-size globe on the thick end is probably a pearl, encrusted by age. The Romans loved pearls.

No, it belonged to me, I decided, maybe not in law but then law is only an opinion.

It would be reasonable to ask who owned the metal ore that was mined and melted in the making of the pin? Didn't the maker really own the pin that he created? Or did it belong to the girl who wore it in her hair nearly 2,000 years ago? Or did it belong to the council who owned the allotments? Or the finder? Or Dad, who kept it safe?

No, it belonged to me. It was a small thank-you gesture to Dad for granting the nation evidence of their history. I "inherited" it and, as owner, I could dispose of it as I pleased.

My first thought was to send it to Grace, as some sort of memorial to our marriage. Something so old, so rare and so special went some way to symbolising what we had once had.

Then I sensed that the gesture might have rekindled feelings that – like my memories of Grace – were now embers, losing heat with the passing months. I just took it that she was healing, looking ahead, just as I had been forced to do.

Then I thought: perhaps a special wedding day memento for Jill? She would have appreciated the unique nature of the gift but probably would not have felt the special magic of the link with antiquity, something so redolent of ancient times.

Finally I decided that I would give the pin to Lucy, while Jill is out with her surgery friends having a wedding-eve meal. I wanted the pin to be symbolic reassurance that I was permanently part of Lucy's life, that I'd be making up for what had gone before. It would also be affirmation that her mum and me were dedicating our lives to each other.

Lucy was up and about now but languid and still puffy round the eyes. Her paleness made her spottiness quite startling but she was gamely pretending to be better than she really was so that there was no risk that she would miss the wedding.

She left the meal I'd made untouched and gone up to her room. She was propped against the bed-head, surrounded by soft toys, earphones in, diary open, pen poised when I walked in having tapped on her door.

I was carrying the wicker box and she looked at it expectantly but carried on soundlessly mouthing the words of the song she was listening to on the pink plastic contraption she was clutching.

"Greetings!" she shouted over the music only she could hear.

I signalled for her to take the earphones out and, when she did, I said: "You, young lady, will be deaf by the time you're my age."

"Pardon Kyff?" she said.

"I said that you will....."

She threw her head back and laughed as I got the joke. She had her mother's eyes with exactly the same mischievous glint.

"I got mum with that one," she said with the hoarse giggle that had arrived with the measles.

There was an immediate awkwardness. She rearranged her soft toys, put away her diary with the rhinestone border. I opened the box and took out the photo.

"Just thought you might like to see two or three of the people who'll be there tomorrow. My old gardening friends." She didn't reply and I could tell that she knew the photo was a pretext for something else.

"Right", I said, holding up the photo, "that man, the one with the long frizzy hair, is the cleverest person you'll ever meet, so get a really difficult question ready to ask him. He knows everything!"

She held on to the edge of the picture and said: "Is that man at the back standing on something?"

"No. He really is that size. He's called Yeti."

"Yeti?"

"Another name for Big Foot. The Abominable Snowman. A sort of enormous wild man."

"He looks like the Jolly Green Giant. Anyway, why is he dressed like that?"

"That's just Yeti. You'll love him. And that lady – she's Madge. Kind as can be."

I reached into the box and pulled out the cylinder of tissue paper. Lucy's face brightened, but I knew at that moment that she would be bitterly disappointed with the gift she was about to receive.

I needed to convey the uniqueness of the present but knew it was impossible. To a child's eyes the pin would seem to be no more than a rusty old nail.

In the end, I hurried things. I told Lucy I wanted her to have something special to remember a really important day for all three of us, and that although I could have bought something new, that gift had to be amazing. That's why I was giving her something that had come from a girl like her who lived more that 1,700 years ago.

Lucy blushed. She took the crinkly package and unfolded the paper, but was hesitant about lifting the pin out.

"Go on," I said, "it won't break."

She looked up from the hairpin to me and was about to say something when we heard the key turn in the front door lock and Jill shout: "I'm back!"

Simultaneously, down in the hall the phone began to ring. I called down: "I'll get it Jill! Come up and see the patient!"

As I hurried downstairs, Jill was striding up. We stopped fleetingly, and kissed each other almost violently without exchanging a word.

As I picked up the phone I could hear Lucy saying excitedly: "Mum - just look what Kyff's given me!"

The caller was Madge. She would be coming by train, she said, and wanted to know how far the church was from the station.

"I've splashed out on a new hat," she said. "Honestly Kyff, it's an absolute riot of colour. I'll look like a Bird of Paradise. I only hope Jill doesn't think I'm trying to steal the show."

I told her that she had always brightened things up. I didn't tell her that it was expected that she would try to steal the show.

She was concerned that she hadn't bought us what she called a real present. She'd been stumped, she said.

"I'm giving a token so you can choose a luxury together."

"That's kind Madge," I said.

"Well, you'll be short of nothing I expect," she said.

"You're right, Madge," I replied. "We've everything we need."

ACKNOWLEDGEMENTS

Thanks...

...to my wife Linda, who assured me that The Healing Hut was a tale worth telling, read it, and asked the right questions...

To my children, Adele (for invaluable criticism), Lauren (professional proof-reading) and Keir (encouragement).

Also grateful thanks to Sue Hunter, Sue John and book editor Linne Matthews for much-appreciated feedback and John and Indira McLoughlin for urging me on.

Also thanks to...

Eirlys Evans for kindly providing colloquial Welsh translation,

... and to Sharon Reid (design and technological hand-holding to get the words on to paper).

About the author...

Neil Patrick is a retired journalist and former editor of the national magazine Yours. He has written thousands of articles in a career covering 50 years and is now a columnist for Choice magazine. He was co-author, with Edmund Hockridge, of Hey There, the biography of the Canadian star of West End musicals.

Lightning Source UK Ltd.
Milton Keynes UK
UKOW05f1636060114

224048UK00002B/4/P